A. L. O. E.

Hebrew Heroes

A Tale Founded on Jewish History

A. L. O. E.

Hebrew Heroes
A Tale Founded on Jewish History

ISBN/EAN: 9783337120702

Printed in Europe, USA, Canada, Australia, Japan

Cover: Foto ©Andreas Hilbeck / pixelio.de

More available books at **www.hansebooks.com**

A CRITICAL MOMENT

Page 185

HEBREW HEROES.

A TALE FOUNDED ON JEWISH HISTORY.

BY

A. L. O. E.,

AUTHOR OF "THE TRIUMPH OVER MIDIAN," "RESCUED FROM EGYPT,"
"EXILES IN BABYLON," ETC.

WITH TWENTY-EIGHT ILLUSTRATIONS.

London:
T. NELSON AND SONS, PATERNOSTER ROW.
EDINBURGH; AND NEW YORK.

1886.

Preface.

HERE are few portions of the world's history which, to my own mind, afford subjects of such thrilling interest as that which I have selected for the groundwork of the following story. I have tried, in the main, to adhere closely to facts, though I have ventured somewhat to compress the length of time which actually elapsed between the rising against Syrian tyranny at Modin, and the restoration of the Temple. I may also have been inaccurate in representing Antiochus Epiphanes as being still in Jerusalem at the period when the battle of Emmaus took place. Such trifling deviations from history seem to me, however, by no means to interfere with that fidelity to its grand outlines which an author should conscientiously observe. No historical character has been wilfully misrepresented in these pages. If I have ventured to paint one of the noblest of Judah's heroes with the feelings and weaknesses common to man, I trust that even his most enthusiastic Hebrew admirer will not deem that they lower his dignity as commander, or patriot prince.

The exploits of Judas Maccabeus might seem to be a theme more befitting the pen of one of his own race than mine ; yet would I fain hope that a work which it has been a labour of love to a Christian to write, may not be altogether despised even by the descendants of Hebrew heroes who shared the Asmonean's toils and triumphs in the land for which he conquered and died.

A. L. O. E.

Contents.

———◦———

HEBREW HEROES.

CHAPTER I.

FAITHFUL TO THE DEATH.

HE sun was setting gloriously over the hills which encompass Jerusalem, pouring its streams of golden light on the valleys clothed with the vine, pomegranate, and olive, sparkling on the brook Kedron, casting a rich glow on flat-roofed dwellings, parapets, and walls, and throwing into bold relief from the crimson sky the pinnacles of the Temple, which, at the period of which I write, crowned the height of Mount Zion. Not the gorgeous Temple which Solomon had raised—that had long ago been given to the flames—nor yet the Temple as adorned by King Herod : the building before us stands in its simple majesty as erected by the Hebrews after their return from Babylon under the leadership of Zerubbabel and Jeshua. Not the might

of the powerful, nor the gold of the wealthy, but the
earnest zeal of a people down-trodden and oppressed had
built that Temple ; and its highest adornment was the
promise which Haggai's inspired lips had uttered : *The
Desire of all nations shall come: and I will fill this
house with glory, saith the Lord of hosts* (Haggai ii. 7).
*The glory of this latter house shall be greater than that
of the former* (Haggai ii. 9).

The fulfilment of that promise was still a subject for
faith ; and seldom had faith had to breast a fiercer storm
of persecution than that which was sweeping over God's
ancient people at the time when my story opens—about
167 years before the Christian Era. The Roman had
not yet trodden the soil of Palestine as a conqueror ;
but a yoke yet more intolerable than his lay on the
necks of the sons of Abraham. Antiochus Epiphanes,
king of Syria, one of the most merciless tyrants that
ever existed, bore rule in the city of David. He had
deluged the streets of Jerusalem with blood, he had
plundered and polluted the Temple, offered the unclean
beast upon God's holy altar, and set up the image of
Jupiter Olympus in the place dedicated to the worship
of the Lord of Sabaoth. It was a time of rebuke and
blasphemy, of fiery persecution against the one pure
faith ; and if some shrank back from the trial, other
Hebrews showed that the spirit of Shadrach and his
brethren still lived amongst the people of Judæa.

On the evening which I am describing, a young man was wandering among the clumps of hoary olive-trees which shaded a valley on the eastern side of Jerusalem. The red sunbeams pierced here and there between the gray branching stems and through the foliage, and shone full on the figure of Lycidas the Athenian. No one could have mistaken him for a Hebrew, even had the young man worn the garb of a Jew instead of that of a Grecian. The exquisitely-formed features of the stranger were those which have been made familiar to us by the masterpieces of antiquity treasured in our museums. Lycidas might well have served as model to Phidias for a statue of Endymion. His form was of faultless proportions, remarkable rather for symmetry and grace than for strength; and his face might have been deemed too feminine in its beauty, but for the stamp of intellect on it. That young brow had already worn the leafy crown in the Olympic contest for poetic honours. Lycidas had read his verses aloud in the arena to the critical ears of the Athenians, his fellow-citizens, and thousands from other parts of Greece, and had heard their plaudits ringing through the air at the close. That had been a proud moment for the youthful Athenian, but his ambition had not been satisfied by this his first great success. Lycidas was his own severest critic, and regarded himself as being rather at the starting-point than as at the goal. He had resolved on writing a poem, the fame of which should emulate that of the Iliad, and had chosen as the theme of his verse THE HEROISM OF VIRTUE. Lycidas would draw his pictures from history, choose his models from men, and not from the so-called deities with which superstition or fancy had peopled Olympus. The Athenian had an innate love of the pure and true, which made him intuitively reject fables, and which, amongst his countrymen, exposed him to the charge of scepticism. Lycidas could laugh with Aristophanes at legends of gods and demigods, whom their very priests represented as having more than the common infirmities and vices of mortal men. Had Lycidas reared an altar, it would have been like that which was seen two centuries later in his native city, with the inscription, TO THE UNKNOWN GOD. The Greek knew of no being above earth whom he could intelligently worship; and his religion consisted rather in an intense admiration for virtue in the abstract, than in anything to which his more superstitious countrymen would have given the name of piety.

To collect materials for his poem on THE HEROISM OF VIRTUE, Lycidas had travelled far and wide. He had visited Rome, then a powerful republic, and listened with keen interest to her annals, so rich in stories of patriotism and self-devotion. The Athenian had then turned his course eastward, had visited Alexandria, ascended the Nile, gazed on the Pyramids, even then— more than two thousand years ago—venerable from their antiquity. After seeing the marvels of the land of the Pharaohs, Lycidas had travelled by the way of Gaza to Jerusalem, where he was now residing. He was an occasional guest at the court of the Syrian monarch, to whom he had brought a letter of introduction from Perseus, king of Macedonia.

It was not to indulge in pleasant poetic reveries that Lycidas had on that evening sought the seclusion of the olive-grove, if the direction of the current of his thoughts might be known by the index of his face, which wore an expression of indignation, which at times almost flashed into fierceness, while the silent lips moved, as if uttering words of stern reproof and earnest expostulation. No one was near to watch the countenance of the young Greek, until he suddenly met a person richly attired in the costume worn at the Syrian court, who came upon him in a spot where the narrowness of the path precluded the two men from avoiding each other without turning back, and so brought about a meeting which, to the last comer at least, was unwelcome.

" Ha! my Lord Pollux, is it you!" exclaimed Lycidas, with courteous salutation. "I missed you suddenly from my side to-day at that—shall I call it tragedy? for never was a more thrilling scene acted before the eyes of man."

" I was taken with a giddiness—a touch of fever," replied the courtier addressed by the name of Pollux. He looked haggard and pale as he spoke.

"I marvel not—I marvel not if your blood boiled to fever-heat, as did mine!" cried Lycidas.   "No generous

AN UNWELCOME MEETING.

spirit could have beheld unmoved those seven Hebrew brethren, one after another, before the eyes of their mother, tortured to death in the presence of Antiochus, because they refused to break a law which they regarded as divine!"

"Nay," replied Pollux, forcing a smile; "their fate

was nothing to me. What cared I if they chose to throw away their lives like fools for an idle superstition!"

"Fools! say rather like heroes!" exclaimed Lycidas, stopping short (for he had turned and joined Pollux in his walk). "I marvel that you have so little sympathy for those gallant youths—you who, from your cast of features, I should have deemed to be one of their race."

Pollux winced, and knitted his dark brows, as if the remark were unwelcome.

"I have looked on the Olympic arena," continued Lycidas, resuming his walk, and quickening his steps as he warmed with his subject; "I have seen the athletes with every muscle strained, their limbs intertwined, wrestling like Milo, or pressing forward in the race for the crown and the palm, as if life were less dear than victory. But never before had I beheld such a struggle as that on which my eyes looked to-day, where the triumph was over the fear of man, the fear of death, where mortals wrestled with agony, and overcame it, silent, or but speaking such brave words as burned themselves into the memory—deathless utterances from the dying! There were no plaudits to encourage these athletes, at least none that man could hear; there was no shouting as each victor reached the goal. But if the fortitude of suffering virtue be indeed a spectacle on which the gods admiringly look, then be assured that

the invisible ones were gazing down to-day on that
glorious arena, ay, and preparing the crown and the
palm. For I can as soon believe," continued the
Athenian, raising his arm and pointing towards the
setting sun, "that that orb is lost, extinguished, blotted
out from the universe, because he is sinking from our
view, as that the noble spirits which animated those
tortured forms could perish with them for ever!"

Pollux turned his head aside. He cared not that his
companion should see the gesture of pain with which he
gnawed his nether lip.

"It is certain that the sufferers looked forward to
existence beyond death," continued the young Athenian.
"One of the brothers, as he came forward to suffer, fixed
his calm, stern gaze on Antiochus (I doubt not but that
gaze will haunt the memory of Syria's king when his
own dying hour shall arrive), and said—I well remember
his words—'Wicked prince, you bereave us of earthly
life; but the King of heaven and earth, if we die in
defence of His laws, will one day raise us up to life
eternal.' The next sufferer, stretching forth his hands
as if to receive the palm rather than the executioner's
stroke, said, with the same calm assurance, 'I received
these limbs from Heaven; but I now despise them, since
I am to defend the laws of God, from the sure and stead-
fast hope that He will one day restore them to me.' Is
it possible that these men believed that not only souls

(349)

but bodies would rise again—that some mysterious Power could and would restore them to life eternal? Is this the faith of the Hebrews?" The last question was impatiently repeated by Lycidas before it received an answer.

"Some of them hold such a wild faith," said Pollux.

"A sublime, mysterious faith," observed Lycidas; "one which makes the souls of those who hold it invulnerable as was the body of Achilles, and without the one weak point. It inspires even women and children with the courage of heroes, as I witnessed this day. The seventh of the Hebrew brethren was of tender years and goodly. Even the king pitied his youth, and offered him mercy and honours if he would forsake the law of his God. Antiochus swore that he would raise the youth to riches and power, and rank him amongst his favoured courtiers, if he would bend to the will of the king. I watched the countenance of the boy as the offer was made. He saw on the one side the mangled forms of his brethren, the grim faces of the executioners; on the other, all the pomps and glories of earth, and yet he wavered not in his choice."

Pollux could hardly suppress a groan, and listened with ill-concealed impatience as the Athenian went on with his narrative.

"Then the king bade the mother plead with her son, obey the promptings of nature, and bid him live for her

sake. She had stood through all the fearful scene, not
like a Niobe in tears, but with hands clasped and eyes
upraised, as one who sees the invisible, and drinks in
courage from words inaudible to other ears than her own.
She heard the king, approached her young son, laid her
hand on his shoulder, and gazed on him with unutterable
tenderness. Faith with her might conquer fear, but
could only deepen love. She conjured her child, by all
that she had done and suffered for him, firmly to believe,
and to fear not. 'Show yourself worthy of your
brethren,' she said, 'that, by the mercy of God, I
may receive you, together with your brothers, in
the glory which awaits us.' And the fair boy smiled
in her face, and followed in the glorious track of
those who had suffered before him, praying for his
country as he died for his faith. Then, in cruelty
which acted the part of mercy, the mother—last of
that heroic band—was reünited to them by death. But
I could not stay to look upon *that* sacrifice," said
Lycidas, with emotion; "I had seen enough, and
more than enough."

"And I have heard enough, and more than enough,"
muttered Pollux, on whom the description of the scene
given by Lycidas had inflicted keen anguish—the anguish
of shame and remorse.

"You pity the sufferers?" observed the Athenian.

"Pity! I envy," was the thought to which the

blanched lips of a renegade dared not give utterance. Pollux but shook his head in reply.

"I would fain know more of the religion of the Hebrews," said Lycidas. "I have heard marvellous stories —more sublime than any that our poets have sung—of a Deity bringing this people out of Egypt, making a path for them through the depths of the sea, reining back its foaming waves as a rider his white-maned steed; giving to the thirsty—water from the rock, to the hungry —bread from the skies ; and scattering the foes of Israel before them, as chaff is driven by the wind. I have heard of the sun's fiery chariot arrested in its course by the voice of a man, speaking with authority given to him by an inspiring Deity. Tell me what is the name of the Hebrews' powerful God ?"

Pollux pressed his lips closely together; he dared not utter the awful name of Him whom he had denied. The courtier laid his hand on the jewelled clasp which fastened his girdle. Perhaps the movement was accidental ; perhaps he wished to direct the attention of his companion to the figures of Hercules and the Nemean lion which were embossed on the gold. "You forget," observed Pollux, "that I am a worshipper of the deities of Olympus, that I sacrifice to the mighty Jove."

" I asked not what was your religion," said Lycidas ; " my question regarded that held by the Hebrews, of which you can scarcely be ignorant. What is the name of that God whom they would not deny, even to save themselves from torture and death?"

"I cannot tarry here longer, noble stranger," was the hurried reply of Pollux. "The sun has sunk; I must return to the city; Antiochus the king expects my attendance at his banquet to-night."

"I am bidden to it, but I go not," said the young Athenian. "Slaughter in the daytime, feasting at night —blood on the hands, wine at the lips—I hate, I loathe this union of massacre and mirth. Go you and enjoy the revel in the palace of your king. Were I present, I should see at the banquet the shadowy forms of that glorious matron and her sons; I should hear above the laughter, the shout, and the song, the thrilling tones of voices confessing unshaken confidence in the power and mercy of their God, and the glorious hope of immortality where the oppressor can torture no more."

And with a somewhat constrained interchange of parting courtesies, the free Greek and the sycophant of a tyrant went on their several ways.

CHAPTER II.

THE MIDNIGHT BURIAL.

HE scene which he had witnessed had left the mind of Lycidas in an excited and feverish state. The cooling breeze which whispered amongst the leaves of the olives, and the solitude of the secluded place where Pollux had left him, were refreshing to the young Greek's spirit. He threw himself on the grass beneath one of the trees, leaned against its trunk, and gazed upwards at the stars as, one by one, they appeared, like gems studding the deep azure sky.

"Are these brave spirits now reigning in one of these orbs of beauty?" thought the poet; "or are the stars themselves living souls, spirits freed from the chains of matter, shining for ever in the firmament above? I must know more of that Hebrew religion, and seek out those who can initiate me into its mysteries, if it be lawful for a stranger to learn them."

And then the thoughts of Lycidas turned to his poem, and he tried to throw into verse some of the ideas suggested to his mind by the martyrdoms which he had witnessed, but he speedily gave up the attempt in despair.

"Poetic ornament would but mar the grand outlines of such a history," he murmured to himself; "who would carve flowers upon the Pyramids, or crown with daisies an obelisk pointing to the skies!"

Gradually sleep stole over the young Greek, his head drooped upon his arm, his eyelids closed, and he slumbered long and deeply.

Lycidas was awakened by sounds near him, low and subdued, the cautious tread of many feet, the smothered whisper, and the faint rustle of garments. The Athenian opened his eyes, and gazed from his place of concealment behind the thick branching stem of the olive on a strange striking scene.

The moon, full and round, had just risen, but the foliage of the trees as yet obscured most of her light, as her silver lamp hung near the horizon, casting long black shadows over the earth. Several forms were moving about in the faint gleam, apparently engaged in some work which needed concealment, for none of them carried a torch. Lycidas, himself silent as the grave, watched the movements of those before him with a curiosity which for a time so engrossed his mind as to take away all sense of personal danger, though he soon became aware that the intrusion of a stranger on these mysterious midnight proceedings would not only be unwelcome, but might to himself be perilous.

The group of men assembled in that retired spot were evidently Hebrews, and as the eyes of Lycidas became accustomed to the gloom, and the ascending moon had more power to disperse it, he intuitively singled out one from amongst them as the leader and chief of the rest. Not that his tunic and mantle were of richer materials than those of his comrades ; plain and dusty with travel were the sandals upon his feet ; and he wore the simple white turban which a field-labourer might have worn. But never had turban been folded around a more majestic brow, and the form wrapped in the mantle had the unconscious dignity which marks those born to command. The very tread of his sandalled feet reminded the Athenian of that of the desert lion, and from the dark deep-set eye glanced the calm soul of a hero.

"Here be the place," said the chief, if such he were, pointing to the earth under the branches of the very tree against the trunk of which, on the further side, the temple of Lycidas was pressed, as he bent eagerly forward to watch and to listen.

Not a word was uttered in reply ; but the men around, after laying aside their upper garments, set to work to dig what appeared to be a wide trench. The

leader himself threw off his mantle, took a spade, and
laboured with energy, bringing the whole force of his
powerful muscles to bear on his humble toil. All worked
in profound silence, nor paused in their labour except
now and then to listen, like men to whom danger had
taught some caution.

Whilst the men went on with their digging, Lycidas
strained his eyes to distinguish the outlines of a group
at some paces' distance, which doubtless, though separated from them, belonged to the same party as those
so actively employed before him. Two forms appeared
to be seated on the ground in a spot evidently chosen
for its seclusion; one of them was clothed in dark garments, the other was shrouded in a large white linen
veil. Other figures in white seemed to be stretched
upon the ground in repose. Lycidas watched this silent
group for hours, and all remained motionless as marble,
save that ever and anon the dark female figure slightly
swayed backwards and forwards with a rocking motion,
and that several times the veiled head was turned with
a quick movement, as of alarm, when the breeze rustled
in the olives a little more loudly than usual, or bore
sounds from the city to the woman's sensitive ear.

Meanwhile the work of digging proceeded steadily,
and the mound of earth thrown out grew large, for the
arms of those who laboured were strong and willing, and
no man paused either to rest or to speak save once. It

was almost a relief to Lycidas to hear at last the sound of a human voice from one of those phantom-like toilers by night. He who spoke was the fiercest-looking of the band, with something of the wildness of Ishmael's race on features whose high, strongly-marked outlines showed the Hebrew cast of countenance in its most exaggerated type.

"There's more thunder in the air," he observed, resting for a minute on his spade, and addressing himself to him whom Lycidas had mentally named "the Hebrew prince," on account of his commanding height and noble demeanour, and the deference with which his order had been received.

No answer was returned to the remark, and the wild-looking Jew spoke again,—

"Have you heard that Apelles starts to-morrow for Modin, charged with a mission from the tyrant to compel its inhabitants to do sacrifice to one of his accursed idol-gods?"

"Is it so? then ere daybreak I set out for Modin," was the reply.

"It may be that the venerable Mattathias would rather have you absent," observed the first speaker.

"Abishai, when the storm bursts, a son's place is by the side of his father," said the princely Hebrew; and as he spoke he threw up a spadeful of earth from the pit which Lycidas doubted not was meant for a grave.

Again the work proceeded in silence. The moon had risen above the trees before that silence was once more broken, this time by the leader of the band,—

"It is deep enough now, and broad enough ; go ye and bring the honoured dead."

The command was at once obeyed. All the men present, excepting the chief himself, who remained standing in the grave, went towards the group which has been previously mentioned. Interest chained Lycidas to the spot, though it occurred to his mind that prudence required him to seize this favourable opportunity of quietly making his escape.

The Greek remained, watching in the shadow, as on the rudest of biers, formed by two javelins fastened by cross-bars together, the swathed forms of the dead, one after another, were borne to the edge of the pit. They were followed by the two female mourners that had kept guard over the remains while the grave was being prepared. The first of these was a tall, stately woman, with hair which glistened in the moonbeams like silver, braided back from a face of which age had not destroyed the majestic beauty. Sternly sad stood the Hebrew matron by the grave of the martyred dead ; no tear in her eyes, which were bright with something of prophetic fire. So might a Deborah have stood, had Sisera won the victory, and she had had to raise the death-wail over Israel's slain, instead of the song of triumph to hail the conquerors' return.

The other female form, which was smaller, and exquisitely graceful in its movements, remained slightly retired, and still closely veiled. Lycidas remarked that the eyes of the leader watched that veiled form, as it approached, with a softened and somewhat anxious expression. This was, however, but for some moments, and the Hebrew then gave his undivided attention to the pious work on which he was engaged.

Still standing in the grave, the chief received the bodies, one by one, from the men who had borne them to the place of interment. He took each corpse in his powerful arms, and unaided laid it down in its last resting-place, as gently as if he were laying down on a soft couch a sleeper whom he feared to awaken. Lycidas caught a glimpse of the pale placid face of one of the shrouded forms, but needed not that glimpse to feel certain that those whose remains were thus secretly interred by kinsmen or friends at the peril of their lives, were the same as those whose martyrdom he had so indignantly witnessed. The Athenian knew enough of the Syrian tyrant to estimate how daring and how difficult must have been the feat of rescuing so many of the bodies of his victims from the dishonour of being left to the dog or the vulture. The devotion of the living, as well as the martyrdom of the dead, gave an interest to that midnight burial which no earthly pomp could have lent. The spirit of the young Athenian glowed with

generous sympathy; and of high descent and proud
antecedents as he was, Lycidas would have deemed it an
honour to have helped to dig that wide grave for the
eight slaughtered Jews.

The burial was conducted in solemn silence, save as
regarded the Hebrew matron, and her deep thrilling
accents were meeter requiem for the martyrs than the
loudest lamentations of hired mourners would have been.
As the chief received each lifeless form into his arms, the
matron uttered a short sentence over it, in which words
of the ancient Hebrew spoken by her fathers blended
with the Chaldee, then the language commonly used by
the Jews.   Her thoughts, as she gave them utterance,
clothed themselves in unpremeditated poetry; the
Athenian could neither understand all her words, nor
her allusions to the past, but the majesty of gesture, the
music of sound, made him listen as he might have done
to the inspired priestess of some oracle's shrine.

"We may not wail aloud for thee, my son, nor rend
our garments, nor put on sackcloth, nor pour dust upon
our heads.   He who hath bereaved thee of life, would
bereave thee even of our tears; but thou art resting on
Abraham's bosom, where the tyrant can reach thee no
more.

"Thou art taken away from the evil.   Thou seest no
longer Jerusalem trodden by the heathen, nor the abomi-
nation of desolation set up in the sanctuary of the Lord.

"Even as Isaac was laid on the altar, so didst thou yield thy body to death, and thy sacrifice is accepted.

"As the dead wood of Aaron's rod, cut off from the tree on which it had grown, yet blossomed and bare fruit; cut off as thou art in thy prime, thy memory shall blossom for ever.

"The three holy children trod unharmed the fiery furnace seven time heated. He who was with them was surely with thee; and the Angel of Death hath bidden thee come forth, naught harmed by the fire, save the bonds of flesh which thy free spirit hath left behind.

"To touch a dead body is counted pollution; to touch thine is rather consecration; for it is a holy thing which thou hast freely offered to God."

With peculiar tenderness the matron breathed her requiem over the seventh body as it was laid by the rest.

"Youngest and best-beloved of thy mother; thou flower of the spring, thou shalt slumber in peace on her bosom. Ye were lovely and pleasant in your lives, in your deaths ye are not divided."

It was with calm chastened sorrow that the last fare-well had been spoken as the bodies of the martyred brethren had been placed in their quiet grave; but there was a bitterness of grief in the wail of the Hebrew woman over their mother, which made every word seem to Lycidas like a drop of blood wrung from the heart of the speaker.

"Blessed, oh, thrice blessed art thou, Solomona, my sister, richest of mothers in Israel! Thou hast borne seven, and amongst them not one has been false to his God. Thy diadem lacks no gem—thy circle of love is unbroken. Blessed she who, dying by her martyred sons, could say to her Lord: *Lo, I and the children whom Thou hast given me;*" and as the matron ended her lament, she tore her silver hair, rent her garments, and bowed her head with a gesture of uncontrollable grief.

All the bodies having been now reverentially placed in the grave, the chief rose from it, and joined his companions. Abishai then thus addressed him,—

"Hadassah hath made her lament. Son of Phineas, descendant of Aaron the high-priest of God, have you no word to speak over the grave of those who died for the faith?"

The chief lifted up his right hand towards heaven, and slowly repeated that sublime verse from Isaiah, which to those who lived in that remote period must have seemed as full of mystery as of consolation,—" *Thy dead shall live! My dead body shall they arise! Awake and sing, ye that dwell in dust: for thy dew the dew of herbs, and the earth shall cast out the dead.*" *

The sound of that glorious promise of Scripture seemed to rouse Hadassah from her agonizing grief; she lifted

* Isaiah xxvi. 19.   It will be observed that interpolated italics are omitted.

up her bowed head, calm and serene as before. Turning
to the veiled woman near her, she said, "We may not
burn perfumes over these our honoured dead, but you,
Zarah, my child, have brought living flowers for the
burial, and their fragrance shall rise as incense. Cast
them into the grave ere we close it."

Obedient to the command of her aged relative, the
maiden whom Hadassah had addressed glided forward to

THE MIDNIGHT BURIAL.

the brink of the grave, and threw down into it a fragrant shower of blossoms. The movement threw back
her veil, and there flashed upon Lycidas a vision of

loveliness more exquisite than the poet had ever beheld
even in his dreams, as the full stream of moonlight fell
on the countenance of the fairest of all the daughters of
Zion.   Her long dark lashes drooped, moist with tears,
as she performed her simple act of reverence towards her
dead kinsmen ;   then Zarah raised her eyes with a
mournful sweet expression, which was suddenly exchanged for a look of alarm—she started, and a faint
cry escaped from her lips.   The maiden had caught
sight of the stranger crouching in the deep shadow, her
eyes had met his—concealment was over—Lycidas was
discovered !

CHAPTER III.

"SPY! a traitor! cut him down—hew him to pieces!" such were the cries, not loud, but terrible, that, as thunder on flash, followed that exclamation from Zarah. Cold steel gleamed in the moonlight; Lycidas, who had scarcely before thought of his own personal danger, found himself in a moment surrounded by a furious band with weapons upraised to take his life. With the instinct of self-preservation the young Athenian sprang forwards, clasped the knees of the leader, and exclaimed, "No spy—no Syrian—no foe! as ye would find mercy in the hour of death, only hear me!" Then, ashamed at having been betrayed into showing what might look like cowardly fear, the Greek stood erect, but gasping, expecting that ere he could draw another breath he should feel the dagger in his side, or the sword at his throat.

3

"Hold—let him speak ere he die!" cried the leader; and, at his gesture of command, uplifted blades were arrested in air, and, like leopards crouching in act to spring, the Hebrews surrounded their prisoner, to prevent the possibility of his making his escape.

"What would you say in your defence, young man?" asked the leader, in tones calm and stern. "Can you deny that you have been present as a spy at a scene to have witnessed which places the lives of all here assembled in your hands?"

"I am a Greek, an Athenian," said Lycidas, who had recovered his self-possession, and who intuitively felt that he was at the mercy of one who might be sternly just, but who would not be wantonly cruel. "I am here, but not as a spy—not to look with prying eyes upon your solemn and sacred rites. Led by chance to this spot, sleep overtook me under this tree. I would forfeit my right hand, nay, my life, rather than betray one engaged in the noble act which I have accidentally witnessed to-night."

"Will you hear him, the heathen dog, the son of Belial, the lying Gentile!" yelled out Abishai, his gleaming white teeth and flashing eyes giving to him an almost wolf-like ferocity of aspect, that well accorded with his cry for blood. "He was present—I know it—when our martyred brethren were slain; ay, he looked on their dying pangs!—tear him to pieces—set your heel on his neck—he has rejoiced at the slaughter of the just."

"No!" cried Lycidas with vehemence; "I call to witness the—"

"Stop his blaspheming tongue with the steel!" exclaimed Abishai furiously; "let him not profane our ears with the names of the demons whom he worships. Cut him off from the face of the earth—that grave will hold one body more—the blood of our brethren cries out for vengeance!"

Several voices echoed the fierce appeal, but amongst the wild cries for revenge, the ear of Lycidas, and the ear of the leader also, caught the maiden's faint exclamation, "O Judas, have mercy; spare him!"

Still the extended hand of the chief alone kept back the fierce band who would have cut down their defenceless victim. But there was painful doubt on the brow of the leader; not that he was influenced by the demand for blood from Abishai and his fierce companions, but that he was aware of the extreme risk of setting the captive free. Lycidas felt that his fate hung on the lips of that calm princely man, and was almost satisfied that so it should be; a thought rose in the mind of the Greek, "If I must die, let it be by his hand."

"Stranger," began the son of Mattathias, and at the sound of his voice the tumult was hushed, and all stood silent to listen; "I doubt not your word, I thirst

not for your blood—were my own life only at stake,
not a hair of your head should be harmed. But on
your silence as to what you have seen this night
depends the safety of all here assembled, even of these
daughters of Zion, for the tyrant spares not our women.
We have no power to detain in captivity—we have but
one way of ensuring silence ; would you yourself—with
the grave of those martyrs before you—be able to
reproach us with cruelty should we decide on taking that
way ? "

Lycidas met without blenching the calm sad eyes of
the speaker, but he could not answer the question. He
knew that under like circumstances neither Syrian nor
Greek would feel hesitation before, or remorse after, what
would be deemed a stern deed of necessity. The
eloquent lips of the poet had no power to plead now for
life.

"Why waste words!" exclaimed fierce Abishai;
"why do you hesitate, Judas? One would scarce deem
you to be the descendant of that Phineas who won
deathless fame by smiting Zimri and Cosbi through with
a dart. 'Thine eye shall not pity, nor thine hand
spare.' Guilt lies on your head if you let Agag go.
Was not the Canaanite to be rooted out of the land?
Who dare bid us draw back when the Lord hath delivered the prey to our swords?"

"I dare—I do!" cried Hadassah, advancing with

dignity to the edge of the grove which separated her and her grand-daughter Zarah from the Hebrew men and their captive. "Shame on you, Abishai, man of blood! Yea, though you be the husband of my dead daughter, I repeat, shame on you to bring the name of the Lord to sanction your own thirst for vengeance! Hear me, son of Mattathias; ye men of Judah, hear me. The Merciful bids me speak, and I cannot refrain from speaking the words which He puts into my mouth."

The matron was evidently regarded with reverence by those who were present. Judas was related to her by blood, Abishai by marriage; two of the other five Hebrews had been her servants in her more prosperous days. But it was chiefly the dignity of Hadassah's character that gave weight to her speech; the widowed lady was regarded in Jerusalem almost as a prophetess, as one indued with wisdom from on high. Her pleading might not be effectual, but would at least be listened to with respect.

"The Canaanite was swept from the land," said Hadassah; "Zeba and Zalmunna were slain; Cosbi and Zimri were smitten through with a dart; but these were sinners whose cup of iniquity was full, and the swords of Israel executed God's righteous vengeance upon them, even as the waves of the sea overwhelmed Pharaoh, or the flood a world of transgressors. But the God of justice is the God also of mercy, slow to anger and

plenteous in goodness. He calleth vengeance—though
His work—His *strange work* (Isa. xxviii. 21). He hath
given command, by His servant the Preacher, *If thine
enemy be hungry, give him bread to eat; and if he be
thirsty, give him water to drink* (Prov. xxv. 21).
*Rejoice not when thine enemy falleth; and let not thine
heart be glad when he stumbleth*" (Prov. xxiv. 17).

"An enemy born of the house of Israel, not a vile
Gentile," muttered one of the men who were present.

"Is the Lord the Maker only of the Jew; made He
not the Gentile also?" cried Hadassah. "*Thou shalt
not oppress a stranger*, saith the Lord, *seeing ye were
strangers in the land of Egypt* (Ex. xxiii. 9). Did not
Hobab the Midianite dwell among the people of Israel;
was not Achior the Ammonite welcomed by the elders
of Bethura; was not the blood of the Hittite required at
the hand of David, and Ittai the Gittite found faithful
when Israelites fell away from their king? God said of
Cyrus the Persian, *He is my shepherd* (Isa. xliv. 28),
and Alexander of Macedon was suffered to offer sacrifices
to the Lord God of Jacob. Yea, hath not Isaiah the
prophet declared that He, the Holy One, the Messiah, for
whose coming we look, *shall bring forth judgment to the
Gentiles* (Isa. xlii. 1), shall be *a light of the Gentiles*
(Isa. xlii. 6), that He will lift up His hand to the Gentiles
(Isa. xlix. 22), so that their kings shall be nursing-
fathers, and their queens nursing-mothers to His people

(Isa. xlix. 23)? Ay, a time is coming—may it speedily come!—when *the idols He shall utterly abolish* (Isa. ii. 18), when the Lord's house shall be established, and all nations shall flow into it (Isa. ii. 2), when *the earth shall be filled with the knowledge of the glory of the Lord, as the waters cover the sea*" (Hab. ii. 14).

The noble features of the aged matron kindled as with inspiration, and as she raised her hand towards heaven, she seemed to call the Deity to confirm His glorious promises of mercy to the people yet walking in darkness.

A confused murmur rose amongst the listeners; if Hadassah's appeal had impressed some, it had stirred up in others the fierce jealousy which made so many Jews unwilling that the Gentiles should ever share the privileges of Abraham's race. The captive's life hung upon a slender thread, and he knew it.

"Hadassah," said the chief, addressing the widow with respect, "do you then require that we should trust this stranger, when—if he prove false—so many Hebrew lives will be the forfeit of confidence misplaced?"

"I require that you should trust Him who hath said, *Thou shalt do no murder;* who hath ordained that *whoso sheddeth man's blood, by man shall his blood be shed.* We show little faith when we think to find safety in transgressing the law of our God."

Again rose a fierce, angry murmur. Lycidas heard
the words, "folly, madness, tempting Providence,"
mingled with imprecations on "dogs of heathen,"
"idolaters," "the polluted, the worshippers of graven
images."

Judas laid hold on his javelin, which he had placed
against the trunk of the olive when he had exchanged
the weapon for the spade. The heart of Lycidas
throbbed faster; he read his own death-warrant in the
movement, but he braced his spirit to fall bravely, as
became a fellow-citizen of Miltiades. Again there was
profound silence, all awaiting what should follow that
simple action of the leader.

"Time passes, every minute that we linger here is
fraught with peril; our decision must be prompt," said
Judas, and he motioned to Hadassah and Zarah to join
the company of men on the side of the grave nearest to
the stem of the tree. When they had done so, the son
of Mattathias cast his javelin down on the ground.
"Let those who would let the captive go free, those
who would trust his gratitude and honour, pass over
my javelin," cried Judas. "If the greater number cross
it, we spare; if they remain here, we slay. Are you
content?" he inquired.

There was a murmured "Content" from most of those
present. The chief then turned his glance on Lycidas,
and with stern courtesy repeated his question to the

Greek. The young captive bowed his head, folded his arms, and answered "Content."

"The women shall not vote!" exclaimed Abishai.

"They shall vote," said the chief, with decision; "their peril is equal to ours, and so shall their privilege be."

It was with strangely mingled emotions that Lycidas beheld, as it were, the balance raised, one of the scales of which was weighted with his freedom and life! Fear was scarcely the predominating feeling. A cloud for a few moments darkened the face of the moon, but through the shadow he could see the stately dark figure of Hadassah as she crossed over the javelin, and the flutter of Zarah's white veil. As the silver orb emerged from the cloud, the women were followed by the two Hebrews who had once been servants to Hadassah.

"Four on that side—five on this—he dies!" cried Abishai eagerly; but even as the exclamation was on his lips, Judas with a bound sprang over the javelin, and stood at the side of Zarah.

"He lives—the Merciful be praised!" cried Hadassah. Abishai, with a muttered curse, thrust back his thirsty blade into its sheath.

"Captive, depart in peace," said the son of Mattathias; "but ere you quit this spot, solemnly vow silence as to what you have witnessed here."

Lycidas instantly obeyed. "May I share the torments of those whose grave—but for your mercy—I should have shared, if I ever prove false to my oath!" cried the Greek.

THE DECISION.

The chief waved his hand to bid him depart, and leave the Hebrews to complete the solemn work which his appearance had interrupted.

Lycidas, however, showed no haste to escape. He glanced towards Hadassah and Zarah. "May I not speak my gratitude," he began, advancing one step towards them ; but the widow by a gesture forbade his nearer approach.

"Live your gratitude, speak it not, stranger," said she. "If ever you see son or daughter of Abraham in peril, remember this night; if ever your enemy stand defenceless before you, remember this night. And when next you would bow down before an idol, and pray—as your people pray—to the deaf wood and the senseless stone, pause and reflect first upon what you have learned on this sacred spot of the faith of the Hebrews,"— Hadassah pointed to the open grave as she spoke,— "how it can nerve the weak to suffer, and induce the strong to spare!"

CHAPTER IV.

FOLLOWING BEHIND.

S he quitted that place of burial, which he had little expected to leave alive, Lycidas felt like one under an enchanter's spell. Joy at almost unhoped-for escape from a violent death was not the emotion uppermost in his mind, and it became the less so with every step which the Athenian took from the olive-grove. Strange as the feeling appeared even to himself, the young poet could almost have wished the whole scene acted over again, notwithstanding the painfully prominent part which he had had to play in it. Lycidas would not have been unwilling to have heard again the fierce cries and execrations, and to have seen once more the flashing weapons around him, for the sake of also hearing the soft appeal, "Have mercy! spare him!" and to have had another glimpse of Zarah's form and face, as, with a halo of moonlight and loveliness around her, she dropped her tribute of living flowers into the grave of the dead.

"These Hebrew women are not as the women of earth, but beings that belong to a higher sphere," thought Lycidas, as he pursued his way towards the city. "That aged matron has all the majesty of a Juno, and the maiden is fair as—nay, to which of the deities of Olympus could I compare one so tender and so pure? Venus! the idea were profanation—chaste Dian with her merciless arrows—Pallas, terrible to her enemies? —no! Strange that it should seem an insult to the women to compare her to the goddess!"

Lycidas gazed upwards at the exquisite blue of that Eastern sky, and around him at the fair landscape of hills and valleys calmly sleeping in moonlight. A thrilling sense of beauty pervaded his soul.

"O holy and beneficent Nature," he murmured, "hast thou no voice to explain to men through thy visible glories the mysteries of the invisible! Dost thou not even now whisper to my soul, 'purity and goodness are the attributes of Divinity, for they are stamped upon the works of creation; and so must purity and goodness be the badge of the Divinity's true worshippers on earth!' There is a spirit stirring within the breast that echoes this voice of Nature, that repeats, 'purity and goodness, not power and might, give the highest dignity to mortal or immortal!' But if it be so, if my hand have touched the mighty veil which shrouds the truth from man's profane gaze, if I have a glimpse of the sacred mystery beyond, how far from that truth, in what a mist of error must all the nations of earth be wandering now!" Lycidas unconsciously slackened his steps, and raised his hand to his brow. "Perhaps not *all*," he reflected; "from what I hear it appears that this Hebrew nation, this handful of conquered people groaning in bondage, hold themselves to be the sole guardians of a faith which is lofty, soul-ennobling, and pure. They deem themselves to be as a beacon on a hill set on high, throughout ages past, to show a dark world that there is still light, and a light which shall yet overspread the earth *as the waters cover the sea:* those were the words of Hadassah. And she spake also of One who should come, One looked for by the Jews, who shall bring judgment unto the Gentiles. Do the Hebrews hope for the advent of a Deity upon earth, or only that of a prophet? I would that I could see Hadassah again; and I *will* see her—I will never give up the search for one who can guide unto knowledge. Come what may, I will look upon her and on that beauteous maiden again!"

Absorbed as he was by such thoughts, there is little wonder that the young Athenian missed his way, and that he unconsciously wandered in a direction different from that which he had intended to take. The moonlight also failed him, clouds had arisen, and only now and then a fitful gleam fell on his path. Lycidas became at last uncertain even as to the direction in which

Jerusalem lay. The young Athenian was weary, less from physical fatigue than from the effects of strong excitement upon a sensitive frame. Sometimes he fancied now that he heard a stealthy step behind him, and stopped to listen, then felt assured that his senses must have deceived him, and went on his way, groping through the darkness. What a strange episode in his existence that night appeared to the Greek—scarcely a mere episode, for it seemed to him that it absorbed into itself all the true poetry of his life as regarded the past, and gave him new aspirations and hopes as regarded the future. To Lycidas the remembrance of his poetical triumph in the Olympic arena, the plaudits which had then filled his soul with ecstatic delight, was little more than to a man is the recollection of the toys which amused his childhood. The Greek had been brought face to face with life's grand realities, and what had strongly excited his ambition once appeared to him now as shadows that pass away.

"And yet," mused the young poet, "I would fain once more win the leafy crown, that I might lay it at Zarah's feet. But what would such a trophy of earthly distinction be to her? not worth one of the flowers, hallowed by her touch, which she cast into the martyrs' grave! Ha! again I fancied that I heard a rustle of garments behind me! How powerful is the imagination, that mirage of the mind, that makes us fancy the existence of things that are not!"

Lycidas had now reached a part of the road which bordered an abrupt descent to the left, the hill along whose side the path wound appearing to have been scarped in this place, probably to leave wider space for some vine-clad terrace below. Lights were gleaming in the far distance, marking the position of the city in which the guests of Antiochus, preceded by torch-bearers, were wending their way back to their several homes. Sounds of wild mirth, from those reeling back from the revels, were faintly borne on the night breeze from the distant streets.

Lycidas, however, when he reached the point whence the lights were visible, was not left a moment either to gaze or to listen.

"Dog of a Gentile—I have you!" hissed a voice from behind; and Lycidas was instantly engaged in a life or death hand-to-hand struggle with Abishai the Jew, who, as soon as he could steal away from his companions at the grave, had followed and dogged the steps of the Greek. It was almost a hopeless struggle for the young Athenian; his enemy surpassed him in strength of muscle and weight of body, wore a dagger, and was determined to use it, though some wild sense of honour had prevented Abishai from stabbing the unconscious youth without warning, when he stole upon him from behind. But the love of life is strong, and desperation gives almost supernatural power. Lycidas felt the keen blade strike him once and again, he felt his blood gushing

warm from the wounds, he caught the arm uplifted to
smite, with despair's fierce energy he endeavoured to
wrench the murderous weapon away. The two men
went wrestling, struggling, straining each sinew to the
utmost, drawing nearer, inch by inch, to the brink of
the steep descent. Abishai dropped his dagger in the
struggle, and could not stoop to attempt to recover it in
the darkness, but he grasped with his sinewy hand the
gasping youth by the locks, and, with a gigantic effort,
hurled him over the edge.

With dilating eyeballs and a look of fierce triumph,
Abishai leaned over the brink, trying to distinguish
through the deepening gloom the lifeless form of his
victim.

"I have silenced the Gentile once and for ever!" cried
the fierce Hebrew through his clenched teeth. "I said
not 'Content' when the question was put, but I say it
now!" He drew back from the edge, wiped the
moisture from his heated brow, and left a red stain
upon it.

"Ere I go to rest," said the stern Jew, "I will let
Hadassah know that my arm has achieved that safety
for her and our brave companions which her wild folly
would have sacrificed. I marvel that Judas, son of Mattathias, a bold man, and deemed a wise one, should have
let himself be swayed from his purpose by the idle words
of a woman. But I trow," added Abishai with a grim

smile, "that a glance from Zarah went further with him than all the pleadings of Hadassah. It is said amongst us, their kinsmen, that these twain shall be made one; but this is no time for marrying and giving in marriage, when the unclean swine is sacrificed on God's altar, and the shadow of the idol darkens the Temple, and the sons of Abraham are given but the alternative to defile themselves or to die. The day of vengeance is at hand! may all the enemies of Judah perish as that poor wretch has perished this night!"

Abishai sought for his dagger, and found it; he then left the scene of his act of ruthless cruelty, with a conscience less troubled by so dark a deed than it would have been had he rubbed corn between his hands on the Sabbath, or neglected one of the washings prescribed by the traditions of the elders.

CHAPTER V.

THE DREAM.

AT sunrise on the following morning two women were seated on the ground in the back part of a small flat-roofed house, situated in a very secluded spot amongst the hills, not a mile from Jerusalem. They sat opposite to each other, engaged, after the manner of the East, in grinding corn, by moving round, by means of handles, the upper mill-stone upon the nether one.

The room in which they were—if room it could be termed—was a narrow place on the ground-floor, partitioned off from a larger apartment, and devoted to holding stores, and other such domestic uses. Here corn was ground, rice sifted from the husk, and occasionally weaving carried on. Large bunches of raisins hung on the walls, jars of olive-oil and honey were neatly ranged on the floor; nor lacked there stores of millet, lentiles, and dried figs, such being the food on which

chiefly subsisted the dwellers in that lonely home. A
curtain, now drawn aside, divided this store-place from
the larger front room, which opened to the road in front.
It had a door communicating with a small patch of
cultivated ground behind, in which were a few flowers
tended by women's hands, the fairest clustering round a
bright little spring which gushed from the hill on whose
steepest side the small habitation seemed to nestle.

One of the women, busy with the laborious task of
grinding, was a Hebrew servant, past the prime of her
days, but still strong to work; the other was fair and
young, her delicate frame, her slender fingers, looking
little suited for manual labour. With a very sad countenance and a heavy heart sat Zarah that morning at the
millstone engaged in her monotonous task. It was not
that she was unwilling to spend her strength in humble
toil, or that she murmured because her grandmother
Hadassah had no longer men-servants and but one maid-
servant to do her bidding. Zarah had too much of the
spirit of a Ruth to shrink from work, or to complain of
poverty, if shared with one who was to her as a mother;
nay, her cheerfulness at labour was wont to gush forth
in song. It was not a personal trial that now made the
tears flow from Zarah's lustrous eyes as she slowly turned
round the millstone; no selfish sorrow drew heavy sighs
from her bosom as she murmured to herself, "Oh, cruel
—cruel!"

" Peace be unto you, my child. You are early, and it was late ere you could retire to rest," said the voice of Hadassah, as, pale and sad in aspect, the widow lady entered the apartment.

Zarah arose from her humble posture, approached her grandmother, first meekly kissed the hem of her garment, and then received her tender embrace.

" I could not sleep," faltered the maiden ; " I dared not close my eyes lest I should dream some dream of horror. O ruthless Abishai, most cruel of men ! Will not the All-merciful, who cares for the stranger, require that young Greek's blood at his hand ?" Zarah covered her face and wept.

" His was an unrighteous and wicked deed," said Hadassah.

"And it was I who betrayed the stranger," sobbed Zarah. " It was my start and exclamation which directed the murderer's eyes to his place of concealment. I shall never be happy again."

" Nay, you did no wrong, my white dove," said Hadassah, tenderly drawing the maiden closer to her bosom ; " the guilt lies on the head of Abishai, and on his head alone. Had he not been the beloved of my dead Miriam, my only daughter, never more should that man of blood cross the threshold of Hadassah."

" I never wish to look on Abishai again !" cried Zarah, with as much of anger as her gentle nature was

capable of feeling flashing from under her long dark
lashes. "He might have trusted one whom Judas
could trust. The face of that Greek was a face which
could not deceive;" and the maiden added, but not
aloud, "the stranger—when he stood with folded arms,
so calm, so beauteous, so noble, and bowed his head, and
said, 'Content,' when his life was trembling in the
balance—looked to me as one of the goodly angels that
came to Sodom at eve. Better, if he must needs die,
that the Greek should have fallen by the javelin of my
brave kinsman Judas, than by the dagger of Abishai.—
Mother!" cried Zarah, suddenly raising her head, and
looking into the face of Hadassah with an earnest,
pleading gaze, "may we not hope that the stranger's
soul has found mercy with God? How could the young
Gentile worship One whom he knew not? His blindness
was inherited from his parents; he did not wilfully turn
away from the light. Oh, say that you think that the
All-merciful has had compassion on the murdered Greek!
Did not the Lord spare Nineveh? pitied He not even
the little ones and the cattle?"

"I do think it—I do firmly believe it," said Hadassah,
raising her eyes towards heaven. "Verily the dream
that visited me last night must have been sent to assure
me of this."

"Tell me your dream, mother," cried Zarah, who
always addressed by this title the parent of her father.

"Come with me into the front room, my child. Leave Anna to prepare our pottage of lentiles, and I will tell you my dream," said Hadassah, leading the way into what might, in a European dwelling, have been called the sitting-room. This, with the place which they had just quitted, and two sleeping-apartments above, which were reached by a rough stair on the exterior of the dwelling, constituted all the accommodation of Hadassah's small house, if we except the flat roof, surrounded by a parapet, often used by the ladies as a cool and airy retreat.

Hadassah and her grand-daughter seated themselves in a half-reclining posture upon skins that were spread on the tiled floor, and while Zarah listened with glistening eyes, the Hebrew widow told her dream to the maiden.

"Methought, in the visions of the night—for I snatched a brief hour of repose after our return from the burial—I beheld two women before me. They were both goodly to look upon, with a strange spiritual beauty not seen on this side of the tomb. The feet of the women rested not on the earth, but they gently floated above it. The air seemed purpled around them, and fragrant with the odour of myrrh. The first woman bore in her hand a scarlet cord, the other a bundle of golden corn.

"'Hadassah,' said the first, 'I am Rahab, of the doomed race of Canaan, yet received as a daughter of

Abraham. For the sake of David, born of my line, and for the sake of Him who was the Root of Jesse (Isa. xi. 10), and shall be the Branch (Isa. xi. 1), have pity upon the stranger.'

"And the second woman, who was exceeding fair, spoke to me in like manner : ' Hadassah, I am Ruth, of the guilty race of Moab, yet received as a daughter of Abraham. For the sake of David, born of my line, and for the sake of Him who was the Root of Jesse, and shall be the Branch, have pity upon the stranger.' And so the two bright visitants vanished, and I awoke."

" Would that your dream had been sent to Abishai !" exclaimed Zarah ; " then might he not through life have borne the brand-mark of Cain !"

"Hark !" cried Hadassah suddenly " was that a groan that I heard ?"

Zarah had heard the sound also, and was on her feet and at the door before Hadassah had ended the sentence.

"O mother ! it is he—the stranger—he is dying !" exclaimed Zarah, trembling as she bent over the form of Lycidas, which lay stretched on the ground, close to the threshold.

The injuries which the young Greek had received from the dagger and the fall, though severe and dangerous, had not proved fatal. The fresh morning air had restored him to consciousness. Unable to rise, Lycidas had yet managed to drag himself feebly along for some distance, till, as he reached the nearest dwelling, the strength of the Athenian had utterly failed him, and he had swooned at the door of Hadassah.

"Bear him in—he bleeds!" said Hadassah; and after calling the strong-armed Anna to aid them, the Hebrew ladies themselves carried the senseless form of the stranger into the house, and beyond the curtain-partition into that back portion of the dwelling described in the beginning of this chapter.

For some time undivided attention was given to efforts to restore consciousness to the wounded man. Hadassah, like many of her countrywomen, had knowledge of the healing art. Zarah brought of the balm of Gilead and reviving wine; Anna dragged into the inner room mats and skins, that the sufferer might have something softer to rest upon than the hard floor. Zarah and the servant then retired, by the order of Hadassah, leaving her to examine and bind up the wounds of Lycidas, which she did with tenderness and skill. When all had been done which could be done, Hadassah drew aside the curtain-screen, and rejoined Zarah and Anna in the front apartment, where the latter was engaged in removing the crimson stains left by the wounded Greek on the floor and threshold.

"Go on the road, Anna," said the widow; "carefully efface any marks by which a wounded man could be tracked to my dwelling. No one must know that the stranger is here."

"If Abishai heard of it, even your roof would not protect the youth," said Zarah, turning pale at the thought

THE WOUNDED GREEK.

of a repetition, in the sacred precincts of home, of the horrible scene of the previous night. "O mother, think you that the stranger will live?"

"He may. Youth can swim through stormy waters," replied Hadassah; "but—may I be forgiven the inhospitable thought!—I would that the Greek had come to any other house rather than to mine."

"So few visitors ever seek this spot—so few strangers ever pass it—we lead lives so retired—we can, better than most, conceal a guest," observed Zarah.

The brow of Hadassah was clouded still. In that small dwelling, with a fair girl under her care, the widow lady was unwilling to harbour for weeks, or more probably months, a man, and that man a Gentile. Anxiously she resolved the matter in her mind, but no other course seemed to open before her. She could not be guilty of the cruelty of turning the helpless sufferer out to die.

"On Abishai's account," said Hadassah, "I dare not seek out the friends of the Greek—if friends he have in Jerusalem, and ask them to bear him thence. To do that, after Abishai's murderous attempt on his life, would be to deliver over Miriam's husband to the executioner's sword. This young man is bound alike by honour and gratitude to preserve silence as to what passed by the grave ; but there is nothing to prevent him from seeking, and much to induce him to seek, retribution on a would-be assassin, who violated the pledge of safety given to the Greek. Would, 1 repeat, that this stranger had come to any house rather than mine."

" Mother, remember your dream !" exclaimed Zarah, who, in the secret depths of her heart, did not share Hadassah's regret. Compassion for the suffering, admiration for the beautiful and brave, combined to awaken in the maiden strong interest in the fate of the stranger. Zarah was well-pleased that her grandmother's hospitality should be to him some reparation for a deep wrong sustained from one of her family.

"Yes," said Hadassah thoughtfully; "that dream must have been sent to prepare me for this. The Lord hath given me a work to perform, and He will not let His servant suffer for striving to do His bidding. The wounded stranger, Gentile though he be, needs hospitality, and I dare not refuse it. If the Lord hath guided him to the home of Hadassah, the Lord will send a blessing with him." And trying to stifle her misgivings, the widow lady returned to her guest.

CHAPTER VI.

THE JOURNEY HOME.

EFORE the sun had risen above the horizon on that day, Judas, son of Mattathias, of the noble family of the Asmoneans, started on his long homeward journey. He had not reëntered Jerusalem during the night; almost as soon as he, with the assistance of Joab and Isaac, two of his companions, had filled up with earth the grave of the martyrs, he had skirted the city from the east to the west, and turned his face towards Modin.

It would scarcely have been deemed by any one who might have seen the princely Hebrew ascending the western hill with his quick, firm tread, that the greater part of the preceding night had been spent by him in severe toil and none in sleep. His soul, filled with a lofty purpose, so mastered the infirmities of the flesh, that the Asmonean seemed to himself scarcely capable of feeling fatigue, and set out, without hesitation, on a journey which would have severely tasked the powers of a strong pedestrian after long uninterrupted repose.

As he reached the highest point of one of these hills which stand round Jerusalem, like guardians of the holy and beautiful city, Judas paused and turned round to take what he felt might be a last look of Zion, over which the sun was about to rise. He gazed on the fair towers, the girdling walls, the sepulchres in the valleys, the Temple crowning the height, with that intense love which glows in the bosom of every Hebrew deserving the name, a love in which piety mingles with patriotism, glorious memories with still more glorious hopes. From the Asmonean's lips burst the words in which the Psalmist has embalmed that love for all generations,— *Beautiful for situation, the joy of the whole earth, is Mount Zion, the city of the great King. Mark ye well her bulwarks, consider her palaces; that ye may tell it to the generations following. Pray for the peace of Jerusalem: they shall prosper that love thee. Peace be within thy walls, and prosperity within thy palaces. If I forget thee, O Jerusalem, let my right hand forget her cunning; if I do not remember thee, let my tongue cleave to the roof of my mouth.*

Faith was to the Asmonean as the rosy glow preceding the sunrise, which then flushed the eastern sky. His eye rested on the Temple, now desecrated, defiled, abandoned to the Gentile, and he remembered the promise regarding it : *The Lord, whom ye seek, shall suddenly come to His Temple, even the Messenger of the Covenant, whom ye delight in* (Mal. iii. 1). Then the Hebrew's gaze wandered beyond to a fair hill, clothed with verdure, and his faith grasped the promise of God : *Then shall the Lord go forth...... and His feet shall stand in that day upon the Mount of Olives* (Zech. xiv. 3, 4). Hope and joy were kindled at the thought. As surely as the hill itself should remain, so surely should a Temple stand on Mount Zion, till the Messiah should appear within it. *God is not a man, that He should lie: neither the son of man, that He should repent: hath He said, and shall He not do it?* (Num. xxiii. 19).

"Oh, that the Messiah might come in my day!" exclaimed the Asmonean; "that my eyes might behold the King in His beauty; that my voice might join the united acclamations of Israel, when the Son of David shall be seated on the throne of His fathers, and His enemies shall be made His footstool! That I might see the whole world worshipping in the presence of the Seed of the woman who shall bruise the serpent's head!" (Gen. iii. 15.) The Hebrew grasped his javelin more firmly, and his dark eye dilated with joy and triumph. "But the night is not yet past for Israel," he added, more sadly ; "the voice is not yet *heard in the wilderness, Prepare ye the way of the Lord* (Isa. xl. 3); we may have yet much to do and to suffer ere the Sun of Righteousness arise."

Then a softened expression stole over the features of the Asmonean, as he gazed in another direction, but still with his face turned towards the east. He could not see a white dwelling nestling under the shadow of a hill, but he knew well where it lay, and where she abode to whom he had bidden on that night a long, perhaps a last farewell. The Asmonean stretched out his hand, and exclaimed, "Oh! Father of the fatherless, guard and bless her! To Thy care I commit the treasure of my soul!" And without trusting himself to linger longer, Judas turned and went on his way.

It was the month of Shebet, answering to the latter part of our January, and Palestine was already bright with the beauty of early spring. The purple mandrake was in flower, the crocus, tulip, and hyacinth enamelled the fields, with the blue lily contrasting with thousands of scarlet anemones. The almond-tree and the peach were in flower, and fragrant sighed the breeze over blossoms of lemon and citron. The winter had this year been mild, and some figs left from the last season still clung to the boughs yet bare of foliage. The vine on the terraced hills was bursting into leaf, and already in the fields the rising corn showed its young blades above the ground. But Judas was too much absorbed with his own thoughts to pay much attention to the landscape around him; with Israel the spiritual winter was not over, her time for the singing of birds had not come.

Onwards pressed the traveller without resting, till at about noonday he reached the valley of Ajalon. There was a fountain by the side of the road, and here the weary man slaked his thirst, and sat down for awhile to rest beneath the shade of some date-palms. The Asmonean took from the scrip which he carried his simple repast of dried figs, laved his brow and hands in the cooling water, blessed God for his food, and began to eat.

Ere many minutes had elapsed, a woman in the widow's garb of mourning, bearing a child of about six years old on her back, dragged her weary steps to the fountain by which the traveller was seated. She placed her boy on the ground, drank of the water herself, and gave to her son to drink. Her appearance denoted extreme poverty, and the child was evidently suffering from sickness.

Judas divided his slender supply of provisions into three portions, and with the courteous salutation of " Peace be with you," offered one to the widow, and one to the boy.

" The blessing of the God of Abraham be with you!" exclaimed the poor woman; " your servant hath not tasted food since sunset." And, seated on the turf not far from Judas, the widow and her son partook of the dried figs with the eagerness of those who are well-nigh famished.

"Your child looks ill," observed the Asmonean, regarding with compassion the wasted, shrunken frame of the boy.

"He will not suffer long," replied the widow, with the calm apathy of despair. "I laid his father's head in the grave last month, and I shall lay Terah's head beside him this month. The seal of death is upon him; I shall soon be alone in the world."

"Nay, despair not,—God is good; the child may yet live," said Judas.

"Why should I wish him to live?" murmured the widow. "His father was taken from the evil to come, the boy will be taken from the evil to come. Jerusalem is defiled, the land is in bondage, Israel is given a prey to the heathen! The faithful are few in the land, and persecution will sweep these few away. There is no resting-place but under the sod, no freedom but in the grave. The name of Judah will soon be blotted out from amongst the nations!"

"Never!" exclaimed Judas, with energy; "never, while the God of Truth lives and reigns! Judah can never perish. The vine that was brought out of Egypt may be broken, her branches torn away, her fruit scattered, the boar out of the wood may waste it, and the wild beast of the field devour, but yet *Israel shall blossom and bud, and fill the face of the world with fruit* (Isa. xxvii. 6). Were but one man left of God's chosen people, yet from that one man should spring the Deliverer who shall yet speak peace to the nations, and reign for ever and ever!"

"Could I but hope—" faltered the widow.

"Can you not *believe?*" exclaimed the Asmonean. "See yonder—look to the east—there is Gibeon, over which the sun stayed at the voice of Joshua; over this valley of Ajalon hung the moon arrested in her course in the day when the Amorites fled before Israel. He who raised up Moses, Joshua, and Gideon, can by human instruments, or without them, repeat the miracles wrought of old, and again deliver His people."

As he concluded the last sentence the Asmonean rose to continue his journey; he could give his weary limbs but little time for rest, for long was the distance which he yet had to traverse.

"My home is but a furlong further on," said the widow, also rising, "and I have again strength to go forward."

She was about to lift up her boy, but Judas prevented her. "I can relieve you of that burden," he said, and raised the child on his shoulders.

They had proceeded for some way in silence, the widow pondering over the speech of the wayfaring man, when from behind was heard the clatter of hoofs and the

JUDAS AND THE WIDOW'S SON.

jingle of steel.   The child, whom the Asmonean was
carrying, turned to gaze, and exclaimed in fear, as he
grasped the locks of his protector, " See—horsemen in
bright armour, with banners and spears!—fly, fly!—the
Syrians are coming!"

Judas did not turn nor alter his pace, he merely went
closer to the side of the cactus-bordered road, to give
more space to the horsemen to pass him.   On rode the
Syrians in goodly array, their steel glittering in the sunlight, the dust rising like a cloud around the hoofs of

their horses. In the centre of the line was a gorgeous arabah, or covered cart with curtains, to which the troop of soldiers appeared to form an escort. There was an opening in the roof of this arabah, evidently for the convenience of accommodating within it a figure too high to be otherwise carried in the conveyance, for out of the opening appeared a white marble head of Grecian statuary Judas and his companion regarded it with the aversion and horror with which the sight of an idol always inspired pious Jews.

When the Syrians had passed the travellers, and the clatter of their arms had died away in the distance, the widow wrung her hands and exclaimed, " Yonder ride Apelles and his men of war to Modin, to do the bidding of the tyrant; and they bear the accursed thing with them, to be set up on high and worshipped. Alas! they will compel all the Hébrews at Modin to bow down to their idol of stone."

" Perhaps not," said Judas calmly.

"All men will be forced to offer sacrifice," cried the woman ; "there will be no way of escaping the pollution."

"Solomona and her sons found one way," observed the Asmonean, "and God may provide yet another."

The traveller had now reached the door of the widow's humble dwelling. Judas set down his living burden, and the mother thanked the kind stranger, and asked him to come in and rest.

"I cannot abide here," replied Judas; "a long journey is yet before me; I must be at Modin this night."

"At Modin!" exclaimed the astonished woman, glancing up at the worn, weary countenance of the speaker. "Why, the horsemen will scarcely reach Modin this night, unless, indeed, the king's business be urgent."

"My King's business is urgent," said the Asmonean, as he tightened his girdle around him, and with a grave, courteous salutation to the woman, he went on his way.

The widow watched his princely form for some time in silence, then exclaimed, "That can be none other than Judas, the son of Mattathias; there is not a second Hebrew such as he. Ah, my Terah," she added, addressing herself to her son, "there is a man whom the Syrians will not frighten."

"He will rather frighten the Syrians," said the boy.

Many a time was that childish saying repeated in after-days, as if it had been prophetic, when Judah had long had rest from her foes, and Terah himself was an old man. When he sat beneath his own vine and fig-tree, no man making him afraid, he never wearied describing to his grand-children that form which had made the earliest impression which his memory had retained. He would speak with kindling enthusiasm of the princely man who had taken him in his arms and carried him on his shoulders—who had been as tender to a sick child, as he had afterwards been terrible to Israel's foes.

The sun had just sunk when the foot of the Asmonean trod the green valley of Sharon. It was well that from thence every step of the way was familiar to Judas, for he had soon no light but that of the stars to guide him. The wind was rising; it rustled amidst the tamarisks, and shook the leafy crests of the evergreen palms; it bore to the ear of the almost exhausted traveller the wild howl of the jackals, rising higher and higher in pitch, like the wail of a human being in distress. Weary indeed and footsore was the Asmonean, but still he bravely pressed forward, till at length he heard the welcome sound of the waves of the Mediterranean lashing the coast near which stood Modin, about an English mile from the town of Joppa.

Thankful was Judas to reach his father's home, where, the heavy strain upon his powers being for awhile relaxed, he slept the deep sweet sleep of the weary, after a journey which could have been accomplished on foot in a single day only by a man possessing great powers of endurance, as well as physical strength.

CHAPTER VII.

THE arrival of Apelles, the emissary of Antiochus Epiphanes, had thrown the town of Modin into a state of great excitement. A proclamation was made in the morning of the following day, that all the inhabitants, men, women, and children, should assemble in the market-place at noon, to obey the mandate of the king, by worshipping at an altar of Bacchus, which was erected at that spot. "Curses, not loud but deep," were muttered in many a Hebrew home. Some of the Syrian soldiers had been quartered for the night with the inhabitants of Modin. The fatted calf had to be killed, the best wine poured out, for idolatrous guests whose very presence polluted a banquet. The Syrians repaid the reluctant hospitality of their hosts by recital of all the horrors of the persecution in Jerusalem. They told of the barbarities perpetrated on Solomona and her sons; shuddering women clasped their children closer to their bosoms as they heard how two mothers had been flung from the battlements at the south side of the Temple, with their infants hung round their necks, because they had dedicated those martyr-babes to God in the way commanded by Moses. Such examples of cruelty struck terror into the hearts of all whose faith and courage were not strong. It was evident that Antiochus was terribly in earnest, and that if his wrath were aroused by opposition, the horrors which had been witnessed at Jerusalem might be repeated at Modin. The plea of terrible necessity half silenced the consciences of many Hebrews who secretly abhorred the rites of the heathen. A quantity of ivy was gathered, and twined by unwilling hands, to be worn in honour of the false deity whose worship was to be forced upon a reluctant people.

A lofty shrine on which was raised a marble image of the god of wine, with his temples crowned with ivy, a bunch of grapes in his hand, and sensuality stamped on every feature, was erected in the centre of the market-place. Before it was the altar of sacrifice, and around this, as the hour of noon approached, collected a motley crowd. There were the white-robed priests of Bacchus, with the victims chosen for sacrifice. Men of war, both on foot and on horseback, formed a semicircle about the shrine, to enforce, if necessary, compliance with the decree of the Syrian monarch. Apelles himself, magnifi-

cently attired, with tunic of Tyrian purple, jewelled
sandals, and fringes of gold, sat on a lofty seat on the
right side of the altar, awaiting the appointed time when
the sun should reach his meridian height. Numbers of
people filled the market-place, of both sexes, and of every
age, for the soldiery had swept through Modin, forcing
all the inhabitants to quit their dwellings and assemble
to offer sacrifice upon the altar of Bacchus.

Directly opposite to the altar there was one group of
Hebrews conspicuous above all the rest, and towards this
group the eyes of the assembled people were frequently
turned. There stood Mattathias, with snowy beard de-
scending to his girdle—a venerable patriarch, surrounded
by his five stalwart sons. There appeared Johannan,
the first-born; Simon, with his calm intellectual brow;
Eleazar, with his quick glance of fire; Jonathan; and
Judas, third in order of birth, but amongst those illustrious brethren already first in fame. In stern silence the
Asmonean family watched the preparations made by the
Syrian priests to celebrate their unhallowed rites. Not
a word escaped the lips of the Hebrews; they stood
almost as motionless as statues, only their glances be-
traying the secret indignation of their souls.

Mattathias, as a direct descendant of Aaron through
Phineas, and a man of great wisdom and spotless in-
tegrity, possessed great influence within his native city
of Modin. Disputes were referred to his decision, his

judgment was appealed to in cases of difficulty, and his example was likely to carry with it greater weight than that of any other man in Judæa. Apelles was perfectly aware of this. "Mattathias once gained, all is gained," the Syrian courtier had said to the king before departing on his mission to Modin; "the old man's sons have no law but his will, and if the Asmoneans bow their heads in worship, all Judæa will join in offering sacrifice to your gods."

Anxious to win over by soft persuasions the only Hebrews whose opposition could cause any difficulty in the execution of the king's commands, when the hour for offering sacrifice had almost arrived, Apelles descended from his seat of state, and approached the Asmonean group. This unexpected movement of the Syrian awakened eager attention amongst the assembled crowds.

"Venerable Mattathias," said Apelles, saluting the old man with stately courtesy, "your high position, your wide-spread fame, entitle you to the place of leader in performing the solemn act by which Modin at once declares her fealty to our mighty monarch, Antiochus Epiphanes, and her devotion to the worship of Bacchus. Now, therefore, come you first and fulfil the king's commandment, like as all the heathen have done, yea, and the men of Judah also, and such as remain at Jerusalem; so shall you and your house be in the number of the king's friends, and you and your children shall be

MATTATHIAS BEFORE APELLES.

honoured with silver and gold and many rewards."
When the Syrian had ceased speaking, the silence
amongst the expectant people was so profound
that the roll of the billows on the beach, and the

scream of a white-winged sea-bird, could be distinctly heard.

Sternly the old man had heard Apelles to the end; then fixing upon him the keen eyes which flashed under the white overhanging brows, like volcano fire bursting from beneath a mountain crest of snow, he replied, in tones so loud that they rang all over the market-place, "Though all the nations that are under the king's dominion obey him, and fall away every one from the religion of their fathers, and give consent to his commandments, yet will I and my sons and my brethren walk in the covenant of our fathers. God forbid that we should forsake the law and the ordinances! We will not hearken to the king's words to go from our religion, either on the right hand or the left."

Hardly had the brave words died on the ears of those who heard them, when, in strange contrast, there sounded a hymn in honour of Bacchus, and, gaily dressed and crowned with ivy, a wretched apostate Jew, eager to win the king's favour by being the first to obey his will, came forward singing towards the altar. All the blood of Phineas boiled in the veins of his descendant; was the Lord of Hosts to be thus openly insulted, His judgments thus impiously defied! Forward sprang the old Asmonean, as if once more endowed with youth, one moment his dagger glittered in the sunlight, the next moment the apostate groaned out his soul upon the altar of Bacchus!

To execute justice in this summary manner, and before all the people, was indeed to draw the sword and throw the scabbard away. A fierce shout for vengeance arose from the Syrian soldiers, and their ranks closed around Mattathias, but not around him alone. Not for a minute had his sons deserted his side, and now, like lions at bay, they united in the defence of their father. Nor were they to maintain the struggle unaided. There were Hebrews amongst the assembled crowds to whom the voice of Mattathias had been as the trumpet-call to the war-horse; there were men who counted their holy faith as dearer than life. These, with shouts, rushed to the rescue, and the market-place of Modin became the scene of a hand-to-hand desperate struggle, where discipline and numbers on the one side, devotion, heroism, and a good cause on the other, maintained a fearful strife. Though sharp, it was but a brief one. The fight was thickest near the altar—around it flowed the blood of human victims; there the powerful arm of Judas laid Apelles lifeless in the dust. This was the crisis of the struggle, for at the fall of their leader the Syrians were seized with sudden panic. The horses, whose trappings had glittered so gaily, were either urged by their riders to frantic speed, or dashed with emptied saddles through the throng, to carry afar the news of defeat. Flight was all that was left to the troops of Antiochus or the priests of Bacchus, and few succeeded in making their escape, for many Jews who had stood aloof from the struggle joined in the pursuit. The very women caught up stones from the path to fling at the flying foe; children's voices swelled the loud shout of triumph. The altar of Bacchus was thrown down with wild exultation; the idol was broken to pieces, and its fragments were rolled in the blood-stained dust. Those Jews who had shown most fear an hour before, now by more furious zeal tried to efface from other minds and their own the memory of their former submission. One spirit seemed to animate all—the spirit of freedom! Modin had arisen like Samson, when he snapped the green withes and went forth to the fight with the strength of a giant.

But this was an ebullition of zeal likely to be more fiery than lasting. Mattathias little trusted that courage which only follows in the train of success. The old man knew that the struggle with the power of Syria was only commencing; that it would probably be long protracted, and that it would be impracticable to defend Modin against the hosts which would soon be sent to assail it. The patriarch stood in the centre of the market-place, with his foot on the fragments of the broken altar, and once more his loud clear voice rang far and wide. "Whosoever is zealous of the law, and maintaineth the Covenant, let him follow me! Let us away to the mountains, ye men of Judah!"

How many of the inhabitants of Modin obeyed the

call? how many resolved to leave city and home, to dwell with the beasts in the caves of the mountains? History relates that but a little band of *ten*, inclusive of the Asmoneans, by retiring to the fastnesses of the mountains, formed the nucleus of that brotherhood of heroes who were to wrest victory after victory from the hosts of Syria, and win that unsullied fame which belongs only to those who display firm endurance and devoted courage in a righteous and holy cause.

CHAPTER VIII.

HADASSAH'S GUEST.

IN no place were the tidings of the rising at Modin received with greater exultation than in the lonely dwelling of Hadassah. The Hebrew widow could hardly refrain from taking down the timbrel from the wall, and bursting, like Miriam, into song. *"Sing unto the Lord, for He hath triumphed gloriously! He hath dashed to pieces the enemy!"*

Constant information of what was occurring, every rumour, true or false, whether of victory or of failure, was brought to Hadassah by her son-in-law, Abishai, who little dreamed that every word which he uttered was overheard by the wounded Athenian, from whom he was divided but by the partitioning curtain!

In one of his visits to Hadassah, Abishai told how Judas had in the mountains raised a standard, which bore the inscription, "Who is like unto Thee among the gods, O Jehovah!"

" It is said," observed Abishai, " that from the initial
letters of this inscription the word MACCABEUS is formed,
and that by this new title Judas is commonly called;
it is a name which the Syrians will soon have cause to
dread."

" It is a well-chosen name!" cried Hadassah.   " Let
the Asmonean be called *Makke-baiah* (a conqueror in the
Lord), for doubtless the God whom he serves will give
to him the victory!"

The triumphant joy of the patriotic Hadassah received
a painful check when she heard some time afterwards
from Abishai of the grievous sacrifice of the lives of a
thousand faithful Hebrews, who had taken refuge in a
cave at no great distance from Jerusalem.   Being attacked there on the Sabbath-day by the Syrians, these
Hebrews had actually let themselves be slaughtered without resistance, rather than incur sin (as they thought) by
breaking the Fourth Commandment!   Grieved at this
waste of precious life, it was a relief to Hadassah to
learn that such a sacrifice to a mistaken sense of duty
would not be repeated; for when the tidings had reached
Mattathias and his sons, they had bitterly mourned for
their slaughtered countrymen, and had said one to another, " If we all do as our brethren have done, and
fight not for our lives and laws against the heathen,
they will quickly root us out of the earth."   A decree,
therefore, was sent forth from the camp in the moun-

tains, that to Hebrews attacked on the Sabbath-day, self-defence was lawful and right.

In the meantime, under the care of Hadassah, the wounds of Lycidas were gradually healing. Never to any man had confinement and suffering been more sweetened, for was he not near to Zarah; did he not hear the soft music of her voice, breathe the same air, even see her light form gliding past the entrance of his hiding-place, though the maiden never entered it? The necessity of concealing the presence of Lycidas, above all from the blood-thirsty Abishai, compelled the closing during the daytime of the door at the back of the dwelling which opened on the small piece of ground behind. Peasants or travellers would occasionally, though rarely, come to fill their pitchers or slake their thirst at the little fountain gushing from the hill, and had the door of what Lycidas playfully called his "den" been open, there would have been nothing to prevent strangers from seeing or entering within. The whole ventilation of the confined space occupied by the invalid depended therefore during the daytime on its communication with the front room, which might be called the only public apartment, and in which not only food was now prepared and taken, and the occasional guest received, but in which the Hebrew ladies pursued their daily avocations. Here Zarah would pursue her homely occupation of spinning, and Hadassah copy out on rolls of vellum

portions from the Law and the Prophets. This latter
occupation was fraught with peril; and had Hadassah
been discovered in the act of transcribing from the sacred
pages, it might have cost her her life. Antiochus had
eagerly sought to destroy all copies of the Scriptures, or
to profane them by having vile pictures painted on the
margins. To possess—far more to copy out—God's
Holy Word was now a capital offence. But the faith of
Hadassah seemed to raise her above all personal fear;
the peril connected with her pious labours made her but
more earnestly pursue them. The presence of the young
Gentile in her dwelling was a source of far greater un
easiness to the widow than any danger which threatened
herself.

Had Hadassah been able to seclude her patient entirely, she would willingly have discharged the duties of
hospitality towards him; but such seclusion the scanty
accommodation of her dwelling would have rendered
impossible, even had Lycidas been willing to submit to
perfect isolation. But this was by no means the case.
Not only did he require the curtain frequently to be
drawn back to enable him freely to breathe; but the
Greek, as his strength increased, was eager to be seen
as well as to see, and to speak as well as to listen. No
anxious warnings of danger to be apprehended from the
sudden entrance of Abishai could prevent Lycidas from
dragging his languid limbs beyond the limits which the

curtain defined, and joining in social converse. Lycidas resolutely shut his eyes to the fact that, to his hostess at least, his presence was unwelcome. He deceived himself into the belief that he was rather repaying the kindness which he had received, by lightening the dulness of the secluded lives led by the Hebrew ladies. The young

SOCIAL CONVERSE.

Athenian drew forth for their amusement all the rich stores of his cultivated mind. Now he recited wondrous tales of other lands; now gave vivid descriptions of adventures of his own; poetry flowed spontaneously from his lips like a stream—now sparkling with fancy, now deepening into pathos: Lycidas had in Athens been compared to Apollo, as much for his mental gifts as his singular personal beauty.

To the brilliant conversation of the stranger, so unlike what she ever had heard before, Zarah listened with innocent pleasure. She was ever obedient to her aged relative, and often did Hadassah's bidding in the upper rooms of the dwelling, even when it seemed to the maiden that she was sent on needless errands; but the light form, in its simple blue garment, with the long linen veil thrown back from the graceful head, was always returning to the apartment, to which it was drawn by a new and powerful attraction. If Hadassah sometimes appeared irritable and imperious towards the fair young being whom she loved, it was because her mind was disturbed, her rest broken by anxieties which she could impart to no one. The aged lady scarcely knew which evil she most dreaded: the discovery of Lycidas by Abishai—a discovery which would inevitably stain her threshold with blood—or the long sojourn under her roof of the dangerous stranger, whom she had unwillingly admitted, and now more unwillingly retained in her home.

CHAPTER IX.

DEATH OF MATTATHIAS.

WILD was the life led by Mattathias and his followers in the mountains—a life of danger and hardship; danger met manfully, hardship endured cheerfully. Amongst wild rocks, heaped together like the fragments of an elder world torn asunder by some fearful convulsion of Nature, the band of heroes found their home. Where the hyæna has its den, and the leopard its lair, where the timid wabber or coney hides in the stony clefts, there the Hebrews lurked in caves, and manned the gigantic fastnesses which no human hands had reared, and from which it would be no easy task for any enemy to dislodge them.

The small band that had rallied round Mattathias when he withdrew from Modin, had been soon joined by other bold and zealous sons of Abraham, and the mountains became a place of refuge to many who fled

from persecution.   As numbers increased, so did the
difficulty of procuring means of subsistence.   The Asmoneans and their followers chiefly lived upon roots.
The less hardy of the band suffered severely from the
chill of the frosts, the keenness of the sharp mountain
air, the sharp winds that blew over snow-clad heights.
But no voice of complaint was heard.   Frequent forays
were made into the plains; idol-altars were thrown
down, forts were burned, detachments of Syrians cut
off.   None of the enemy within many miles of the
rocky haunts of the Asmoneans lay down to rest at
night feeling secure from sudden attack during the hours
of darkness; and oft-times the early morning light
showed a heap of smouldering ruins where, on the evening before, the banners of Syria had waved on the walls
of some well-manned fortress.

To the bold spirit of Maccabeus there was something
congenial in the adventurous kind of existence which he
led, and yet he was not one who would have adopted a
guerrilla life from choice.   As even in a hard and rocky
waste there are spots where rich vegetation betrays some
source of hidden nourishment below, and they who dig
deep enough under the surface find a spring of bright
pure living waters,—so deep within the Asmonean's
heart lay a hidden source of tenderness which prevented
his nature from becoming hardened by the stern neces-
sities of warfare.   This secret affection made the warrior

more chivalrous to women, more indulgent to the weak, more compassionate to all who suffered. In the moment of triumph, " Will not Zarah rejoice ? " was the thought which made victory more sweet; in preservation from imminent danger, the thought, " Zarah has been praying for me," made deliverance doubly welcome. When the evening star gleamed in the sky, its pure soft guiding orb seemed to Judas an emblem of Zarah ; as he gazed on it, the warrior would indulge in delicious musings. This desperate warfare might not last for ever. If the Lord of Sabaoth should bless the arms of His servants, might not the time come when swords should be beaten into ploughshares, when children should play fearlessly in pastures which no oppressor's foot should tread, and the sound of bridal rejoicings be heard in the land of the free ? Hopes so intensely delightful would then steal over the Asmonean's soul, that he would suddenly start like a sentinel who finds himself dropping asleep on his post. How dared the leader of Israel's forlorn hope indulge in reveries which made him feel how precious a thing life might be to himself, when he had freely devoted that life to the service of God and his country ? When David was engaged in rescuing his flock from the lion and the bear, did he stop to gather the lilies of the field ? " It is well," thought Judas Maccabeus, " that I have never told Zarah what is in my heart ; if I fall, as I shall probably fall, on

the field of conflict, I would not leave her to the grief
of a widow."

An event was at hand which was felt as a heavy
blow by all to whom the cause of Israel was dear, but
more especially so by the Asmonean brethren, who from
their childhood had regarded their father with reverence
and affection.

Mattathias was an aged man, and though his spirit
never sank under toil and hardship, his constitution soon
gave way under their effects. The patriarch felt that
his days, nay, that his hours were numbered, and sum-
moned his sons around him to hear his last wishes, and
to receive his parting blessing.

In a cave near the foot of a mountain, stretched upon
a soft couch of skins of animals slain in the chase, lay
the venerable man. The pallor of death was already on
his face, but its expression was tranquil and calm. The
aged pilgrim looked like one who feels indeed that he
has God's rod and staff to lean on while he is passing
through the valley of the shadow of death. The full
glare of noonday was glowing on the world without, but
softened and subdued was the light which struggled into
the cave, and fell on the form of the dying man, and the
stalwart figures of the Asmonean brothers bending in
mute sorrow around their honoured parent.

Mattathias bade his sons raise him a little, that he
might speak to them with more ease. Jonathan and

Eleazar, kneeling, supported him in their arms; while their
three brothers, in the same attitude of respect, listened
silently at his side to the patriarch's farewell address.

MATTATHIAS' FAREWELL ADDRESS.

I shall not dare to add words of my own to those
which the historian has preserved as the dying utterances of this noble old man—a hero, and the father of
heroes.   I give them as they fell upon the ears of Judas
Maccabeus and his brothers, who received them as Joseph
received the parting blessing of Israel.

"Now hath pride and rebuke gotten strength, and
the time of destruction, and the wrath of indignation.

Now, therefore, my sons, be ye zealous for the law, and give your lives for the covenant of your fathers. Call to remembrance what acts our fathers did in their time, so shall ye receive great honour and an everlasting name.

"Was not Abraham found faithful in temptation, and it was imputed unto him for righteousness. Elias, for being zealous and fervent for the law, was taken up into heaven. Ananias, Azarias, and Misael, by believing were saved out of the flame. Daniel, for his innocence, was delivered from the mouth of the lion. And thus, consider ye, throughout all ages, that none that put their trust in Him shall be overcome. Wherefore, ye my sons, be valiant, and show yourselves men in behalf of the law; for by it ye shall obtain glory."

The old man paused, as if to gather strength, and then stretching forth his wasted hand towards Simon, his second son, he went on:

"Behold, I know that your brother Simon is a man of counsel; give ear unto him alway; he shall be a father unto you."

Then the hand was again extended, and this time laid on the bowed head of Maccabeus:

"As for Judas Maccabeus," said the dying man, in firmer accents, as if the very name inspired him with vigour, "he hath been mighty and strong, even from his youth up; let him be your captain, and fight the battle of the people."

There was no murmur of dissent, not even a glance of jealousy from the eye of the generous Johannan, when his younger brothers were thus preferred before him, as superior in those qualities with which leaders should be endowed. Johannan knew, and was content to acknowledge, that the wisdom of Simon and the military talents of Judas far exceeded his own; he would serve with them, and serve under them, cheerfully submissive to the will of God and the counsels of his father. We find not the slightest trace of jealous rivalry amongst that glorious band of brethren, who all shared the privilege of suffering—three of dying—for their country.

Then, after solemnly blessing his five sons, Mattathias departed in peace, as one who has fought a good fight, and kept the faith to the end. Great lamentation was made throughout Judæa for him in whom the nation had lost a parent. The sons of Mattathias carried his body to Modin, and buried it in the sepulchre of his fathers.

In after-times of prosperity and peace Simon raised a fair monument of marble, in the form of seven lofty pillars, which could be seen from afar by those sailing over the blue waters of the Mediterranean. The Asmonean prince placed this memorial there in honour of his parents and their five sons, after Jonathan, Eleazar, and Judas Maccabeus had sealed with their brave blood the testimony of their devotion to the cause of faith and of freedom.

CHAPTER X.

CONCEALMENT.

WE will now return to the quiet dwelling-place of Hadassah, where Lycidas day by day was becoming more hopelessly entangled in the silken meshes which kept him a willing captive in the Hebrew home. The very danger of his position served to add to its charms. It was with keen gratification that the Greek marked the anxiety which Zarah felt on his account. Whenever Lycidas emerged from his "den," Zarah kept careful watch as she sat at her wheel near the front entrance of the dwelling, ready to give timely notice of the approach of any intruder. The wave of the maiden's hand gave sufficient warning to the Greek. The view from the doorway commanded a long enough tract of road to render it impossible for any visitor to enter the house so suddenly as to prevent Lycidas, thus warned, from having time to retreat behind his curtain.

An occasion, however, arose when the gentle sentinel was at last found off her guard. Resting on his arm, with his form half reclining on the floor, Lycidas was giving to Hadassah an account of the defence of Thermopylæ, while his eyes were fixed on Zarah, who sat listening with her whole attention absorbed by the thrilling tale, when Abishai, breathless with excitement, rushed so suddenly into the house that Zarah was not aware of his coming in time to give her accustomed signal. It was Hadassah who heard the sound of rapid footsteps, though not till they had almost crossed the threshold. With great presence of mind the widow flung over Lycidas a large striped mantle of goat-hair, which she was preparing for Judas Maccabeus, should any opportunity arise of conveying it to the Asmonean leader. Hadassah then shifted her position, so as to interpose her own form between her guest and the door. These movements were so rapid as to take less time in the action than the narration.

"Why, child, you look as much startled and terrified as if the Syrians were upon you!" exclaimed Abishai to Zarah, catching sight of her look of terror. His own eyes were flashing with triumph, and his gestures betrayed his excitement as he continued, "I bring you tidings of victory—glorious victory—achieved by our hero, Judas Maccabeus. Apollonius—may the graves of his fathers be polluted!—Apollonius, who tore down the dwellings near Mount Zion to make fortifications of the stones, he himself is laid low! The murderer, the oppressor, the instrument of a tyrant, and almost more hateful than the tyrant himself, now lies in his gore, and his mighty army has fled before the warriors of Judah!"

"The Lord of Hosts be praised!" exclaimed Hadassah. "Tell us, my son, of the fight," and she motioned to Abishai to take his seat beside her, so that his back should be turned towards Lycidas. The Jew seated himself so near to the Greek that the folds of his upper garment touched the mantle under which Lycidas lay crouched. If Abishai but moved his hand a few inches, he must feel that a warm and living form was concealed under the goat-hair stripes.

"How your cheek changes colour, child!" exclaimed Abishai, surveying with surprise his young niece, who could not disguise her terror, nor prevent her knees from trembling beneath her as she stood in the doorway. "You have no cause to fear; Maccabeus is not even wounded. Apollonius met him in fight, and fell by his hand. Henceforth Judas, it is said, declares that he will always use as his own the sword which he took from the vanquished Syrian. As David said when he grasped that of Goliath, 'There is no weapon like that.'"

Zarah scarcely heard the words addressed to her. One thought possessed her mind to the exclusion of every other—the peril of the wounded Athenian. Should any sound or movement betray his presence to her fanatic uncle, she knew that the doom of Lycidas would be sealed, for he was yet by far too weak to defend himself with the faintest chance of success, and his recumbent position rendered him utterly helpless.

Hadassah anxiously watched the countenance of Zarah, and read the thoughts passing within. Fearing that the maiden would faint where she stood, Hadassah motioned to her to come closer to her and take her seat at her feet. Zarah obeyed, taking care to be near enough to Abishai to catch him by the knees, and with what little strength she possessed at least to impede his movements should he discover the presence of the Greek.

"Judas has brought great honour to our race," exclaimed Abishai, who attributed the emotion of his niece to a cause very different from the real one. "In his acts he is like a lion, and like a lion's whelp roaring for his prey. He has pursued the wicked, and sought them out; he has destroyed the ungodly, thrown down their altars, and turned away wrath from Israel."

"He is a mighty instrument in the hands of the Lord," said Hadassah.

"Is he not something more?" exclaimed Abishai, his manner becoming yet more excited; "may not the time for the great deliverance be come, and the great Deliverer be amongst us, of whom it is written, *Mine own arm brought salvation unto Me; and My fury, it upheld Me.*

And I will tread down the people in Mine anger, and make them drunk in My fury, and I will bring down their strength to the earth" (Isa. lxiii. 5, 6). Wild hope gleamed in the Hebrew's fierce eyes as he spoke, and he started upright on his feet.

"Shame to you, son of Nathan," said Hadassah with dignity, "you speak like one who knows not the writings of the Prophets. He that shall come, the Messiah, is to be of the tribe of Judah, not that of Levi (Isa. xi. 1), shall be born at Bethlehem, not at Modin (Mic. v. 11). Nor have the prophetical weeks of Daniel yet run out. *Know therefore and understand, that from the going forth of the commandment to restore and to build Jerusalem unto the Messiah the Prince shall be seven weeks, and threescore and two weeks* (Dan. ix. 25). The set time is not come."

The wild animation of Abishai sank under the calm rebuke of one who as much excelled him in knowledge and intellectual power as he surpassed her in physical strength. He looked abashed at being convicted of ignorance of prophetic writings.

"You know, O Hadassah," said the Hebrew, "that I have been from my youth a man of the sword rather than of the book. Nor can I now study if I would. You are aware how Antiochus has sought out our holy writings to destroy or pollute them. Save the copy of the Scriptures which I occasionally see at the house of the elder, Salathiel, when we meet there by stealth to worship God on the Sabbath, my eyes never so much as look on the roll of the holy Word."

"I have a complete copy of the Psalms and Prophets, and am making from it another," said Hadassah, intuitively lowering her tone, and glancing at the door.

"A noble but dangerous work!" cried Abishai.

"Go and look yonder, my son, glance up the path to the right and the left, see whether any of the heathen be near," said Hadassah, pointing to the door as she spoke. "If none of the enemy be in sight, I will show you the sacred treasure which I hold at risk of my life."

Abishai instantly left the dwelling, half closing the door behind him.

"Now, Lycidas! oh, haste!" exclaimed Zarah in an eager whisper. She was terrified lest the opportunity of retreat which Hadassah had given should be lost by one moment's delay.

There was no need to repeat the word. Lycidas instantly drew back into his retreat behind the curtain, and the Hebrew ladies could breathe more freely again. Zarah gave a bright joyous glance at Hadassah, but it met no answering smile. The widow's features wore a sad, almost indignant expression, the sight of which shot a keen pang through the gentle heart of Zarah. What had she done, what had she said, that her venerated relative should look on her thus? Had there been

aught in her conduct unseemly? She had called the
Gentile by his name; could it be that which had drawn
upon her the unwonted displeasure of Hadassah?

As she asked herself such questions, the cheek of
Zarah became suffused with crimson. She scarcely knew
what caused the painful embarrassment which she felt.
She seemed to herself like one detected in doing evil,
and yet her conscience had nothing wherewith to reproach her as concerned her conduct towards her grandmother's guest. So uneasy was the maiden, however,
that on Abishai's return she did not stay to hear the
conversation which ensued between him and Hadassah,
but glided up the outer stair to the roof of the house,
where, seated alone on the flat roof, with only heaven's
blue canopy above her, she could commune with her own
heart, and question it regarding the nature of the dangerous interest which she felt in the Gentile stranger.

CHAPTER XI.

WHEN Abishai re-entered the dwelling of Hadassah, he found her drawing forth, from a secret receptacle in the wall, a long roll of parchment, covered with writing in Hebrew characters within and without. The lady pressed it reverentially to her lips, and then resumed her seat, with the sacred roll laid across her knees. Abishai regarded with respect, almost amounting to awe, a woman to whom had been given the talent, wisdom, and courage to transcribe so large a portion of the oracles of God. He felt as Barak may have done towards Deborah, and stood leaning against the wall, listening with respectful attention to the words of this "mother in Israel."

"These Scriptures, my son," said Hadassah, "have been my study by day and my meditation by night; and most earnestly have I sought, with fasting and prayer, to penetrate some of their deep meaning in regard to Him that shall come. I am yet as a child in knowledge, but the All-wise may be pleased to reveal

THE ROLL OF SCRIPTURE.

something even to a child. It has seemed to me of late that I have been permitted to trace one word, written as in gigantic shadows—now fainter, now deeper—on Nature, in History, on the Law, in the Prophets. That single word is SACRIFICE. Wherever I turn I see it. It seems to me as a law of being—yea, as the very essence of religion itself."

"I do not understand you," said Abishai. "How is the word Sacrifice written on Nature?"

"See we it not on all things around us?" replied

Hadassah. "Does not the seed die that the corn may spring up? doth not the decaying leaf nourish the living plant? doth not one creature maintain its existence by the destruction of others? There is a mystery of suffering in this fair world, some stern necessity for what we call evil, though from it a merciful God is ever evolving good. These things distressed and perplexed me, till I could dimly trace that word Sacrifice as written by God's finger upon His works: death the parent of life, pain and sorrow—of joy."

"The primeval curse is on Nature," observed the Hebrew.

"Linked with the primeval blessing," said Hadassah. "And now when I turn from natural objects to the history of our race, sacrifice and suffering are still ever before me. Isaac is devoted as a burnt-offering before he becomes the father of the chosen race; Joseph is sold for pieces of silver ere he can redeem his family from destruction; the storm is only stilled by Jonah's being cast out into the deep; Samson triumphs over the enemy by the sacrifice of his own life. All these historical facts seem to me as types, dim and shadowy indeed, yet legible to the eye of faith, and Sacrifice is the word which they form."

"Dim and shadowy," repeated Abishai, to whom Hadassah's views on the subject appeared somewhat fanciful and vague.

"If so in Nature and history," said the Hebrew lady,
"the lines are clear and distinct enough in our holy law.
Why have countless victims been offered, even from the
time of the fall? Why was the dying lamb of Abel
more acceptable than the bloodless offering of Cain?
Why have thousands of guiltless creatures been slain on
the altar of God; nay, not upon His alone, even on
altars of the heathen who have never heard of His name,
as if there were a deep instinct implanted in the soul of
man, to testify that without shedding of blood there is
no remission of sin? Think we that the All-merciful
can take pleasure in the death of bulls or of goats? Yet
hath He Himself ordained it. Sacrifice, suffering, sub-
stitution, one life accepted as ransom for another,—this
idea pervades the law given by inspiration to Moses—
yea, long before the birth of Moses—to Abraham, to
Noah, to Abel."

"I grant it," Abishai replied. "As man is guilty in
the sight of his Maker, there must be sacrifice for sin as
long as the world shall last."

The light of inspiration seemed to glow in the uplifted eyes of Hadassah, and her lips to breathe words
not her own as she spoke again. "What if all these
sacrifices but point to one great Sacrifice; what if the
deep mystery of suffering be resolved into some deeper
mystery of love; what if God Himself should provide
the substitute, and if on some altar blood be shed which

shall suffice to atone for transgressions past, present, and to come, even to the end of all time? May it not be—*must* it not so be—if we read the Scriptures aright?"

"I cannot divine your meaning," said Abishai.

"What is written here of the coming Messiah?" asked Hadassah, laying her hand on the roll of prophecy, as she turned her earnest, searching gaze upon her companion.

"That He shall rule the nations with a rod of iron, and break them in pieces like a potter's vessel!" exclaimed Abishai with exultation; "is He not named Messiah the Prince?"

"Who shall be *cut off, but not for Himself*" (Dan. ix. 26), said Hadassah, in low thrilling tones that made Abishai start, and look at her with surprise. "You," she continued, "see the PRINCE in prophecy, written as in characters of light; I see the SACRIFICE, ever in letters of deepening shadow. Behold here,"—and as the widow spoke, she opened the roll till her finger could point to the Twenty-second Psalm,—"what means this cry of mysterious sorrow, *My God, my God, why hast Thou forsaken Me?*"

"It is David's cry of anguish," said Abishai.

"Look further on, my son, ponder the subject more deeply," cried Hadassah, and she proceeded to read aloud part of the inspired Word. "*The assembly of the wicked have inclosed Me: they pierced My hands and My feet.*

*I may tell all My bones: they look and stare upon Me.
They part My garments among them, and cast lots on
My vesture* (Ps. xxii. 16–18).   These things never happened to David; the Psalmist speaks not here of himself."

"Of whom then could he be speaking?" said Abishai,
looking perplexed.   "Not surely of the Messiah; not of
the seed of the woman who shall bruise the serpent's
head" (Gen. iii. 15).

"Wherefore not," asked Hadassah, "seeing that He
Himself must be bruised in the conflict? If it be written,
*My Servant shall deal prudently, He shall be exalted
and extolled, and be very high,* the shadow lies close
under the brightness, it is also written, *His visage was
so marred more than any man, and His form more
than the sons of men;* and why? because *so shall He
sprinkle many nations* (Isa. lii. 13–15), it may be—
with His own blood?"

"Yours are strange thoughts," muttered the son of
Nathan.

"They are not my thoughts," replied Hadassah.   "Behold, further on in the roll, what was revealed to the
prophet Isaiah.   Is the note of triumph sounded here?
*He is despised and rejected of men; a Man of sorrows,
and acquainted with grief: and we hid as it were our
faces from Him; He was despised, and we esteemed Him
not.   Surely He hath borne our griefs, and carried our*

sorrows : yet we did esteem Him stricken, smitten of God, and afflicted. But *He was wounded for our transgressions, He was bruised for our iniquities : the chastisement of our peace was upon Him; and with His stripes we are healed. All we like sheep have gone astray ; we have turned every one to his own way ; and the Lord hath laid on Him the iniquity of us all. He was cut off out of the land of the living : for the transgression of My people was He stricken* (Isa. liii. 3–6, 8). Have we not here the Victim, the Substitute, the Sacrifice bound on the altar, bleeding, wounded, dying, and that for sins not His own ?"

"It cannot be. It is impossible—quite impossible—that when the Messiah comes He should be despised and rejected," exclaimed Abishai, to whom this interpretation of prophecy was as unwelcome as it was new. "When He comes, all Israel shall triumph and rejoice, and welcome their King, the Ruler of the world."

Hadassah silently unrolled her parchment until she came to the thirteenth chapter* of the prophet Zechariah.

"Listen to this, son of Nathan," said she. "*Awake, O sword, against my Shepherd, and against the Man that is my Fellow, saith the Lord of hosts*" (Zech. xiii. 7).

"Who is *My Fellow?*" repeated Abishai, in amazement, for that portion of Scripture had never been

---

* Of course, the Hebrew roll was not divided into chapters ; they are but given for facility of reference.

brought to his attention before. "Can you have read the sentence correctly? Were that not written in the Word of God, methinks it were rank blasphemy even to think that the Lord of hosts could have an equal."

"There is mystery in that word which man cannot fathom," cried Hadassah. "The Divine Essence is One: the foundation of our faith is the most solemn declaration, *Hear, O Israel! the Lord our God* is One Lord* (Deut. vi. 4); and yet in that very declaration is conveyed the idea of unity combined with distinction of persons."

"Hadassah, Hadassah, into what wilderness of heresy are you wandering?" Abishai exclaimed.

The Hebrew lady appeared not to hear him, but went on, as if thinking aloud:—

"No man hath seen God at any time, He Himself hath declared—*No man shall see Me, and live*" (Exod. xxxiii. 20). But who, then, visibly appeared unto Abraham? Who was it who wrestled with Jacob? Who spake unto Gideon? On whose glory was Isaiah permitted to gaze? Who was seen to walk in the fiery furnace? Who was He, *like the Son of Man,* who *came with the clouds of heaven, and came to the Ancient of Days?*" (Dan. vii. 13.)

"At one moment you would view Messiah as a Victim; at the next, as a God!" cried the Hebrew.

* "God," in the original, is "Elohim," a *plural* word.

"If God should deign to take the form of Man, to bear Man's penalty, to suffer Man's death, might He not be *both?*" asked Hadassah.

Seeing that Abishai started at the question, she turned to the portion of the roll which contained the prophecy of Isaiah, and read aloud :—

"*Unto us a Child is born.* Here is clearly an announcement of human birth ; yet is this Child revealed to us as *the mighty God, the everlasting Father, the Prince of Peace*" (Isa. ix. 6).

"Such thoughts as these are too high, too difficult, for the human mind to grasp," exclaimed Abishai, pressing his brow. "The frail vessel must burst that has such hot molten gold poured within it. All that I can answer to what you have said is this : I believe not— and never will believe—that when Messiah, the Hope of Israel, shall come, He will be rejected by our nation. Were it so, such a fearful curse would fall upon our race that the memory of the Egyptian bondage, the Babylonish captivity, the Syrian persecution, would be forgotten in the greater horrors of what God's just vengeance would bring upon this people. We should become a by-word, a reproach, a hissing. We should be scattered far and wide amongst the nations, as chaff is scattered by the winds, until—"

Abishai paused, and clenched his hand and set his teeth, as if language failed him to describe the utter

desolation and misery which such a crime as the rejec-
tion of the Messiah must bring upon the descendants of
Abraham. As Abishai did not finish his sentence, Hadassah completed it for him.

"Until," she said, with a brightening countenance —
"until Judah repent of her sin, and turn to Him whom
she once denied. Hear, son of Nathan, but one more
prophecy from the Scriptures. Thus saith the Lord :
*I will pour upon the house of David, and upon the in-
habitants of Jerusalem, the spirit of grace and of supplications : and they shall look upon* ME *whom they have
pierced, and they shall mourn for Him, as one mourn-
eth for his only son, and shall be in bitterness for Him,
as one that is in bitterness for his first-born* (Zech.
xii. 10). *And the Lord shall be King over all the
earth*" (Zech. xiv. 9).

Abishai left the dwelling of Hadassah with a perturbed spirit, unwilling to own to himself that views so
widely differing from his own could have any foundation
in truth. The idea of a rejected, suffering, dying Messiah, was beyond measure repugnant to the soul of the
Hebrew.

"See what comes of concentrating all the powers of
the mind on abstruse study!" Abishai muttered to himself as he descended the hill. "Hadassah is going mad ;
her judgment is giving way under the strain."

CHAPTER XII

TRIALS OF THE HEART.

OR the first time in the course of her life, Zarah dreaded a meeting with Hadassah. Though the season was now so far advanced that the heat of the sun was great, the maiden lingered on the shadeless house-top, leaning her brow against the parapet, listlessly gazing towards Jerusalem, but with her mind scarcely taking in the objects upon which her eyes were fixed. Was it a foreboding of coming sorrow, or a feeling of self-reproach, that brooded over the maiden's soul? Zarah was afraid to analyze her own feelings: she only knew that her heart was very heavy.

Nearly two hours thus passed. The sun had now approached the horizon, and the heat was less oppressive. Zarah heard the slow step of Hadassah ascending the stair, and rose to meet her, but with a sensation of fear. The remembrance of that look of sad displeasure, such as had never been turned upon her before, had haunted the mind of the conscious girl. Was Hadassah angry with her daughter? Would she come to probe a heart which had never from childhood kept a secret from one so tenderly loved. Zarah was afraid to raise her eyes to Hadassah's when they met, lest she should encounter that stern look again; but never had the aged lady's face worn an expression of greater tenderness than it did when, on the house-top, she rejoined the child of her love.

"Have you been here, in the heat of the sun, my dove, letting the fierce rays beat on your unveiled face?" said Hadassah, after printing a kiss on the maiden's brow. "Nay, I must chide you, my Zarah. Seat yourself where yon tall palm now throws its shadow, and I will sit beside you. We will talk of the glorious tidings which Abishai brought to us to-day."

It was a great relief to Zarah to hear that such was to be the subject of the coming conversation. She glanced timidly up into the face of Hadassah; and, quite reassured by what she saw there, took her favourite place at her grandmother's feet.

"Is it not evident," pursued Hadassah, "that the arm of the Lord is stretched out to fight for Judah—that His blessing goes with Judas Maccabeus? Do you not rejoice, Zarah, in the victory which has been won by our Hebrew heroes?"

"I do rejoice; I thank God for it," replied the maiden.

" I hope that the time is coming when we shall go forth, like the women of Israel in olden time, who went singing and dancing to meet Saul and David, after the triumph over the Philistines."

" David, when he slew Goliath and won the hand of a king's daughter, deserved not more of his country than does Maccabeus," observed Hadassah. " Are you not proud of your kinsman, my child ?"

" All Judæa is proud of her hero," said Zarah.

" Happy the woman whom he shall choose as his bride !" cried Hadassah.

The maiden gave no reply.

" Zarah, why should I longer conceal from you what has so long been in my thoughts ?" said the aged lady, after a pause of some minutes' duration. " Why should you not know of the high honour awaiting my daughter ? From your early childhood both Mattathias, our revered kinsman—on whose grave be peace !—and myself have looked forward to the future espousals of my loved Zarah and Judas."

" Judas ! Oh, no, no !" exclaimed Zarah, suddenly withdrawing her trembling hand from that of her grand-mother, in which it had been clasped. " He is wedded to his country ; he will never think of taking a wife." She spoke rapidly, and with some emotion.

" His toils and triumphs may, and I trust will, lead to future peace," said Hadassah. " Then may he enjoy

the happiness which he has earned so well. Will you
not give it to him, Zarah—you, whose very name signi-
fies 'brightness'?"

"I honour Maccabeus as a hero—I could reverence
him as my prince—I would kneel and wash the dust
from his feet, or cut off my long hair to string his bow;
but I cannot be his bride," exclaimed Zarah. "I am so
weak, so unworthy! It would be like mating the eagle
with the sparrow that sits on the house-tops. Maccabeus
is the noblest of men."

"Blessed the wife who can so honour her lord!" said
Hadassah.

"I do honour Maccabeus from the depth of my soul;
but—but I fear him," faltered Zarah.

"Were you a Syrian you might say so," observed
Hadassah, with a faint approach to a smile, "but not as
a daughter of Judah. Terrible as he is to his country's
foes, to armed oppressors, no maiden had ever cause to
dread Maccabeus. The sharp thorns of the cactus make
it an impenetrable fence which the strongest intruder
cannot break through; yet bears it brilliant flowers and
refreshing fruit. The strong war-horse tramples down
the enemy in battle; but in peace the little child unharmed may play with his mane. The bravest are the
most gentle. Judas is no exception to this rule. Pure-
hearted and true, he is one to make a woman happy."

Zarah sighed, and drooped her head.

"Was it not a proud moment for Achsah, when Othniel, after the conquest of Kirjathsepher, claimed her hand as the victor's prize?" asked Hadassah.

"But Achsah was the daughter of a Caleb," said Zarah. Then, raising her head, she suddenly inquired— "Did my father also destine me to be the bride of my kinsman?"

Hadassah winced at the question, as if a painful wound had been touched.

"Oh, my child, have pity on me," she faintly murmured, "and speak not of him!"

Zarah had for long known that there was one subject which she dared never approach. Her grandmother had, as it were, one locked chamber in her heart, which no one might venture to open. Whether Zarah's father were dead or not, the maiden knew not. She faintly remembered a tall, handsome man, who had played with her tresses and danced her in his arms when she was a child, in her early home at Bethsura; but since she had left that home in company with her grandmother, she had never seen him nor heard his name. The slightest allusion to her father by Zarah had caused such distress to Hadassah, that the child had soon learned to be silent, though not to forget. Hadassah often spoke of Miriam, her only daughter, and of Zarah's own gentle mother,— twin-roses, as she would call them, both early gathered for heaven in the first year of their wedded lives; but

of her son she never would speak. A mystery hung
round the fate of Abner—such was his name—which
his daughter vainly longed to penetrate. Her heart re-
proached her now for the unguarded question into which
she had been surprised.

"Oh, forgive me, mother!" said Zarah, kissing the
hand of Hadassah, which was tremulous and cold. "Your
word, your will, shall be enough for me in all things,
except—oh, ask me not to wed my kinsman!"

"Is it, can it be, because another has a nearer place
in your heart?" said Hadassah.

The fair countenance of Zarah became suddenly rosy
as the sunlit cloud, then pale as Lebanon snow, at the
question.

"Oh, then, my fears are too true!" exclaimed Hadassah, in a tone, not of wrath, but of anguish. "Must
the sins of the father be visited upon the innocent child?
A Gentile—a heathen—an idolater! Would I had died
ere this day!"

"Be not angry with me, mother," faltered Zarah,
wetting Hadassah's hand with her tears.

"I am not angry, my poor dove," cried the widow.
"Woe is me that I have been, as it were, constrained to
expose you to this cruel snare! But you will break
through it," she added, with more animation; "my bird
will rise above earth with her silver wings unsullied and
bright. Various are the temptations which the soul's

enemy employs to draw away God's servants from their allegiance. Some he would sway through their fears; others he would win by the love of the world, its wealth and its pleasures; others he would chain by their hearts' strong affections. But the Lord gives strength to His people to resist and to conquer, whether the temptation be from fear or from love. You are the worthy kinswoman of Solomona, who gave life itself for the faith."

" Perhaps the sacrifice of life is not the hardest to make," Zarah dreamily replied.

"Solomona gave her seven sons," said Hadassah.

" Oh, what a mercy-stroke to her was that which let her follow them !" exclaimed Zarah. " Had she been left to survive all whom she loved, Solomona had been the most wretched woman on earth."

" No, not the *most* wretched," said Hadassah, with deep feeling, "for they all died in the faith. Better, ah, far better, to lose seven by death, than one by — by treason against God ! " And in an almost inaudible voice the aged lady added, closing her eyes, " Must I know that misery *twice ?*"

" No, mother, mine own dear mother, you shall never know that misery through me !" exclaimed Zarah with animation. " I will pray, I will strive, I will try to put away, even from my thoughts, all that would come between me and the faith of a daughter of Abraham ; only guide me, help me, tell your child what she should

do." And the maiden passionately kissed again and
again the hand of Hadassah, and then pillowed her aching
head on her parent's bosom. Hadassah folded her there
in a long and tender embrace.

"I would send you to Bethsura, to my aged cousin
Rachel," said the widow ; "only—"

"Oh, send me not away—let me stay beside you!
Your health is failing; I should never know peace afar
from you!" sobbed Zarah, in a tone of entreaty.

"I dare not send my child to Idumea, with no safe
escort, and the Syrians, men of Belial, holding the land,"
said Hadassah. "Better keep her here under my wing,
in the quiet seclusion of my home. But oh, my child,
attend to the voice of your mother! You must avoid
meeting the Gentile stranger. You must be little in the
lower apartments, Zarah, and never save when I am
there also. Your trial will not last long; the Athenian's
wounds are healing. After the Passover-feast, Abishai
will leave Jerusalem to join the patriot band : when he
is once safe beyond the reach of the enemy, I will no
longer for one hour harbour Lycidas under my roof—he
has been here far too long already. Your painful
struggle will now last but a short time, my Zarah."

Zarah thought, though she did not say so, that the
heart-struggle would last as long as her earthly existence.

"You will obey me, my daughter?" asked the

widow; " you will shun the too attractive society of the stranger?"

The maiden bowed her head in assent, and murmured—" Pray for me, mother; I am so weak."

" My life shall be one prayer," said Hadassah.

" Mine — one sacrifice," thought the poor maiden. " Oh, may that sacrifice be accepted!"

CHAPTER XIII

SILENT CONFLICT.

THE maiden kept her silent promise—faithfully she obeyed the hest of Hadassah. Seldom as possible did she enter the room which communicated with the hiding-place of Lycidas, and never save in the company of her aged relative. Zarah's wheel was carried to her sleeping-apartment. Heat and discomfort were made no excuse for leaving the more secluded portions of the small and inconvenient dwelling ; Zarah, a voluntary prisoner, avoiding seeing him who appeared to her to be an embodiment of all that was beautiful in form and brilliant in mind—one whose society resembled the light which glorifies every object on which it may fall.

And Zarah did not—as many maidens in her place might have done—punish Hadassah for throwing her influence into the scale of duty, by showing her the extent of the sacrifice which she had required. The

young girl, while her heart was bleeding, struggled to
maintain a serene and placid mien. Hadassah never
heard Zarah sigh, never surprised her in tears. No duty
was neglected, no work left undone; nay, Zarah spun
more busily than ever, for the support of the stranger
was a drain on the scanty resources of Hadassah, and to
work for him and pray for him was the sole indulgence
which Zarah could allow herself without self-reproach.
She tried—how arduous was the effort!—even to turn
her thoughts from the subject which was to her as the
forbidden fruit was to Eve. The chasm which divided
Abraham's daughter from the heathen was one over
which, as Zarah knew, it would be sinful to throw even
the rainbow bridge of imagination. She must force her
mind from approaching the dangerous brink. How
many of the psalms of David — always those most
mournful in their tone — Zarah repeated to herself, to
bring solace to her spirit by day or sleep to her eyelids
by night! While Judas Maccabeus was maintaining a
gallant struggle against the enemies of his country,
conquering, but through much stern endurance, Zarah,
with the same faith and obedience as animated the warrior, was keeping up a more painful fight against the
heathen in her own gentle heart.

There was one subject of thought, and that a distress-
ing one, to which Zarah's mind most readily reverted
when she would turn it from the channel into which it

was ever naturally flowing. This was the mystery connected with the fate of Abner, her father. The few
words which had escaped Hadassah in an unguarded
moment were as the dull red light which a torch might
throw on the sides of some yawning pit, whose depths
are left in profound darkness. Often had Zarah yearned
to know more of her father: how he had died (for she
had once deemed him dead), where his dear remains had
been laid, — all that concerned him was of deep interest
to his only child. But any attempt to break through
the reserve which sealed the lips of Hadassah had evidently occasioned such acute distress that Zarah had
long since given up the hope of gaining information from
her. Anna had entered the service of Hadassah since
the Hebrew lady had quitted Bethsura: the attendant
knew nothing, and therefore could tell nothing, of what
had previously occurred in the family. Solomona, when
she had paid occasional visits to her kinswomen, had
never given Zarah an opportunity of speaking on so
delicate a subject. Once when Zarah had ventured to
ask the question, "Did you know my father?" Solomona
had appeared not to hear it, and had instantly started
some quite irrelevant topic of conversation. Abishai
doubtless knew much about the brother of his wife, but
Zarah shrank from questioning him : from his fierce
impetuosity of character, he was not one to draw out
the confidence of a gentle and timid girl. Zarah almost

felt as if her uncle disliked, and, for some reason which she understood not, regarded her with mingled pity and contempt.

Thus the daugater of Abner, cut off from all means of gaining reliable information, was thrown back on her own conjectures. A vague doubt which had lately arisen in Zarah's mind, but which had always heretofore been repelled as treason to a parent's memory, was given form and substance by the faint exclamation which grief had wrung from Hadassah, *"Must I know that misery twice?"* Many slight circumstances then recurred to Zarah's memory to confirm her suspicions, especially the anguish which Hadassah had betrayed at the burial of Solomona, when a strange pang of envy had seemed to intensify that of bereavement. Zarah was as one bending lower and lower over that pit of which she longed, yet dreaded, to sound the depths, straining her eyes to penetrate the darkness, while trembling to think what horrors that darkness might hide.

"Is it possible that my father may yet be breathing on earth, living—the life of an apostate?" The idea haunted Zarah like a spectre. There was only one hope which had power to lay it: "If living, he may be spared for repentance. God is merciful; He judgeth not severely; He delighteth in receiving his wanderers back. Did not Nathan say to penitent David, 'Thou shalt not surely die'? Was not even the guilty Manasseh restored to his throne? Oh, the son of the pious Hadassah, a woman of such faith and prayer, can never be lost!" After such meditations, the burdened heart of Zarah would find relief in fervent supplications for her father. Her filial affection came to the aid of her religious obe-

SINGING TO HADASSAH.

dience. "God will not hear prayers," thought Zarah, "from one in whose heart an idol is enshrined. For my father's sake, as well as my own, let me strive to give unreserved obedience to my Lord."

So, endeavouring to overcome one grief by the help of

another, and to cast a veil over both, Zarah passed weary day after day, letting no murmur mar her offering of meek submission. She would even speak cheerfully to Hadassah, and sing to her songs of Zion, which the aged lady delighted to hear. There was one song especially dear, in which Hadassah had herself woven prophetic promises into verse. The rhymes might be rude, and altogether unworthy of their theme; but when softly warbled by Zarah's melodious voice, they appeared to the aged listener like the very breathing of hope.

LAY OF ZION.

"Jerusalem! thou sittest in the dust;
   God's heavy judgment on thy children lies:
   But He in whom their fathers put their trust
   Shall bid thee yet, as from the grave, arise!*
     O Zion, discrowned Queen!
      A throne awaits for thee;†
     For glorious thou hast been,
     All glorious shalt thou be.‡

"Behold, the white-winged ships from Tarshish strand §
   Shall bear thy sons and daughters o'er the wave;
   All nations call thee blessed, delightsome land,‖
   Which God of old to faithful Abraham gave.¶
     O Zion, &c.

"Ephraim with Judah God shall then restore;**
   The Hand that severed now uniteth them:
   Ephraim shall envy, Judah vex, no more;††
   All shall rejoice in thee, Jerusalem!
     O Zion, &c.

* Isa. lx. 1. † Isa. xxii. 23. ‡ Isa. lx. 13, 14. § Isa. lx. 9. ‖ Mal. iii. 12. ¶ Gen. xiii. 15. ** Ezek. xxxvii. 16, 17. †† Isa. xi. 13.

" Assyria, Egypt, shall with Israel join *
    (The land where Daniel trod the lions' den,
  The land where Pharaohs bowed at Apis' shrine);
    Oppressors once, but more than sisters then.
        O Zion, &c.

" God shall a wall of fire round thee abide,†
    To guard thee as the apple of the eye;‡
Rejoicing as the bridegroom o'er the bride,§
  For He hath pardoned thine iniquity.‖
      O Zion, &c.

" The mountains may depart, the hills may shake,¶
    But nought thy Saviour's love from thee shall sever;
The mother may her sucking child forsake,
  God thy Redeemer shall forsake thee never. **
      O Zion, discrowned Queen!
        A throne still waits for thee;
      For glorious thou hast been,
      All glorious shalt thou be.

* Isa. xix. 24. † Zech. ii. 5. ‡ Zech. ii. 8. § Isa. lxii. 5. ‖ Isa. xliv. 22. ¶ Isa. liv 10. ** Isa. xlix. 15.

CHAPTER XIV

A CRISIS.

YCIDAS, in the meantime, was chafing in wild impatience under the trial of Zarah's almost perpetual absence. He could no longer watch her, no longer listen to her, except when his straining ear caught the faint sound of her music floating down from an upper apartment. Why was she away? why should she shun him? she whose presence alone had rendered not only tolerable but delightful the kind of mild captivity in which he was retained, while the state of his wounds rendered the Greek unable, without assistance, to leave the dwelling of Hadassah. Lycidas had none of the scruples of Zarah regarding union with one of a different race and religion. The Greek had resolved on winning the fair Hebrew maid as his bride; he was conscious of possessing the gift of attractions such as few young hearts could resist, and asked fortune only for an opportunity of exerting all his powers to the utmost to secure the most precious prize for which mortal had ever contended.

Lycidas beguiled many tedious hours by the composition of a poem, of singular beauty, in honour of Zarah. Most melodious was the flow of the verse, most delicate the fragrance of the incense of praise. The realms of nature, the kingdom of art, were ransacked for images of beauty. But Lycidas felt disgusted with his own work before he had completed it. He seemed to himself like one decorating with gems and hanging rich garments on an exquisite statue, in the attempt to do it honour only marring the perfection of its symmetry and the grace of its marble drapery. A few words which the Greek had heard Hadassah read from her sacred parchment appeared to him to include more than all his most laboured descriptions could convey. Lycidas had thought of Zarah when he had listened to the expression, *the beauty of holiness.*

"I will not stay a prisoner here, if I am to be shut out in this stifling little den not only from the world, but from her who is more than the world to me," thought the Greek. After months of suffering and weakness, strength, though but slowly, was returning to the frame of Lycidas; and when no one was near to watch him, when the door to the west was closed, and the curtain to the east was drawn, he would occasionally try how far that strength would enable him to go. He would raise himself on his feet, though not without a pang from his wounded side. Then the Greek would take a few steps, from one end of his prison to the other, leaning for support against the wall. This was something for a beginning; youth and love would soon enable him to do more. But Lycidas carefully concealed from Hadassah and Anna that he could do as much. They never saw him but reclining on the floor. He feared that measures might be taken to clip the wings of the bird if it were once guessed how nearly those wings were fledged.

The day before the celebration of the great feast of the Passover, Hadassah was far from well. Whether her illness arose from the state of the weather, for the month of Nisan was this year more than usually hot, or the effect of long fastings and prayer upon a frame enfeebled by age, or whether from secret grief preying on her health, Zarah knew not,—perhaps from all these causes combined. The maiden grew uneasy about her grandmother, and redoubled her tender ministrations to her comfort.

On the day mentioned, Anna had gone into Jerusalem to dispose of flax spun by the Hebrew ladies, and procure a few necessary articles of food. Hadassah never suffered her beautiful girl to enter the walls of the city, nor, indeed, ever to quit the precincts of her home, save when on Sabbath-days and feast-days she went, closely

veiled, to the dwelling of the elder Salathiel, about half
a mile distant from that of Hadassah, to join in social
worship. Hadassah with jealous care shrouded her white
dove from the gaze of Syrian eyes.

The aged lady had passed a very restless night. With
thrilling interest Zarah had heard her moaning in her
sleep, " Abner! my son! my poor lost son!" The
sealed lips were opened, when the mind had no longer
power to control their utterance. Hadassah awoke in
the morning feverish and ill. She made a vain attempt
to rise and pursue her usual avocations. Zarah entreated
her to lie still. For hours the widow lay stretched on
a mat with her eyes half closed, while Zarah watched
beside her, fanning her feverish brow.

" Let me prepare for you a cooling drink, dear mother,"
said the maiden at last, rising and going to the water-
jar, which stood in a corner of the apartment. " Alas!
it is empty. Anna forgot to replenish it from the spring
ere she set out for the city. I will go and fill it
myself."

Zarah lifted up the jar, and poising it on her head,
lightly descended the rough steps of the outer stair, and
proceeded to the spring at the back of the house. The
spring was surrounded by oleanders, which at this time
of the year in Palestine are robed in their richest bloom.
But the season had been singularly hot and dry, the latter
rains had not yet fallen, and the spring was beginning

to fail. Zarah placed her jar beneath the opening from which, pure and bright, the water trickled, but the supply was so scanty that she could almost count the drops as they fell. It would take a considerable time for the jar to be filled by these drops.

"Ah! methinks my earthly joys are even as this failing spring!" thought the maiden, sadly, as she watched the slow drip of the water. "All will be dried up soon. My loved grandmother's strength is sinking; she will be unable to-morrow to keep the holy feast in Salathiel's house, though her heart will be with the worshippers there. How different, oh! how different is this Passover from that which we celebrated last year! Then, indeed, there was an idol in the Temple of the Lord, and holy sacrifice could not be offered in the appointed place, but the fierce storm of persecution had not arisen in all its terrors. Then around the table of Salathiel how many gathered whom I never again shall behold upon earth! Solomona, my kinswoman, and her seven sons all met in that solemn assembly; the bright-eyed Asahel, the fearless Mahali, young Joseph, who was my merry playmate when ten years ago we came from Bethsura hither! I remember that when Hadassah looked on that cluster of brothers she said that they were like the Pleiades—they are more like those star-gems now, for they shine not on earth but in heaven! And Solomona looked proudly on her boys—her noble sons, and said

that not one of them had ever raised a blush on the
cheek of their mother; and then, methinks, she regretted
having uttered the boast, and I fancied that I heard a
stifled sigh from Hadassah. Was it that the spirit of
prophecy came upon her then, that she foresaw the
terrible future, or was it—alas! alas! I dare not think
wherefore she sighed! And old Mattathias, he who now
sleeps in the sepulchre of his fathers, he and his sons
kept that Passover-feast with Salathiel, having come up
to Jerusalem to worship, according to the law of Moses.
How venerable looked the old man with his long snowy
beard! it seemed to me that so Abraham must have
looked when his earthly pilgrimage was well-nigh ended.
Mattathias laid his hand on my head and blessed me,
and called me daughter. Ah! can it be that he thought
of me then as his daughter indeed! The princely Judas
stood near, and when I raised my head I met the gaze
of his eyes, and I thought—no, I never then fully grasped
the meaning expressed in that gaze, it was to me as the
tender glance of a brother. Mattathias is gone; Solomona and her children are all gone; Judas, with his
gallant band, is like a lion at bay with the hunters
closing in an ever-narrowing circle around him. Apollonius has been vanquished, Seron defeated by our hero;
but now Nicanor and Giorgias, with the forces of Ptolemy,
upwards of forty thousand men, are combining to crush
him by their overwhelming numbers. What can the

devotion of our patriots avail but to swell the band of martyrs who have already laid down their lives in defence of our faith and our laws! Alas! theirs will be a stern keeping of the holy feast; other blood will flow besides that of the Paschal lamb! And a sad keeping of the feast will be mine; I shall see scarce a familiar face, that of no relative save Abishai; and I owe him but little affection. And, oh! worst of all, I fear me that I have an unholy leaven in my heart, which I in vain seek to put entirely away. I am secretly cherishing the forbidden thing, though not wilfully, not wilfully, as He knows to whom I constantly pray for strength to give up all that is displeasing in His sight!"

The jar was now full; Zarah turned to raise it as the last thought passed through her mind, and started as she did so! Lycidas, with all his soul beaming in his eyes, was close beside her! The maiden uttered a faint exclamation, and endeavoured to pass him, and return to the house.

"Stay, Zarah, idol of my soul!" exclaimed the Athenian, seizing her hand; "you must not fly me, you shall listen to me once—only once!" and with a passionate gush of eloquence the young Greek laid his hopes, his fortunes, his heart at her feet.

Zarah turned deadly pale; her frame trembled. "O Lycidas, have mercy upon me!" she gasped. "It is sin in me even to listen; it were cruelty to suffer you to

hope.   Our law forbids a daughter of Abraham to wed
a Gentile; to return your love would be rebellion against
my God, apostasy from the faith of my fathers; better
to suffer—better to die!"—and with an effort releasing

THE CRISIS.

her icy-cold hand from the clasp of the man whom she
loved, Zarah sprang hurriedly past him, and with the
speed of a frightened gazelle fled up the staircase,

and back into the chamber in which she had left Hadassah.

Lycidas stood bewildered by the maiden's sudden retreat. He felt as if the gate of a paradise had been suddenly closed against him.

CHAPTER XV.

THE TWO CAMPS.

WHILE the scenes lately described had been occurring in the neighbourhood of Jerusalem, Maccabeus, in the mountains, had been preparing for the deadliest shock of war. Like wave upon wave, each swelling higher than the one before it, successive armies hurled their strength against the devoted band that held aloft the banner of the truth, as a beacon-light gleaming on high amidst the fiercest fury of the tempest. The mighty Nicanor, son of Patroclus, a man honoured with the king's peculiar favour, had gathered together a powerful force "to root out the whole generation of the Jews," and with him was joined in command Giorgias, a general of great experience in war.

A large camp was formed by the Syrians at Emmaus, about a Sabbath-day's journey from Jerusalem. The hills were darkened with their goats'-hair tents, the roads thronged with soldiers, and with a multitude of merchants who brought much silver and gold to purchase Hebrew captives as slaves for their markets. For so confident of victory was Nicanor, that he had beforehand proclaimed a sale of the prisoners whom he would reserve from slaughter; nay, had fixed the very price which he would demand for his vanquished foes! Ninety of the Hebrew warriors should be sold for a talent, so ran Nicanor's proclamation.

"These bold outlaws," said the haughty Syrian, "shall spend their superfluous strength, as did their Samson of old, in grinding corn for their victors, or in tilling the fields which they once called their own, with the taskmaster's lash to quicken their labours. Ha! ha! it were good subject for mirth to see the lorldly Maccabeus himself, with blinded eyes, turning the wheel at the well, and bending his proud back to serve as my footstool when I mount my Arab steed! This were sweeter vengeance, a richer triumph, than to hew him to pieces with the sword which he took from the dead Apollonius. Let the Asmonean fall into my hands, and he shall taste what it is to endure a living death!"

Maccabeus, on his part, had led his forces to Mizpeh, where they had encamped. Here a day of solemn humiliation was appointed by the Asmonean chief; he and his warriors fasted, put on sackcloth, and united in prayer to the God of Hosts.

The leader then more perfectly organized his little
army, dividing it into bands, and appointing captains
over the divisions. While Divine aid was implored,
human means were not neglected.

Early in the morning of the succeeding day, Maccabeus
and Simon, his elder brother, held grave consultation together. The scene around them was historic; the very
heap of stones upon which the chiefs were seated marked
the spot where the last leave of Laban had been taken
by Jacob their forefather, when returning to his aged
parent.

But few months have elapsed since Judas stood, as
the reader first saw him, by the grave of the martyrs,
but these eventful months have wrought a marked change
upon the Asmonean leader. Fatigue, hardship, the burden of care, the weight of responsibility, added to the
sorrow of bereavement, have left their stamps on his ex-
pressive features. Maccabeus looks a worn and a weary
man; but there is increased majesty in his demeanour,
that dignity which has nothing to do with pride; for
pride has its origin in self-consciousness, true dignity in
forgetfulness of self.

"This will be our sharpest conflict; the enemy is
strong," observed Simon, glancing in the direction of the
Syrian hosts, which lay between them and Jerusalem.

"With the God of Heaven it is all one to deliver
with a great multitude or with a few," said Maccabeus.

"What is the number of our forces?" asked Simon.

"Six thousand, as given by yesterday's returns," was the reply; "but to-day I will make proclamation that they who are planting vineyards or building houses, or who have lately married wives, have full leave to retire if they will it, and then—ha! Eleazar returned already!" cried the leader, interrupting himself, as a young Hebrew, dressed as a Syrian merchant, with rapid step ascended the little eminence on which the Asmonean brothers were seated.

"I have been in the midst of them!" exclaimed Eleazar; "ay, I have stood in their tents, heard their songs, listened to their proud boastings, been present when the sons of Mammon bartered for the limbs and lives of the free-born sons of Abraham! They may have our bodies as corpses," added the young Asmonean, with a proud smile, "but never as slaves; and even as corpses, they shall purchase us dearly."

"Know you the numbers of the Syrians?" inquired Simon, whose quiet, sedate manner formed a strong contrast to that of the fiery young Eleazar.

"Nicanor has forty thousand footmen and seven thousand horse," was the reply; "to say nothing of those who hang round his camp, as vultures who scent the carnage from afar."

"More than seven to one," observed Simon, slightly shaking his head

"Hebrews have encountered worse odds than that," cried the young man.

"Ay, when all were stanch," his elder brother rejoined.

"Do you then doubt our men!" exclaimed Eleazar.

"Many of them will be faithful unto death; but I know that in some quarters there are misgivings—I may call them fears," was the grave reply of Simon. "Not all our troops are tried warriors; some in the camp have spoken of submission."

"Submission!" cried Eleazar, clenching his hand; "I would lash the slaves up to the conflict as I would lash dogs that hung back in the chase."

"On the contrary," said Maccabeus, who had hitherto listened to the conversation in silence, "I shall proclaim that whoso is fearful, has my free permission to depart from us in peace."

"Were that well?" asked Simon doubtfully; "we are already so greatly outnumbered by the foe."

"It is according to the law," replied Judas, calmly; "it is what Gideon did before encountering Midian. We can have no man with us who is half-hearted; no one who will count his life dear in the struggle which is before us."

"If we are to fall in the struggle," observed Simon, "half our number will indeed suffice for the sacrifice." He spoke without fear, but in the tone of one who felt the full extent of the threatening danger.

"See you yon stone, my brother?" asked Maccabeus, pointing to a pillar on the way to Shen, which was clearly visible against the background of the deep blue sky. "Yonder is Ebenezer, *the stone of help*, which Samuel set up in remembrance of victory over the Philistines, when God thundered from heaven, and discomfited the foes of Israel."

"Ay, I see it," replied Simon ; "and I see the power and faithfulness of the Lord of Hosts written on that stone. We are in His hand, not in that of Nicanor."

"Let God arise, and let His enemies be scattered!" exclaimed Eleazar.

"My brother, give order that the trumpets be sounded," said Maccabeus, "and let our proclamation be known through the camp—that all who fear may retire at once, nor remain to shame us by turning their backs in the day of battle."

The commands of the leader were at once obeyed ; the proclamation was issued, and its alarming effects were speedily seen. The small force of Maccabeus began to melt like a snow-wreath under the beams of the sun. One man remembered the tears of his newly-wedded bride, another the helpless state of a widowed mother ; the hearts of not a few were set on their flocks and herds, while many of their comrades found in the state of crops needing the sickle an excuse to cover the fear which they would have blushed to own as their motive for deserting the cause of their country. Long before

JUDAS ADDRESSING HIS TROOPS.

the evening had closed in, the forces under Maccabeus
had been reduced to one-half their number.

"They have judged themselves unworthy to share the

glory that awaits their brave brethren," cried the indignant Eleazar, as, leaning on his unstrung bow, he watched a long line of fugitives wending their way towards the west.

Undismayed, though perhaps somewhat discouraged by the defection of half his troops, Maccabeus made before sunset a brief address to those who remained. "Arm yourselves," he said, "and be valiant men ; and see that ye be in readiness before the morning, that ye may fight with these nations that are assembled together to destroy us and our sanctuary. For it is better for us to die in battle than to behold the calamity of our people and our sanctuary. Nevertheless, as the will of God is in heaven, so let Him do."

So, with stern resolution to conquer or die, the Hebrews retired to their appointed places in the small camp till morning light should arouse them to the desperate conflict.

CHAPTER XVI.

UT the struggle was not to be deferred till the morning. Night had just spread her veil of darkness over earth, and Simon, prudently reserving his strength for the expected fatigues of the coming day, had wrapped himself in his mantle, and stretched himself on the ground to snatch some hours of repose, when he was roused by the touch of a hand on his shoulder. Opening his eyes, Simon saw, by the red light of a torch which the armour-bearer of Judas was holding aloft, that Maccabeus was before him.

"Awake, arise, my brother! this is no time for sleep," said the leader.

Simon was on his feet in a moment, an attentive listener, as Maccabeus continued:

"A scout has just brought in tidings from the Syrian camp that Nicanor has detached five thousand of his foot-soldiers and a thousand chosen horsemen. under the command of Giorgias, to attack us this night, and take us by surprise."

" They will find us prepared," said Simon, as he girded on his sword.

" Nay ; they will find their prey flown," replied Maccabeus, his features relaxing into a stern smile. " We will fall on the Syrian camp in their absence, teach the enemy his own lesson, and transfer the surprise to our foes."

" Well thought of," exclaimed Simon. " Darkness also will serve to hide the weakness of our force."

" Our brethren are now marshalling our warriors," said Judas. " All, under God, depends upon silence, promptitude, decision. We fight for our lives and our laws."

The leader turned to depart, but as he did so accidentally dropped something on the ground. He stooped to raise and twist it rapidly round his left arm, under the sleeve. The incident was so very trifling that it scarcely drew the notice of Simon ; though the thought did flit across his mind that it was strange that his brother on the eve of battle could pause to pick up anything so utterly valueless as a slight skein of unbleached flax. It was valueless indeed, save from the associations which, in the mind of him who wore it, were entwined with every thread. That flax had been once used to tie

together some flowers long since dead : the flowers had
been dropped into a grave of martyrs ; the light skein
had fallen on the upturned sod, unnoticed save by the
eyes of one.   Perhaps it was from remembrance of the
dead, or perhaps it was because hopes regarding the living (hopes brighter and sweeter than the flowers had
been) seemed now bound up in that flaxen strand, that
Maccabeus fastened that skein round his arm as a precious
thing, when he would not have stooped to pick up a
chaplet of pearls.

By the exertions of the five Asmonean brethren, the
little Hebrew army was rapidly put under arms, and
prepared for the night attack.   The whole force was
united as one forlorn hope.   As moves the dark cloud
in the sky, so darkly and silently moved on the band of
heroes ; and, like that cloud, they bore the thunderbolt
with them.

Most of the Syrians on that eventful night were sunk
in sleep—but not all : in their camp some kept up their
revels till late.   All the luxuries which fancy could de-
vise or wealth could purchase were gathered together at
Emmaus to hide the grim front of war, so that the camp
by daylight presented the motley appearance of a bazaar
with the gay magnificence of a court.   There sherbet
sparkled in vases of silver, and the red wine was poured
into golden cups, chased and embossed, in tents stretched
out with silken cords.   Garments bright with all the

varied tints of the rainbow, rich productions of Oriental
looms, robes from Tyre, shawls from Cashmere, blended
with instruments of warfare—swords, spears, and buck-
lers, the battle-axe and the helmet. The sentry pacing
his rounds paused to listen to wild bursts of merriment,
the loud oath and light song from some gay pavilion,
where young Syrian nobles were exchanging jests and
indulging in deep carousals. Yonder in the glaring
torchlight sat a group of officers, engaged in some game
of chance, and their stakes were the captives whom they
were to drag at their chariot-wheels on the morrow.
Each throw of the dice decided the fate of a Hebrew;
at least, so deemed the merry gamesters.

But the destined slaves were coming to the market
sooner than their expectant masters dreamed or desired,
and the price for each Hebrew would be exacted, not in
gold, but in blood. Suddenly the gamesters at their
play, the revellers at the board, the slumberers on their
couches, were startled by the blare of trumpets and a
ringing war-cry, "The sword of the Lord and Maccabeus!" The full goblet was dashed from the lip, the
dice from the hand. There were wild shouts and cries,
and rushing to and fro—soldiers snatching up weapons,
merchants flying hither and thither for safety, stumbling
over tent-ropes in the darkness. There were confused
noises of terror, trampling of feet, snorting of horses,
calls to arms, clashing of weapons, with all the horrors

of sudden panic spreading like an epidemic through the
mighty host of Syria. The few remained to oppose the
unseen assailants; the many took to flight. The ground
was soon strewn with treasure dropped by terrified fugitives, and weapons thrown down by warriors who had
not the courage to use them. Tents were speedily blaz-
ing; and horses, terrified by the sudden glare and maddened by the scorching heat, prancing, plunging, rushing
wildly through the camp, added to the fearful confusion.
Maccabeus, with the sword of Apollonius in his hand,
pressed on to victory over heaps of prostrate foes. Terror
was sent as a herald before him, and success followed
wherever he trod. It seemed as if the Lord of Hosts
were fighting for Israel, as in the old days of Gideon.

Hot was the pursuit after the flying Syrians. Maccabeus and his warriors followed hard on their track to
Gazera, Azotus, and Jamnia, and that southern part of
Judæa lying between the Red Sea and Sodom, to which,
from its having been colonized by Edomites, had been
given the name of Idumea. For many a mile the track
of the fugitives was marked by their dead. But as the
morning dawned after that terrible though glorious night,
the trumpets of Maccabeus sounded to call his troops
together. The leader had not forgotten—though some
of his eager followers might have done so—that Giorgias,
with an army of chosen warriors, doubling their own in
number, and comparatively fresh, was yet to be encoun-

tered. With stern displeasure, Maccabeus saw his own men, grim with blood and dust, loading themselves with

GREEDY OF THE SPOILS

the rich plunder which lay on the road, like fruit under orchard-trees after a wild tornado.

"Be not greedy of the spoils," cried the leader, "inasmuch as there is a battle before us; but stand ye now against our enemies, and overcome them, and after this ye may boldly take the spoils."

It is a more difficult task to call hounds off the prey that they have run down, than to let them slip from the leashes when the quarry first is in sight. It needed

such moral influence over his men as was possessed by
Maccabeus to enforce instant obedience when wealth was
at their feet, and needed but the gathering up. It was
speedily seen, however, that the warning of the Asmonean chief had not been unnecessary.· But a few
minutes elapsed after the utterance of that warning,
when the vanguard of the forces of Giorgias appeared on
the crest of a hill at some distance, the livelong night
having been spent by them in a vain attempt to discover
the camp of the Hebrews. After a long, tedious march,
Giorgias found himself on a commanding height, from
whence at dawn he had an extensive view of the surrounding country.

"The slaves have fled—they have made their escape
to the mountains," exclaimed Giorgias, as he dismounted
from his weary war-horse, when the first bar of golden
light appeared in the orient sky.

"Then they have left marks of their handiwork behind them," said a horseman, pointing in the direction
in which lay what had been the camp of Nicanor, now
suddenly visible to the Syrians from the summit of the
hill. "See you yon smoke arising from smouldering
heaps? There has been a battle at Emmaus. The lion
has broken through the toils. Maccabeus has not been
sleeping through the night."

"Nay, my Lord Pollux; it is impossible. The Hebrews would never dare to attack a force so greatly out-

numbering their own," exclaimed Giorgias, unwilling to believe the evidence of his own senses. But as the light more clearly revealed the tokens of flight and disaster in the far distance, where the smoke of ruin was rising into the calm morning air, conviction of the terrible truth forced itself on the general's mind, and with mingled astonishment and dismay he exclaimed, "Where are the hosts of Nicanor?"

"Yonder are those who can give an account of them," said Pollux, turning to the south, where in a valley the Hebrews might be seen marshalled around their leader. "There, I ween, is the insolent outlaw who has been making a shambles of our camp. See you the glitter of the spears? Maccabeus is setting his men in battle array. There is but a handful of them. Shall we charge down upon them, and sweep them from the face of the earth?"

Giorgias glanced again northward at Emmaus and the smoking ruins of the Syrian camp; then southward, where the little compact force in the valley was clustering round the standard of Maccabeus. Though the troops under the command of Giorgias doubled the Hebrews in number, he dared not try the issue of battle with those who had so lately discomfited Nicanor's formidable hosts. Had the Syrian leader been animated by such a fearless spirit as characterized his opponent, in all human probability the victory of the night might have been, to Judas and his gallant little band, succeeded by the defeat of the morning. But Giorgias showed an unusual amount of caution on the present occasion; and Pollux, though he assumed a tone of defiance, was secretly by no means desirous to measure swords with Maccabeus.

The Hebrews were weary with conquering and pursuing. Their spirit was unbroken, but their strength was exhausted. It was with some anxiety that the eagle eye of Judas watched the movements of the enemy on the heights, momentarily expecting an attack which he knew that his band of heroes was so little able to sustain.

"They will be down upon us soon," said Simon, as he leaned wearily on his spear.

"Nay; behold, they are vanishing over the crest of the mountain!" triumphantly exclaimed Eleazar. "The cowards! only brave over the wine-bowl! Not a stain on their swords! not a dint on their shields! They are fleeing when no man pursues. Oh, that we had but strength to follow, and chase the dastards even up to the walls of Jerusalem!"

"God hath put fear into their hearts; to Him be the glory!" said Maccabeus, as he sheathed his heavy sword.

And after this—to transcribe the words of the ancient Hebrew historian, describing the triumphs of his countrymen—"they went home, and sung a song of thanksgiving, and praised the Lord in heaven, because He is good, because His mercy endureth for ever."

CHAPTER XVII.

WHEN Zarah, trembling and pale, after her interview with Lycidas, fled to the apartment of Hadassah, she left her water-jar behind her at the spring. The sight of her grandmother, stretched on her low couch, with her eyes closed, and her lips parched and dry, recalled to the remembrance of the poor young maiden the errand for which she had quitted her side.

"The water! the water!" exclaimed Zarah, striking her brow. "She must have it. But oh! I dare not —I dare not go back; for nothing on earth could I go through that terrible struggle again!"

As Zarah stood on the threshold, in a state of painful indecision, to her great relief she heard the voice of Anna below, and called to her to bring up the jar of water which she would find at the fountain. Anna quickly obeyed, and came up the stairs laden, not only with the cooling fluid, but with ripe fruit and vegetables, which she had brought from Jerusalem—the white mulberry and the nebeb, with early figs, cucumbers, and a melon.

Very grateful was the supply to Hadassah ; but more refreshing by far than the draught of cold water were the tidings which Anna had brought from the city. The Jewess was full of eagerness to impart her glorious news.

"I saw them myself—Giorgias and his horsemen— jaded, crestfallen, as they rode through the streets," cried Anna. "I marvel that they dared show their faces : they had not so much as crossed weapons with our conquering heroes !"

"Or they had not lived to tell the tale," exclaimed Hadassah, to whom the news of the victory at Emmaus seemed to give new energy and life.

"We dared not clap our hands and shout," continued the Jewish servant ; "but there is not a Hebrew child that is not wild with joy. We blessed the name of Maccabeus, though we could only breathe it in whispers."

"But a day is coming when the welkin shall ring with that name, and the walls of Jerusalem echo back the sound," cried Hadassah. "O my child," she continued, glancing joyfully at Zarah, "there will be a thankful celebration of the Passover to-morrow. The Lord is giving deliverance to His chosen, even as He once did from the power of the haughty Pharaoh."

"It must be a very quiet keeping of the Feast," observed Anna, shaking her head. "It is said that King Antiochus is raging like a bear robbed of her whelps at the flight of Nicanor and the disgraceful retreat of Giorgias. A courier has ridden off, post-haste, bearer of despatches from the king to Lycias, the regent of the western provinces."

"Is it known what the despatches contain?" asked Hadassah.

"It is reported in the city," said Anna, "that Lycias is to raise a more mighty and terrible army than any that has swept the country before—more mighty than those led by Apollonius, Seron, or Nicanor. King Antiochus has sworn by all his false gods that he will destroy the Asmoneans root and branch."

"What God hath planted, who shall root up? what God prospers, who shall destroy?" cried Hadassah. "Thinks Antiochus Epiphanes that he hath power to strive against the Lord?"

"He has terrible power to use against man," said Anna, who had a less courageous spirit than her mistress. "Sharper measures than ever, it is said, are to be taken to put down our secret worship. Woe unto them who are found keeping the Passover to-morrow! It will be done unto them as it was done to Solomona and her sons."

"Would that God would give me strength to attend

the holy Feast," cried Hadassah, on whom the idea of danger following its celebration appeared to act as a stimulant; "no fear of man should keep me away. But He who withholds the power accepts the will of His servant."

"I will go with my uncle Abishai," said Zarah.

"To rejoice and give thanks," cried Hadassah.

But Zarah's sinking heart could not respond to any accents of joy. She bowed her head on her clasped hands, and faintly murmured,—

"To pray for you, for myself, and—"

No human ear could catch the word which her pale lips inaudibly framed.

"Go to our young Greek guest, Anna," said Hadassah. "Bear to him some of this ripe, cooling fruit, and tell him of the triumphs of Judas. Though Lycidas be but a heathen," she added, as her handmaiden quitted the apartment to do her bidding, "he has a soul to admire, if he cannot emulate, the lofty deeds of our heroes."

In a brief space of time Anna returned to the upper room, with alarm and surprise depicted on her face.

"I can nowhere find the Greek lord," she exclaimed. "He has made his escape from the house. There is nothing left but his mantle, and that had fallen near the spring."

Hadassah glanced inquiringly at Zarah. But the maiden betrayed no surprise, uttered no word. She only trembled a little, as if from cold ; for the sultry heat of Nisan seemed to her suddenly to have changed to the chill of winter. Hadassah made little observation on the flight of Lycidas until Anna had again quitted the apartment, when the widow lady said abruptly,—

"It was strange to leave without a word of farewell, a word of thanks, after having been for months treated as a guest, almost as a son ! "

Zarah, with her cold, nervous fingers, was unconsciously engaged in tearing the edge of her veil into a fringe.

" If I were not uneasy regarding the safety of Abishai," resumed Hadassah—

But here, for the first time in her life, Zarah, with an appearance of impatience, interrupted the speech of her revered relative.

" Have no fear for Abishai," cried the maiden, raising her head, and throwing back the long tresses which, from her drooping position, had fallen over her pallid face. " Have no fear for Abishai," she repeated. " The Greek will never repay your generous hospitality by revenging his private injuries upon your son. I can answer for his forbearance."

" You are right, my child," said Hadassah tenderly. " I did Lycidas a wrong by expressing a doubt. Abishai is secure in his silence ; and, such being the case, I

believe—nay, I feel assured—that it is better that we
harbour the stranger here no longer. I am thankful
that Lycidas has left us, though his manner of departing
seem somewhat churlish."

Was Zarah thankful also? Perhaps she was, though
a miserable void seemed to be left in that young heart,
which she felt that nothing could ever fill up. More an
orphan than the fatherless and the motherless, more desolate than the widow, loving and beloved, yet—save
for one sick and aged woman—alone in the world, it
seemed to Zarah that a slight tie bound her to life,
and that even that tie was gradually breaking. On the
eve of that day of sore trial, the spring behind the
dwelling had quite dried up: not a single drop gushed
forth from the hill to revive the fading oleanders.

Just before sunset a laden mule was driven to the
door of Hadassah's humble retreat. It was led by Joab,
a Jew who had in former years been servant to the lady,
and who had been one of those who had bravely assisted
in digging the grave of the martyrs. His presence,
therefore, in that unfrequented spot excited no alarm.

"Anna," said he, addressing the handmaid who stood
in the doorway (for he knew her by name), "help me to
unload my mule ; and do you bear what I bring to your
mistress."

"From whence comes all this?" asked Anna, with no
small curiosity.

"I met to-day," replied Joab, "the same stranger whom we caught lurking amidst the olives on the night of the burial of Solomona—(that was nigh being his last night upon earth!) He looked ghastly, as if himself new-risen from the grave, and scarcely able to drag his steps along. I helped to raise him on my mule, and it bore him to a house in the city which he mentioned. I doubt whether the Gentile recognized me—his mind seemed to be strangely wandering—till I asked him where he had been since we had met by moonlight under a tree; and then he started, and looked fixedly into my face. He knew me, and did not forget that I had been one to spare his life by stepping over the spear," continued the muleteer, with a grim smile. "The Gentile is not ungrateful. I suppose that he remembered that he owed a debt in another quarter also, for he bade me return in a few hours; and when I did so, charged me to bear these things to the dwelling of the Lady Hadassah—ay, and gave me this purse of silver for her handmaid."

"The Lord Lycidas has a noble heart! Would that he were a son of Abraham!" exclaimed the delighted Anna, as she received the gift of the Greek.

With mingled curiosity and pleasure Anna then carried up what Joab had brought to the house-top, on which the Hebrew ladies were then sitting, for the sake of the cooling breeze of even. At the bidding of Hadassah, Anna

removed the outer wrappings which enclosed what
Lycidas had sent, and drew forth a store of goodly gifts,
selected with exquisite taste—graceful ornaments, em-
broidery in gold, the lamp of delicate workmanship, the
mirror of polished steel. Anna could not forbear uttering exclamations of admiration ; but Hadassah and her

LYCIDAS' GIFTS.

grand-daughter looked on in grave silence, until a scroll was
handed to the former, which she opened and read aloud.

"With these worthless tokens of remembrance, accept
the deep gratitude of one who has learned in a few too
brief months under your roof more than he could else-
where have learned in a life-time, of the loftiness of faith
and the heroism of virtue."

CHAPTER XVIII

THE PASSOVER FEAST.

ERY different was the celebration of the Feast of Unleavened Bread in the days of Antiochus Epiphanes from what it had been in the palmy times when the children of Israel were swayed by their own native kings. There was now no mighty gathering together of the people from Dan to Beersheba ; herdsmen driving their lowing cattle, shepherds leading their bleating flocks from the slopes of Carmel and the pastures beneath the snow-capped heights of Lebanon. Fishermen left not their nets by the shores of the inland lakes, nor their boats drawn up on the coast by the sea, to go up, as their fathers had gone, to worship the Lord in Zion. There were no pilgrims from Sharon's plains or the mountains of Gilead. Jerusalem was not crowded with joyful worshippers, and her streets made almost impassable by the droves and flocks collected for sacrifice, as when Josiah held his never-to-be-forgotten Passover Feast. There were no loud bursts of joyful music, as when the singers, the sons of Asaph, ranged in their appointed places, led the chorus of glad thanksgiving. Groups of Hebrews, by twos and threes, stealthily made their way, as if bound on some secret and dangerous errand, to the few houses in which the owners were bold enough or pious enough to prepare the Paschal feast.

Amongst these dwellings was that of the elder Salathiel—a man who, in despite of threatened persecution, still dared to worship God according to the law as given through Moses. In an upper room in his house all was set ready for the celebration of the feast, in order as seemly as circumstances would permit. The Paschal lamb had been roasted whole in a circular pit in the ground; it had been roasted transfixed on two spits thrust through it, one lengthwise and one transversely, so as to form a cross. The wild and bitter herbs, with which it was to be eaten, had been carefully washed and prepared. On the table had been placed plates containing unleavened bread, and four cups filled with red wine mingled with water.

There had been difficulty in gathering together on this occasion, in the house of Salathiel, even the ten individuals that formed the smallest number deemed by the Hebrews sufficient for the due celebration of the feast. Three of the persons present were females, two of them belonging to Salathiel's own family. The third was Zarah, who, closely shrouded in her large linen veil, came under the escort of Abishai her uncle. The guests arrived late, having had to change their course more than once, from the suspicion that they were dogged by Syrian spies.

Greetings, in that upper chamber, were interchanged in low tones; whispered conversation was held as to the recent events, the tidings of which had thrilled like an electric shock through the heart of Jerusalem. The victories of Judas Maccabeus were in every mind and on every tongue. Glad prophecies were circulated amongst the guests that the next Passover would not be held in secret, and kept with maimed rites like the present; but that ere the circling year brought round the holy season again, the sanctuary would be cleansed, the city free, and that white-robed priests and Levites would gather together in the open face of day, where the smoke of sacrifice should rise from the altar of God's Temple.

Zarah was the most silent and sad of those who met in the house of Salathiel. Many thoughts were flowing through her mind, which she would not have dared to put into words.

"Is it sinful to desire that the blessings of the covenant were not so exclusive?" Thus mused the young Hebrew maid. "Is it sinful to wish that the wall of partition could be broken down, and that Jews and

Gentiles, descended from one common Father, and created by one merciful God, could meet to break bread and drink wine in loving communion together? And, if my mother Hadassah reads Scripture aright, may not such a time be approaching? Precious and goodly is the golden seven-branched candlestick of the Temple; but is not the Sun of Righteousness to arise with healing on His wings (Mal. iv. 2), and will the candlestick then be needed? The candles illumine but one chosen spot; the sun shines from the east to the west, the glory and light of the world. Can God care only for the children of Abraham? Lycidas has told us of far-distant isles in the West, where the poor savages are sunk in darkest idolatry, where they actually offer human sacrifices to their huge wicker-idols. Yet might not God in His loving-kindness have mercy even on such wretches as these? Would it be quite impossible that Britons should receive the light of His Word, even as they receive the light of His sunshine? I would fain cling to this hope; I trust that the hope is not presumptuous. And if even these savage islanders be not quite beyond reach of the mercy of the Great Father, will not that mercy embrace the Greeks, the brave, the noble, the gifted? But my thoughts wander upon dangerous ground. Can there be salvation for any that may not partake of the Paschal lamb? Is not exclusion from this feast exclusion from pardoning grace? Oh, that there could be a Lamb whose blood could take away the sins of all the world—a Sacrifice of such priceless worth, that not in Jerusalem alone, but through all the earth, there might be forgiveness, and hope, and salvation for all who in faith partake of its merits."

The solemn feast now commenced. The bread was blessed by Salathiel, broken, and then distributed around. The first cupful of wine was silently shared; but when the second was passed around, the lesser Hallel, being the 113th and 114th psalms, were chanted in low subdued tones.

Suddenly, in the midst of a verse, every voice was silenced at once, every head turned to listen. The clank of a weapon that had fallen on the paved courtyard below, was to the startled assembly above what the bloodhound's bay is to the deer.

"The Syrians have found us!—we are betrayed!" ejaculated Abishai, starting up and drawing his sword.

"Fly!—fly!" was echoed from mouth to mouth. The apartment in which the Hebrews were assembled had two doors—one communicating by a staircase with the courtyard below; the other, on the opposite side of the room, leading to the roof, which was near enough to other dwellings to afford a tolerable chance of escape to those who should make their way over them under cover of the dusk. It was partly on account of this advantage presented by Salathiel's house that it had been chosen as the scene of the Paschal Feast. The second door, through which escape might thus be effected, had been prudently left wide open, and at the first alarm there was a general rush made towards it.

Terror so often has the effect of confusing the mind, that the impressions made by passing events, though painfully vivid in colouring, are not distinct in their outlines. Zarah could have given no clear account of the scene which followed, which was to her like a horrible dream. The instinct to make her escape was strong; but as she attempted to fly, the maiden's veil caught in something, she knew not what; it was three or four seconds—they seemed as many hours—before she could extricate it. Zarah heard thundering noises at the one door, rushing sounds of flight at the other; then there was a bursting open of the frail barrier which divided her from the enemy, and Zarah felt rather than saw that the place was filled with soldiers. One sight was indelibly stamped on her brain—it was that of Abishai all streaming with blood, his eyes glaring and glazed, his teeth clenched, as he hissed out the word "apostate!" in the last pangs of death. Zarah knew that it was death.

Then rude hands were laid on herself; and the terrified girl felt as the gazelle feels under the claws of the tiger. She was too much alarmed to have breath even to utter a scream.

THE SURPRISE.

"Hold!—harm not the girl!" cried a voice which
sounded to Zarah strangely familiar, though she knew
not where she could possibly have heard it before; and
she saw a tall officer in Syrian dress, the same who has
been introduced to the reader more than once under the
name of Pollux, who appeared to be in command of the
assailing party. Zarah, in her agony of terror, stretched
out her hands for protection to one in whose features,

even at that moment, she recognized the Hebrew type. But Zarah could not appeal for mercy save by that supplicating gesture; horror so overpowered her senses that she swooned away; and had the steel then done its cruel work, she would have felt no pain. But the command of Antiochus had been rather to seize than to slay; and the soldiers, by the order of Pollux, carried off as their only prisoner a senseless maiden, leaving the dead body of Abishai on the floor dyed with his blood.

CHAPTER XIX.

A PRISON.

ROM her long swoon Zarah awoke with a sensation of indescribable horror. The cold drops stood on her brow, and there was a painful tightness at her heart. The poor girl could not at once recall what had happened, but knew that it was something dreadful. The first image that rose up in her mind was that of the expiring Abishai: Zarah shuddered, trembled, raised herself by an effort to a sitting posture, and wildly gazing around her, exclaimed, " Where am I ?—what can have happened ?"

The place in which the maiden found herself was almost quite dark, but as she glanced upwards she could see pale stars gleaming in through a small and heavily-barred window. She knew that she must be in a Syrian prison. Pressing both her hands to her forehead, the young captive recalled the terrible scene of which she had been a witness. " Oh, God be praised that be-

loved Hadassah was not there!" Zarah repeated again
and again to herself, as if to strengthen her grasp on the
only consolation which at first offered itself to her soul.
"Abishai's fate is awful—awful!" Zarah shuddered
with mingled compassion and horror. "But oh, it is
better, far better for him—my poor kinsman—that he
did not fall into the hands of the enemy alive, as I have
done! That would have been more awful still!"

Zarah was no high-spirited heroine, but a timid, gentle,
loving girl, subject to fears, shrinking from danger, peculiarly sensitive to pain, whether physical or mental.
Though related both to Solomona and Hadassah, Zarah
had neither the calm fortitude of the one, nor the exalted spirituality of the other; she deemed herself alike
incapable of uttering the inspired words of a prophetess,
or showing the firm endurance of a martyr.

And it was a martyr's trial that was now looming
before the imprisoned maiden: she would, like Solomona and her sons, have to renounce either her faith or
her life. To Zarah this was a terrible alternative; for
though but a few hours previously the poor maiden had
longed for death to come and release her from sorrow,
the idea of its approach, heralded by such tortures as
Hebrew captives had had to undergo, was unspeakably
dreadful to the tender spirit of Zarah.

"Oh, I fear that I shall never endure to the end;
my courage will give way; I shall disgrace myself, my

country, my race, and draw on myself the wrath of my God!" exclaimed Zarah, starting up in terror, after rehearsing to herself the ordeal to which her faith was likely to be exposed. "Woe is me!—what shall I do—what shall I do—is there no way of escape?" Those massive stone walls, those thick iron bars were sufficient answer to the question. Zarah leant against the wall, and raised her clasped hands towards the glimpse of sky seen between those dark bars.

"Oh, my God, have mercy upon me!" she cried; "feeble, utterly helpless in myself, I cast myself upon Thee! Thou hast said, *When thou passest through the waters, I will be with thee; when thou walkest through the fire, thou shalt not be burned.* Carry the weak lamb in Thy bosom; let me feel beneath the everlasting arms!" The tears were flowing fast down Zarah's cheeks as she sobbed forth her almost inarticulate prayer: "I ask not to be saved from death—not even from torture—if it be Thy will that I should endure it; but oh, save me from falling away from Thee; save me from denying my faith, and breaking the heart of my mother! —And I shall surely be saved!" said Zarah more calmly, her faith gaining strength from the exercise of prayer. "Perhaps the Lord will make the pain tolerable—He to whom all things are possible can do so—or He may even send an angel to protect me, as He sent His bright and holy ones to guard Elisha." The imagination of Zarah pictured a being with glorious wings flying down to her rescue, with a countenance resembling that of Lycidas— to her the type of perfect beauty. "Or the Lord may raise up some earthly friend," continued Zarah. Then fancy again pictured a Lycidas, but this time wanting the wings. The maiden stopped her weeping, and dashed the limpid drops from her eyes. A gleam of brightness seemed to illumine the dark prospect before her. How eagerly do we listen to the voice of hope, even if it be but the echo of a wish—an echo thrown back from the cold hard rock which can only repeat the utterance of our own heart's desires ; it comes back to us like music ! Zarah's prison would have been far more dreary to the maiden, her approaching trial far more dreadful, had she known the fact that Lycidas had gone to Bethlehem, and had heard nothing of the peril of her whom he loved.

In the same unconsciousness of Zarah's imminent peril, another, to whom she was dearer than the sight of the eyes or the breath of life, lay extended on the ground in sleep, many miles from Jerusalem, with no pillow but that stalwart arm, around which was still twined a slight flaxen strand. A monarch might have envied the dream which made the features of the sleeper relax into an expression of happiness which, when waking, they seldom indeed wore. Maccabeus, lying on the parched dry earth, was in thought seated in an Eden of flowers, with Zarah at his side, her small hand clasped in his own.

She was listening, with bashful smile and downcast eyes, to words such as the warrior had never breathed to her, save in his dreams. All was peace within and without, peace deepening into rapture, even as the sky above appeared almost dark from the intensity of its blue! Such was the Hebrew's dream of Zarah! How different the dream from the actual reality! Had Maccabeus known the actual position of the helpless girl, to guard whom from the slightest wrong he would so willingly have shed his life's blood, even that heart which had never yet quailed in the face of peril would have known for once the keenest anguish of fear.

CHAPTER XX

THE COURT OF ANTIOCHUS.

FIERCE had been the rage and disappointment of Antiochus Epiphanes on hearing of the result of the night attack on his forces at Emmaus, and the subsequent retreat of Giorgias without striking a blow. In vain the troops of that too cautious leader endeavoured, by exaggerating the account of the numbers of their enemies, to cover their own shame. Antiochus was furious alike at what he termed the insolence of a handful of outlaws, and the cowardice of his picked troops, who had flaunted their banners and gone forth as if to assured victory, and had then fled like some gay-plumed bird before the swoop of the eagle. Not only the oppressed inhabitants of Jerusalem and its environs had cause to tremble at the rage of the tyrant, but his own Syrian officers and the obsequious courtiers who stood in his presence. And none more so than Pollux, once the chosen companion and special favourite of the Syrian king. Pollux had been so loaded with wealth and honours by his capricious master, as to have become an object of envy to his fellow-courtiers, and especially so to Lysimachus, a Syrian of high birth, who had seen himself passed in the race for royal favour by a rival whom he despised. But there was little cause for envying Pollux, the wretched parasite of a tyrant. Alas, for him who has bartered conscience and self-respect to win a monarch's smile! He has left the firm though narrow path of duty, to find himself on a treacherous quicksand, where the ground on which he places his foot soon begins to give way beneath him!

A few months before the time of which I am writing, Pollux, after a long sojourn in Antioch, then the capital of the Syrian dominions, had rejoined Antiochus in Jerusalem, where the monarch was holding his court in a luxurious palace which he had caused to be erected. It was here that Pollux first experienced the fickleness of royal favour. The courtier had been present at the trial of Solomona and her brave sons without making the slightest effort to save them, though their fate had moved him to something more than pity. But though Pollux could to a certain extent trample down compunction, and force his conscience to silence, he had not perfect command over his nerves. He might consent to the perpetration of horrors, but he could not endure to witness them; and, as we have seen, he had quietly, and, as he hoped, without attracting notice, quitted the chamber of torture.

The keen eye of jealousy had, however, keenly watched the movements of Pollux, and Lysimachus had not failed to make the most of the weakness betrayed by his rival.

"Pollux has sympathy with the Hebrews," observed Lysimachus to the tyrant, when Antiochus was chafing at being baffled by the fortitude of his victims. "Pollux may wear the Syrian garb, and be loaded with favours by the mighty Syrian king, but he remains at heart a Jew."

From that day Pollux found himself an object of suspicion, and having once reached the quicksand, he gradually sank lower and lower, notwithstanding his desperate efforts to save himself from impending ruin. His most costly gifts, his most fulsome flattery, his assurances of deathless devotion to "the greatest, noblest of the kings who sway realms conquered by Alexander, and surpass the fame of Macedonia's godlike hero," met but the coldest response. Pollux had once been wont to delight the king with his brilliant wit; now his forced jests fell like sparks upon water. Antiochus was growing tired of his favourite, as a child grows tired of the toy which he hugs one day, to break and fling aside on the next.

All the more embarrassed from having to simulate

ease, all the more wretched because forcing himself to seem merry, with the sword of Damocles ever hanging over his head, Pollux, in the midst of luxury and pomp, was one of the most miserable of mankind. The court became to him at last an almost intolerable place. In an attempt at once to free himself from its restraints and to win back the favour of the king by military ser vice, in an evil hour for himself, he had volunteered to join the forces of Nicanor. The courtier was incited by no military ardour; he had no desire to fall on the field of victory; Pollux was not a coward, but he clung to life as those well may cling who have forfeited all hope of anything but misery beyond it. Pollux, as we have seen, had accompanied Giorgias when that general led a detachment of chosen troops to make that night attack upon Judas which had proved so unsuccessful. With Giorgias, Pollux had returned to Jerusalem, covered with shame instead of glory. More than his fair share of the obloquy incurred had fallen to the unfortunate courtier.

"Be assured, O most mighty monarch"—thus had Lysimachus addressed the disappointed tyrant—"that had there been no sympathizers with the Hebrew rebels in the army of the king, Giorgias would have returned to Jerusalem with the head of Judas Maccabeus hanging at his saddle-bow."

The insinuation was understood—the instilled poison worked its effect. Antiochus had met his former favourite

with an ominous frown.   He did not, however, consign
Pollux to irremediable ruin ; he gave him a chance of
redeeming his character from the imputation of treachery
towards the Syrian cause.   Pollux received a commission
from Antiochus to attack and seize a party of Hebrews
who, according to information brought by spies, were to
celebrate the Passover Feast in Salathiel's house, in defiance of the edict by which the king had endeavoured
to crush the religion of those who still worshipped the
God of their fathers.

An office more repugnant to the feelings of Pollux
could scarcely have been assigned to him, but he dared
not show the slightest hesitation in obeying the mandate ; nay, the courtier even feigned joy at the opportunity given him of serving the king by rooting out the
religion which, in the secret depths of his heart, Pollux
regarded as the only true one; for he could not obliterate
from memory lessons once learned on his mother's knee.
The poor wretch was, as it were, sunk in the quicksand
up to his lips, and would have clutched at red-hot iron,
had such been the only means of drawing him upwards
out of the living grave in which he was being gradually
entombed.

Wearing the mask of mirth to conceal his misery,
Pollux, before setting out on his hateful mission, jested
in regard to the number of fanatic Jews whom he would
enclose in his toils, and bring to make sport before the

king, to fight wild beasts in the large gymnasium, which had been erected within Jerusalem for games which the Jews regarded as unlawful and sinful. The courtier, in the presence of Antiochus, affected the gay delight of the hunter, trying to cover with a garb of levity the remorse which was gnawing at his heart, and not betray, even by a look, the secret torture which he felt.

We know what followed the attack upon Salathiel's house : the flight of the Hebrews, the fall of Abishai, whose last word and dying look inflicted upon Pollux a pang keen enough to have satisfied the fiercest thirst for revenge.

When tidings were brought to the palace that the result of the boasted exertions of Pollux was the death of a single Hebrew and the capture of one young girl, the wrath of the tyrant Antiochus Epiphanes rose higher than before. His courtiers, catching the infection of the anger of the king, showed something of what would have been the indignant rage of an audience crowding the Coliseum at Rome in the expectation of gloating on the sight of many victims flung to the lions, had the spectacle been reduced to the sacrifice of one.

Antiochus, however, determined to have what sport he could out of the single poor gazelle that had been run down by his hounds. One who—albeit, of the weaker sex—had been venturesome enough to keep the Passover Feast, might make sufficient resistance to his

arbitrary will to afford him a little amusement, when
none more exciting could be had. The monarch, therefore, after he had enjoyed his noonday siesta, gave command that the Hebrew prisoner should be brought into
his presence in his grand hall of audience.

There sat the tyrant of Syria on an ivory throne, his
footstool a crouching silver lion, over his head a canopy
of gold. In front of the king was a splendid altar, on
which fire was constantly burning before a small image
of Jupiter; and the luxurious fragrance of incense, frequently thrown on this fire, filled the magnificent hall.
Many courtiers, in splendid apparel, clustered on either
side below the dais which raised the throned monarch
above them all. Behind these were numerous slaves,
mostly Nubians, richly and gaudily dressed, some of
whom held aloft large fans of the peacock's many-tinted
plumes. The whole scene was one of gorgeous magnificence, the pomp and glory of the world throwing its
false halo of beauty over guilty power.

Antiochus himself wore a robe crusted over with
sparkling jewels, worth the tribute of a conquered pro-
vince. He was, as his appearance has been handed
down to us on coins, a kingly-looking man, with short
curled hair, and regular, strongly-marked features, but a
receding forehead, and an expression cold and hard. No
one would expect from him "the milk of human kindness." Antiochus looked what he was—a stern, merci-

less tyrant. There was at this period no premonitory sign in the appearance of the king of that frightful disease which, within a year's time, was to render him an object of horror and loathing to all who approached him—a disease so exquisitely painful, that it seemed to combine and exceed all the tortures which the tyrant had made his victims endure. Antiochus, glittering on his ivory throne, appeared to be in the prime of health as well as the zenith of power; none guessed how brief was the term of mortal existence remaining to the despot, on the breath of whose lips now hung fortune or ruin, whose angry frown was a sentence of death.

CHAPTER XXI

EFORE this gorgeous assembly—before this terrible king—stood, surrounded by guards, a trembling, shrinking girl, wrapping closer and closer her linen veil around her slight form and drooping head.

"Tear off her veil!" said the king.

The command was instantly obeyed, and, like the painful glare of noonday to one brought suddenly out of darkness, the terrible splendour of the scene before her flashed upon Zarah. Her exquisite beauty, as her face now flushed crimson with shame at having to meet, without the protection of a veil, so many gazing eyes, then turned pale from overwhelming fear, caused an involuntary murmur of admiration to burst from the throng.

"No Herculean task to bend this willow wand," observed Antiochus, even his hard stern countenance relaxing into a smile. "Bring her nearer." The guards obeyed. Zarah approached the king, but with timid, faltering steps; how different from the firm tread with which a captive Maccabeus would have drawn nigh to the oppressor who might slay but never subdue him!

"There is the altar of Jupiter Olympus—that of Venus would have been more appropriate to so fair a votary," said Antiochus, with an oath; "but it little matters which deity receives the homage, so that it be duly paid. Maiden, throw some grains of yon incense into the flame, bend the knee in worship, and I promise you," the king added, with a laugh, "a gay house and a gallant husband, pearls and goodly array, and all else that a young maid's heart can desire."

Zarah did not stir; she did not appear to have even understood or heard the words of the king, only her lips were moving in agonized prayer.

Antiochus repeated more sternly his command to offer the incense.

"Oh, my God, help me; let me not be tried beyond what I can bear!" was the silent ejaculation which rose from the heart of the terror-stricken girl, as she slightly shook her bended head as her only reply.

"What! silent still," cried Antiochus, with displeasure. "Know you not, young mute, that we have workers of miracles here,"—he pointed to some black African slaves who performed the office of executioners;

" these are skilful to bring sounds, and those some of the shrillest, from lips the most closely sealed."

In terror Zarah raised her dark eyes and looked wildly around her, in the vain hope of seeing some one, perhaps Lycidas himself, from whom she might receive protection or pity. But there was not a single countenance amidst the gay throng of courtiers that promised anything but cold indifference to, if not cruel amusement in her sufferings or her degradation; unless, perhaps, that of Pollux formed an exception. Zarah's anxious gaze rested for a moment on his face with an imploring look of entreaty, which might have touched a harder heart than his.

"I brook no more idle delay!" cried Antiochus; "as you love your life, do sacrifice at once to my god."

"I cannot—I dare not!" exclaimed the young maid. Faint as was her utterance of the words, they were heard distinctly, so great was the silence which prevailed through the assembly in that marble hall.

The answer surprised Antiochus and his courtiers.

"Ha! there is some resistance in the willow-wand then, after all!" cried the king, half amused and half angry. "I warrant me tough boughs grow on the tree from which that slender twig has sprung.—Tell me, fair rebel," he continued, "your name and lineage, and the place of your birth."

Zarah had firmly resolved that, come what might, she would betray no friend; above all, that she would never draw down the fire of persecution upon the house of Hadassah. In the midst of all the misery which she was enduring from personal fear, Zarah forgot not this resolution.

"My name is Zarah; I was born in Bethsura; my father was called Abner," faltered forth the young maid.

Pollux involuntarily started and gasped, as if every word had been a live coal dropped upon his bare breast. It was well for him then that all eyes, even those of Lysimachus, were fixed at that moment on Zarah.

"Is your father living?" inquired the king, who, in the common name of Abner, did not recognize the almost forgotten one previously borne by a favourite.

"I know not," was the reply.

"Was he not with you at the rebellious meeting?" asked Antiochus Epiphanes.

"No; I went with my uncle, who was slain: he was my only companion thither," said the trembling maiden, thankful to be able with truth to say what would bring no person into peril.

There was a brief pause, to Zarah inexpressibly awful; then Antiochus Epiphanes, he who had looked on the dying agonies of Solomona and her sons, said in his stern voice of command, "I am not wont to bid thrice, and woe to those who presume to neglect my bidding. Throw incense on that fire, or the consequences be upon your

own head.   Others have experienced ere this what it is
to brave my displeasure and disobey my command."

Bewildered and terrified, Zarah suffered, as if scarcely
conscious of the import of the act, a few grains of incense to
be put into her hand, then, recovering her self-possession,
she flung them from her with a look of aversion and horror.

"Ha! is it so?" thundered Antiochus; "if the incense go not into the fire, the hand that held it shall go.
—Executioners, do your work!"

Four of the fierce black slaves approached the young
Hebrew maiden.   She clasped her hands, and shrieked
out, "Father, save me!"   It was no mortal to whom
she addressed that wild cry for help.

But the cry was answered by a mortal.   Pollux, as if
moved by an irresistible impulse, sprang forward, by a
gesture of his hand arrested the movements of the executioners, and bent his knee before Epiphanes.

"The mighty king," he began, with a great effort to
appear indifferent and at his ease—"the mighty king
has spoken of magicians who have skill to force out
sounds from lips that are dumb.   I dispute not the
power of yonder black magi, but I should deem one
their superior in the mysterious art who could bring
songs rather than shrieks from a Hebrew; who could
subdue the proud will rather than torture the body.
Oh, illustrious monarch of the world, let me but for
twenty-four hours try my potent spells upon this young

rebel, and I will answer for it with my head that, before
the twenty-four hours be past, she shall gladly and
cheerfully do sacrifice to any god in Olympus, feast on
swine's flesh, dance as a Bacchante, or drink wine, like
Belshazzar of old, out of the vessels of the Temple. Try
my powers, O king, and according to my failure or
success, so be the maiden's fate and mine!"

Antiochus hesitated; with a look of keen suspicion
he regarded the kneeling courtier. Zarah watched the
king's countenance with breathless anxiety—a respite
even of twenty-four hours seemed to the poor captive so
priceless a boon. Intense was her relief when she heard
the tyrant's reply to Pollux :—

"Twenty-four hours' delay you have asked, and I
grant. It were a nobler triumph to make a proselyte
than to slay a victim. I myself, as you well know,
Pollux," continued the tyrant, with sarcastic emphasis,
"won such a triumph myself. Take yonder obstinate
Jewess, and work upon her your spells, whatever they
may be; but hear my final decision," the king raised his
hand and uttered a deep oath : "if to-morrow you have
failed in doing what you now undertake to perform, if
the girl be obdurate still, the moment when she refuses to
do sacrifice shall be your last upon earth—she shall go
to the furnace, and her protector to the block."

And then, with an imperious gesture of command,
Antiochus dismissed the assembly.

CHAPTER XXII.

A BREATHING SPACE.

THE captive was not taken back to the prison-chamber which she had occupied during the preceding night, but to an apartment in the palace—one belonging to the suite appropriated to Pollux. She was confined within a room so luxurious, that, save from the door being fastened to prevent her exit, and there being no possibility of escaping through the latticed window, Zarah could scarcely have realized that she was a prisoner still. The floor of the apartment was inlaid with costly marbles; on the walls were depicted scenes taken from mythological subjects; luxurious divans invited to repose; and vases, wreathed with brilliant flowers and filled with rose-water, were surrounded by others loaded with a profusion of fruit and a variety of dainties. The young Hebrew maiden, accustomed to the simplicity of Hadassah's humble home, gazed around in wonder.

When left alone by the guards, the first impulse of the captive was to kneel and return thanks to her heavenly Protector for the merciful respite granted to her. Zarah was young, and hope was strong within her. What might not happen in the space of twenty-four hours to effect complete deliverance! She then laved her face, hands, and arms, and the tresses of her long hair, in the cool, fragrant water, and found great refreshment from her ablutions. It was then with a sense of enjoyment, at which she herself was surprised, that Zarah partook of the fruit before her. Nature had been almost exhausted, not only by the terrible excitement and alarm which the maiden had had to endure, but by sleeplessness and abstinence from food. Coarse bread had indeed been brought to her in her prison, but had remained untouched, not only because the poor captive had had no appetite for eating, but because the bread, being leavened, was not at that season lawful food for a Jewess. Zarah now carefully abstained from any part of the collation which she deemed might contain anything which Moses had judged unclean, and chiefly partook of the fruits, which were pure, as God Himself had made them, and which were, of all kinds of food, that most refreshing to her parched and burning lips.

"How good is my Lord, to spread a table for me thus in this wilderness of trial!" murmured Zarah; and she felt much as the Israelites must have felt when they first saw the glistening bread of heaven lying on the face of the desert. The maiden's spirit was soothed and cheered, as well as her frame refreshed; and, reclining on one of the luxurious divans, she was able with tolerable calmness to review the exciting events of the day.

" How thankful I am that, with all my cowardice and weakness, I was preserved by my Lord from doing anything very wicked !" thought Zarah. " I was not suffered either to betray my friends or to deny my God; and yet my faith almost failed me. I could scarcely endure the terror : how could I endure the pain ? But will not He who supported me under the one sustain me also through the other, if I must die for my faith to-morrow before that terrible king ? I will not weary myself by thinking; I will just trust all to my God. It is so sweet to rest in His love, like a babe on her mother's bosom."

Zarah lay perfectly still for some time, letting her overstrained nerves regain their usual tone. It was such a comfort to be quite alone, with no sound to disturb save the cooing of doves from a garden which separated the palace of Epiphanes from Mount Zion.

The young captive then arose, went to the lattice, and looked forth. Pleasant to the sight was the rich foliage of the juniper and acacia, the terebinth and the palm, the orange, almond, and citron, watered from marble-bordered tanks by artificial irrigation, which counteracted the effects of a season sultry and dry. Here and there fountains threw up their sparkling waters, transformed to diamonds in the sun. But the eyes of the maid of Judah wandered beyond this paradise of beauty, created for the pleasure of a tyrant, and rested on the holy Mount and the sacred Temple on its summit. If the very stones, nay, the dust, of Jerusalem have an interest to Gentile strangers, with what feelings must a child of Abraham regard the spot on which the Temple was reared! As Zarah gazed on the holy pile before her, words of Scripture came into the mind of Hadassah's granddaughter, which filled her with a joy which was indeed nourished by the dew of heavenly hope, but had its root in earthly affection. Slowly and emphatically Zarah repeated to herself: *Also the sons of the stranger, that join themselves to the Lord, to serve Him, and to love the name of the Lord, to be His servants, every one that keepeth the Sabbath from polluting it, and taketh hold of My covenant; even them will I bring to My holy mountain, and make them joyful in my house of prayer: . . . for Mine house shall be called an house of prayer for all people*" (Isa. lvi. 6, 7).

"Oh, blessed promise!" exclaimed Zarah. "Israel has been, like Joseph, the chosen amongst many brethren, to wear the many-coloured robe prepared by his Father, and to go first, through bondage and tribulation, to dignity and honour. But his brethren are not forgotten:

he shall yet be a blessing to them all, even to them who
have hated and sold him. Through Israel shall light
spread throughout the dark world, and with the bread of
life shall the hungry nations be fed."

Zarah was interrupted in her musings by the entrance
of Nubian slaves, who silently replenished the vases,

ZARAH AND THE SLAVES.

lighted silver lamps as the day was closing, placed rich
garments upon the divan, and then retired from her
presence. Their coming had caused a flutter in the
timid heart of the captive; and it was a relief when
they had left her again to that solitude which scarcely

seemed to be loneliness, so sweet were the thoughts which had been her companions. Zarah went up to the divan, and looked admiringly on the silken robes and richly-embroidered veil.

"These are meant for my wear," said the maiden; " but I will not touch them. The Gentiles would allure me, as the serpent allured Eve our mother, by the lust of the eyes and the pride of life. Embroidered robes are not for the prisoner, nor the silver zone for the martyr. This simple blue garment, spun and woven by my own hands, is good enough to die in."

Zarah watched the sun as it sank beneath the western horizon, its last beams lingering on the pinnacles of the Temple.

"Perhaps this will be my last evening on earth," thought the prisoner. " Ere the sun set again, I may have entered into eternal rest." A deep sense of holy peace stole into the maiden's heart, though the expression of her beautiful countenance was pensive as she meditated on the future. " I shall no more join in worship with my brethren below; but perhaps, while they gather together in secret, with perils around them, my eyes shall see the King in His beauty, shall behold the land that is very far off. And will not He for whom I die hear now my feeble prayers for those whom I leave behind? Never have I felt that I could plead with such child-like confidence before Him as I do now; praying not only for myself, but for those who are dearer than self. Oh, may the Lord hear, and graciously answer, the supplications of His child!"

Zarah knelt down, and poured out her simple prayer. First, she besought God for Hadassah; that He would comfort the bereaved one, grant her rest from her tribulation, and give her the desire of her heart. Tears mingled with this prayer, as Zarah thought of the desolation to which the aged widow was left. "Let her not weep long for me," murmured the maiden; "and oh, never let her want a loving one to tend her in sickness and comfort her in sorrow better than I could have done." The Hebrew girl then prayed for her country, and for those who were fighting for its freedom; especially for Judas Maccabeus, that God would be his shield and defender, and cover his head in the day of battle. Zarah forgot not her unknown father. She now pleaded for him more fervently than she had ever pleaded before; and, by some mysterious connection in her mind, thoughts of her lost parent linked themselves to remembrance of the generous courtier to whose intercession she had owed her present respite from torture and death. The young prisoner implored her Lord not to let the Syrian suffer for his kindness to a stranger, but to requite it sevenfold into his own bosom.

Zarah did not yet rise from her knees. Her supplications became yet more fervent as she prayed for another, dearest of all. No fear of displeasing God now marred the comfort which the maiden found in supplication for a Gentile. It was not sinful, she thought, for the dying to love. Her misery might be the means which God would deign to employ in winning Lycidas from the errors of idolatrous worship. She might be permitted, as it were, to beckon to her beloved from the other side of the grave.

Zarah arose from her devotions feeling almost happy. It seemed to her as if the worst bitterness of death were already passed. She again partook, with a thankful spirit, of needful refreshment, and afterwards laid herself down to rest. The prisoner had had no refreshing sleep during the preceding terrible night, and now her eyelids were heavy. Soft slumber stole over Zarah, as the Psalmist's words were on her lips, *I will both lay me down in peace and sleep, for Thou, Lord, only makest me dwell in safety.*

CHAPTER XXIII.

SO profound was the slumber of the weary girl that she heard not the sound of opening the door, nor a step on the marble floor, and lay unconscious of the yearning, anxious, mournful gaze that was fixed upon her as she slept.

"Lovely, most lovely—fairer even than her mother!" murmured Pollux, as he stood beside the couch of Zarah, upon whose slumbering form softly fell the light from a silver lamp. "Even so beautiful and so pure lay my Naomi, when the angel of death had in mercy called her soul away, and bereft me of a gift of which I was so unworthy."

What bitter memories of early years passed through the renegade's soul as he spoke! Happy days, when there was no shame on the brow, no gnawing worm in the conscience—when he had feared the face of no man, and had dared to lift his eyes towards heaven, and his heart to One who dwelt there! Blessed days, never, never to come again!

"Hark! she speaks in her sleep. What says she?"

Pollux bent down his head to listen, and caught the faint murmur, "My poor, poor father!"

The groan which burst from the apostate's lips awoke the sleeper. Zarah started into a sitting posture, and, with a gesture of alarm, threw back the long tresses which had partly fallen over her face.

"Fear not, poor child; I would not harm you," said Pollux, in a gentle, soothing tone, which restored Zarah's confidence at once.

"Oh no; I will not fear you," she cried, recognizing her protector; "it was you—the God of Jacob requite you for it!—it was you who saved me to-day."

"And will do so again," said Pollux, as he seated himself at Zarah's side; "but I cannot save you in spite of yourself. You must let yourself be guided by me."

"What would you have me do?" asked Zarah.

"Bend to the force of circumstances, humour the mighty king, give an outward obedience to his will. I have pledged myself that you should do so. There is nothing so dreadful, after all," continued the courtier, forcing a smile, "in bowing the knee as others do, or in burning a few grains of incense. It is but a little matter."

"A little matter!" repeated Zarah, opening wide her eyes in innocent surprise ; "is it a little matter for me to throw away my soul, and break the heart of Hadassah ? "

Pollux winced on hearing the name, but quickly recovering himself, observed, "The heart of no woman would be thus broken. She would feel a pang less keen at your falling away for a time, than that which would wring her soul should you die by the executioner's hand."

"You have never seen Hadassah ; you do not know her !" exclaimed Zarah with spirit ; "she, has told me herself that she would rather lose seven children by death than one by apostasy from God !"

Pollux bit his nether lip till the blood came. When he resumed speaking, his voice sounded hoarse and strange.

"If you care not for your own danger, maiden, think of my peril ; my head is staked upon your submission," he said.

Zarah looked distressed and perplexed for a moment, then her fair face brightened again. "Even cruel Antiochus," she replied, "would never slay one of his nobles because he failed in persuading a Hebrew girl to violate conscience. You are not—cannot be in peril through me."

"I am, whether you believe it or not," said the courtier. "But methinks, when speaking to a girl like yourself in the morning of life, with so much that might make existence delightful "— Pollux glanced at the luxurious decorations of the apartment—" one might be supposed to need small power of persuasion to convince her that music, dance, and feasting are better than torture ; life than death ; nature's sunshine and earth's love than a nameless grave. The king is munificent to those who oppose not his will; his hand is bounteous and open. Listen to me, fair maiden. Antiochus has promised, if you yield to his commands, to give you in marriage ; it shall be my care that his choice for you shall fall upon one gentle and noble, one who will not deal harshly with you if you choose to follow your own religion, but who will accord to you in the privacy of your home all the freedom of worship which you could desire." Pollux paused, turning over in his mind who would be the noble most likely to fulfil these conditions ; and thinking aloud, he uttered the words, "such a one as Lycidas the Athenian."

How the heart of Zarah bounded at the name ! The temptation was fearfully strong. She beheld life and Lycidas on the one hand ; on the other the cold steel and the glowing flame, and those black fearful ministers of death, the remembrance of whom made her shudder.

Pollux, skilful in the courtier's art of reading the thoughts of men, saw symptoms of yielding in the face of his prisoner, and pushed his advantage. He had ap-

pealed to Zarah's instincts, now he attempted to dazzle
and pervert her reason.   With subtle sophistry he
brought forward arguments with which his mind was
but too familiar.   Pollux spoke of necessity, that artful
plea of the tempter, who would try to make the Deity
Himself answerable for the sin of His creatures, as
having placed them under circumstances where such sin
could not be avoided ; as if strength of temptation were
excuse sufficient for yielding to the temptation.   Then
the courtier spoke of the difference between spiritual
worship, the assent of the soul to a lofty creed, and the
mere outward posture of the body.   The latter might
bow down in the house of Rimmon, Pollux argued, while
the spirit retained its allegiance to the only true God.
Nay, the tempter quoted Scripture (as the devil himself
can quote it) to show that what God demands is the
heart, and that therefore He cares little for the
homage of the knee.   The courtier tried to involve
the artless girl in the meshes of his false philosophy,
but a woman's simple faith and love burst through
them all.

"Leave me—leave me !" cried Zarah passionately, at
the first pause made by Pollux ; "it is sinful, cruel, to
tempt me thus !   You would have tried to persuade the
three children in Babylon to bow down to the image of
gold !   I cannot argue, I cannot reason with one so learned
as you are, but I know that it is written in God's Law,

Thou shalt not bow down nor worship, and that is enough for me."

"But you never can endure the agonies which await you if you madly hold out in your obstinate resistance!" cried Pollux.

"I know that I have no strength of my own; I know that I am a trembling, feeble, cowardly girl, weak as water!" exclaimed Zarah, bursting into tears; "but God—my God—once made a firm wall of water, and He who sends the trial will send the strength to endure it!"

"Zarah, you will drive me to madness!" exclaimed Pollux, alarmed at the constancy shown by so timid and fragile a being; "nay, turn not away, I *will* be heard! I command you to yield obedience to the king, and I have a right to command; Zarah, he who speaks to you is—your father!"

Had not instinct suggested that before, had there not been something in the voice, the face of the courtier of Epiphanes which had reminded Zarah of Hadassah, and had strangely drawn the maiden's heart towards him? Up sprang Abner's daughter with a cry, her arms were around his neck, her head was pillowed on his bosom, his vest was wet with her tears; she sobbed forth, "My father! my father!" forgetting for the moment everything else in the delight of having found the lost one at last, and of being locked in the embrace of a parent.

And Pollux, for a brief space, could thing of nothing but the fact that his child was clasped in his arms. He drew her close to his heart, then held her back that he might gaze upon her face, and press kiss after kiss on the lips of her whom he called his darling, his pride, his beautiful child! But when the first burst of natural emotion was over, Pollux made his daughter sit close beside him, and with his arm round her slight form, resumed the conversation which had been interrupted by his revealing the intimate relationship in which they stood to each other.

"You see, my child," said the courtier, "that you may now yield with an easy conscience. A parent's commands are law to a Hebrew maiden; if there be any sin in what you do, it lies upon me alone."

"And think you that I would bring sin upon your head?" said Zarah. "Oh no, that would be to wrong a parent indeed!"

"I have such a burden of my own to carry," observed Pollux, bitterly, "that I shall scarcely be sensible of so small an addition to its weight. Zarah, it is clearly your duty to submit, for my safety is involved in your submission. If you refuse to obey Antiochus, you seal the doom of your father."

In anguish Zarah clasped her throbbing temples with both her hands; even the path of duty itself seemed dark and uncertain before her. Then a thought, sudden and bright, as if it were an inspiration, came into the young girl's mind.

"Oh no, I will save my father!" she exclaimed; "save him from worse than death! Let us fly together at once," she continued; "no, not together,—I would cumber your flight; but make your escape, O my father, from this wicked court, this barbarous king, this life which, to a son of Hadassah, must be misery and bondage indeed! Oh, fly, fly! be safe, be free! be again what you were once! it is not too late! it is not too late!" There was intense delight to Zarah in the new-born hope that she might draw her wretched parent from this den of infamy, this pit of destruction.

Pollux was startled by the sudden suggestion. "Whither could I fly?" asked the renegade gloomily.

"To Judas Maccabeus, our hero," cried Zarah; "his camp is the rallying-place for all fugitives from oppression."

"Maccabeus!" exclaimed Pollux; "he would loathe —would spurn an apostate!"

"Oh no, he would never spurn the father of Zarah," cried the maiden, for once realizing and exulting in the secret power which she exercised over the leader of the Hebrews; "Judas would welcome you; his brave companions would welcome, coming as you would come to redeem the past, by devoting your sword to your country! God would receive you; and Hadassah," continued

Zarah, her enthusiasm kindling into rapture as she went on—" Hadassah, in her joy, her ecstasy, would forget all her grief; the thought of her long-lost son being with Maccabeus would enable her almost to rejoice at her Zarah being—with God."

" Impossible, impossible," muttered Pollux, rising from his seat as if to depart; but Zarah detected indecision in his tone. She threw herself at his feet, she clasped his knees, she pleaded with passionate fervour, for she deemed that a parent's life and soul were at stake.

" O father, if you would but consent to leave for ever this horrible, horrible place, to return to your people, your mother, your God, I feel as if I could die happy, so happy; we should then meet again in a brighter world, all, all reunited, and for ever !"

It was as the voice of his guardian angel—as if his once fondly-loved wife had been suffered to visit Abner in mortal form, to counsel, warn, entreat; to tell him that there yet might be mercy for him if he would but turn and repent! There was a terrific struggle in the renegade's mind. He could not at once decide on taking so bold and sudden a leap as that to which he was urged, though conscious of the peril as well as misery of his present position at the court. As the deer, driven by wolves to the precipice's brink, hesitates on making the plunge down—though it give him the only chance

PASSIONATE PLEADING.

of escape from the ravening jaws of his fierce pursuers—
so hesitated the wretched Pollux.

He would have felt no indecision had he known that,
at the very time when Zarah was pleading in tears at

his feet, Antiochus was signing, in the presence of the
exulting Lysimachus, a warrant for the execution of
Pollux on the morrow.   His rival had succeeded in
working his ruin ; the only door of safety yet open to
the apostate was that towards which his child, with fervent entreaties, was trying to draw him ; shortly—little
dreamed Pollux how shortly—that door of safety would
be closed.   Unable to form a sudden resolution, to come
to a prompt decision, seeing difficulties and dangers on
every side, fearing to remain where he was, yet afraid
to fly, Pollux wasted the precious time yet given him,
he let the golden moments escape.   In a state of strong
excitement, he at length quitted his daughter's presence,
to seek that solitude in which his perturbed mind might
become sufficiently calm to form a judgment which must
be as the pivot upon which his whole future life would
turn.   Pollux left Zarah still on her knees, nor did she
rise when he had torn himself from her clinging arms
and left the apartment.   When the daughter could no
longer plead with, she pleaded for her father ; she implored that grace and wisdom might be given to him at
this momentous crisis.   There was no more sleep for
Zarah on that eventful night.

CHAPTER XXIV.

DECISION.

TOSSED backwards and forwards on a wild sea of doubt—a vessel without ballast, compass, or rudder—was the mind of the miserable Pollux. The courtier paced for hours up and down a verandah where the cool breeze of heaven could fan him, and where he would be secure from interruption. Ever and anon Pollux tore his beard, or smote his breast; unconsciously giving expression by outward gesture to the inward torture which he felt. Was he to give up all at once—all for which he had bartered his soul—rank, wealth, position—to begin life again on the lowest round of the ladder, with the brand of disgrace, the burden of shame upon him? Could he endure to appear in the presence of Maccabeus, to sue from him the place of hewer of wood and drawer of water; to exchange the pride of power and pomp of wealth for hardship and want, poverty and peril? Pollux felt that he could not

bring his pride to submit to the degradation, or his
worldliness to the loss. The leap to be taken was from
such a height, and into such an abyss, that it seemed as
if he must be dashed in pieces by the fall.

But what was the alternative, if the dreaded leap were
not taken? If Zarah remained firm in the faith, she
must die. Could the father endure to witness the martyrdom of his beautiful child? And his own life—was
it not in danger? Was not instant flight from court
the only means of affording a chance of safety either to
parent or daughter? Was it not the only means of
delivering an apostate from the execrations of his countrymen, the curse of his mother, the impending vengeance
of the Most High? Conscience would no longer be
silenced—Zarah had aroused the sleeper; beside the
faith and purity of his own child, Pollux had regarded
himself almost as a demon!

And Zarah had awakened not only conscience, but
hope. She had clung to the apostate with tenderness,
not shrunk back from him with horror. She had not,
then, been taught to regard her parent as one who had
forfeited all claim to her affection. Zarah had spoken of
the possibility of his yet giving joy to the lofty-souled
mother whom Pollux, in the midst of his guilt, had not
ceased to reverence and love. For many years the apostate had tried to drive from his mind all thought of
Hadassah; now her image came vividly before him, not

in the attitude of uttering a malediction, but as holding out her arms to receive back her prodigal son.

While Pollux was deliberating and Zarah praying, Lysimachus was carousing amidst boon companions in the city. The ruin and approaching execution of his rival gave unwonted zest to the revels of the profligate Syrian.

"Here's to our friend the magnificent Pollux," exclaimed Lysimachus, raising on high a huge goblet of wine. "He is going on a long journey to-morrow; here's to his quick passage over Styx, and welcome at the shadowy court of King Pluto!"

And those who listened were not ashamed to laugh at the jest, or to drink the toast, though they had mixed in familiar intercourse with Pollux, flattered and followed him, when he had basked in the sunshine of royal favour. One of the guests was calculating how he should now get possession of some coveted gem which he had seen sparkling on the girdle of the man to whom he had once sworn unalterable friendship; another fixed on the Arab steed of the ruined courtier as his share of the spoils. There was not one of the sycophants met together at that night-revel who had a word of warning or a thought of pity to give to him who had been the most admired, envied, and flattered of all the nobles who composed the brilliant court of Antiochus Epiphanes!

Stars were paling, the night was waning, the door of

safety was slowly, imperceptibly closing—soon, soon the
decision of Pollux, if made, would be made too late!
When once the course of duty is clear to the mind,
perilous is every minute of delay: while we hesitate, the
enemy steals on; while we doubt, we may find ourselves
under his fangs!

"Zarah shall decide for me!" exclaimed the unhappy
waverer at last. "If I find her resolution immovable,
come what may, I will give my child one chance of
escape from the horrible fate with which she is threatened."

In a few minutes, pale and haggard from his contend-
ing emotions, Pollux re-entered the apartment in which
he had left his daughter.

"Zarah!" he cried, in a hollow tone, as he grasped
the maiden by the wrist, and scanned her countenance
with an almost despairing gaze, "I come to ask what is
your final decision. Are you still insane enough to
choose tortures and death?"

Zarah looked her father full in the face; she was pale,
but she blenched not. In a calm, unhesitating voice she
replied, "I will never deny my faith."

"Then the die is cast!" exclaimed Pollux, almost relieved by being at least freed from the misery of indecision. "We live or perish together!—we will make our
escape before daybreak."

There was little time left for words—none to express

the thankful joy which swelled the heart of Zarah. She was rescuing her father from dishonour and guilt; she was giving him back to his country.

"Put on this dress of a Syrian slave-girl, which I have brought for you," said Pollux. "Take up yon empty water-jar; it must appear as if you went to fill it at the tank. We cannot keep close together; that would awaken suspicion. We shall have guards to pass, and possibly other persons besides, though at this very early hour even slaves will scarcely have commenced their morning toils."

"How shall I find my way, father?" inquired Zarah; "this vast palace is a labyrinth to me."

"You must never quite lose sight of me," Pollux replied; "though following at a sufficient distance to prevent its appearing that your movements are guided by mine. But no, that plan will not answer," he continued, pressing his forehead with his hand; "I should not then have you in view, and, should you be challenged, I should be unable to come to your help. You, my child, must go first."

"Oh, my father, my presence will fearfully increase your danger!" cried Zarah. "Leave me here, I implore, and make your escape alone. No one will challenge you."

Pollux silenced his daughter's expostulation with an impatient gesture of the hand. "Attend to my direc-

tions," he said ; " we have wasted too much time already.
You will follow me through the first court, and then
you will precede me.   Keep to the right till you pass
the first sentries ; then you will find yourself in a garden,
in the centre of which is a tank.   Fill, or make show of
filling, your jar.   Then the long dark passage which you
will see on the left will conduct you to a postern-gate
of the palace ; there will be a guard at that also."

" How shall I pass them ? " asked Zarah, who began
to realize the difficulties and perils of the undertaking
before her.

" I know not; but God, whom you serve, will help
you, my brave and innocent child !   I will be following
at no great distance—every soldier or slave will know
me—call me, and I will come to your aid."

" Father, give me your blessing," faltered Zarah.

" *My* blessing ! " ejaculated Pollux, drawing back ;
" does any one ask a blessing from a wretch from whom
it would seer and blast more than a curse from the lips
of another ! "

" Oh, never say so ! " cried Zarah.   " You are doing
now what is generous—noble—right !   You are casting
in your lot with the people of God ; like Lot, you are
turning your back upon Sodom."

" And you are the angel leading me thence," exclaimed
Pollux.   " O Zarah, Zarah, sainted child of a sainted
woman, you who have been the first to cast a gleam of

hope on the darkness of guilt and despair, if ever I find
mercy from man or from God, if ever I look again on
the face of my mother, if ever I escape the righteous
doom of an apostate, it is owing to you!   Whatever be
the result of our perilous enterprise to-night, remember

GOING FORTH.

that I thank you, I bless you—and you shall be blessed,
O my daughter!"   Pollux laid both his trembling hands
on the head of his kneeling child, and uttered for her
the first prayer to the true God which the apostate had
dared to utter for many guilty, miserable years.

CHAPTER XXV

ADASSAH had, in the meantime, been enduring the martyrdom of the heart.

When Zarah, under the escort of Abishai, left her home to attend the celebration of the holy Feast, Hadassah sent her soul with her, though failing health chained back the aged lady's feeble body. In thought, Hadassah shared the memorial feast; in thought, partook of the sacrifice and joined in the hymns of praise. Her mind dwelt on the circumstances attending the celebration of the first Passover, when, with loins girded and staff in hand, the fathers of Israel had taken their last meal in Egypt, before starting for the Promised Land.

"Is not this the *Promised Land* still?" thought Hadassah; "though those who are as the Canaanites of old now hold it—though unhallowed worship be offered on Mount Zion, and images be set up within the walls of Jerusalem. Yea, it is to Israel the Promised Land, till *every* prophecy be fulfilled; till the King come to Zion, *lowly, and riding on an ass* (Zech. ix. 9); till— oh, most mysterious word!—the thirty pieces of silver be weighed out as the price of the Lord and cast to the potter (Zech. xi. 12, 13); till He shall speak peace to the heathen, and His dominion be from sea to sea, and from the river to the ends of the earth (Zech. ix. 10). Faith looks backward on fulfilled prophecy with grati-tude, on yet unfulfilled prophecy with hope. Zion's brightest days are to come. Her Lord crowned her with glory in the days of old; but in the days which will rise on her yet, He shall Himself be to her as a diadem of beauty!" (Isa. xxviii. 5.)

Absorbed in such high contemplations, with hopes intensified by the victories of Maccabeus—which seemed to her types and pledges of greater triumphs to come— time did not pass wearily with Hadassah until the hour arrived for Zarah's expected return. Even the delay of that return did not at first seriously alarm Hadassah; circumstances might render it safer for the maiden to linger at Salathiel's house; she might even be pressed to remain there during the night, should Syrians be lurking about in the paths amidst the hills. Hadassah had so often attended meetings in the elder's dwelling, with or without her grand-daughter, that habit had made her regard such attendance as less perilous than it was now to be proved to have been.

But Hadassah on this night could not retire to rest. She could not close her eyes in sleep until they had again looked upon her whom the Hebrew lady fondly called her "white dove."

Midnight stole on, and Hadassah's heart, notwithstanding her courage and faith, became burdened with heavy anxiety. She made Anna lie down and rest; while she herself, notwithstanding her state of indisposition, kept watch by the door.

Presently her ear caught the sound of footsteps, hurried yet stealthy. Hadassah heard danger in that sound, and opened the door without waiting to know who came, or whether the steps would be arrested at her threshold. The light which the widow held in her hand fell on a countenance ghastly with fear; she recognized the face of Salathiel, and knew before he uttered a word that he had come as the messenger of disaster.

"The enemy came—we fled over the roofs—Abishai is slain—Zarah in the hands of the Syrians!"

Such were the tidings which fell like a sentence of death on the ear of Hadassah! Salathiel could not wait to tell more; he must overtake his family, and with them flee for his life; and he passed away again into darkness, almost as swiftly as the lightning passes, but, like the lightning, leaving behind a token of where it has been in the tree which it has blasted !

Hadassah did not shriek, nor sink, nor swoon, but she felt as one who has received a death-blow. She stood repeating over and over to herself the latter part of Salathiel's brief but fearful announcement, as if it were too terrible to be true. Had Zarah been taken from her by natural cause, the Hebrew lady would have bowed her head like Job, and have blessed the name of the Lord in mournful submission; but the thought of Zarah in the hands of the Syrians caused an agony of grief more like that of Jacob, when he gazed on the blood-stained garment of his son and refused to be comforted.

For Hadassah loved the young maiden whom she had reared with the intensity of which a strong and fervent nature like hers perhaps alone is capable. Zarah was all that was left to her grandmother in the world, the sole relic remaining of the treasures which she once had possessed. It may be permitted to me here, as a digression, to give a brief account of Hadassah's former life, that the reader may better understand her position at the point reached in my story.

Few women had appeared to enjoy a brighter lot than Hadassah when, beautiful, gifted, and beloved, a happy wife, a rejoicing mother, she had dwelt near Bethsura in Idumea, the possessor of more than competence, and the

dispenser of benefits to many around her.   Hadassah had
in her youthful days an ambitious spirit, a somewhat
haughty temper, and a love of command, which had to
a certain degree marred the beauty of a character which
was essentially noble.

Grief soon came, however, to humble the spirit and
to soften the temper.   Hadassah was early left a widow,
and heavily the grief of bereavement fell upon one whose
love had been passionate and deep.   Two children, however—a daughter and son—remained to console her.
Around these, and especially her boy, the affections of
Hadassah clung but too closely.   Abner was almost
idolized by his mother.   If ambition remained in her
heart, it was ambition for him.   He was her pride, her
delight, the object of her fondest hopes; Abner's very
faults seemed almost to become graces, viewed through
the medium of Hadassah's intense love.

Many years now flowed on, with little to disturb their
even tenor.   Miriam, the only daughter of Hadassah,
was married to Abishai; Abner was united to a fair
maiden whom his mother could receive and love as a
daughter indeed.

The Hebrew widow lived her early days over again in
her children, and life was sweet to her still.

Then came blow upon blow in fearful succession, each
inflicting a deep wound on the heart of Hadassah.   Both
the young wives were taken in the prime of their days,

within a few weeks of each other—Miriam dying child-
less, Naomi leaving but one little daughter behind. But
the heaviest, most crushing stroke was to come!

When Seleucus, King of Pergamos, with the concur-
rence of the Romans, had placed Antiochus on the throne
of Syria, the new monarch had speedily shown himself
an active enemy of the faith held by his subjects in
Judæa. Onias, their venerable High Priest, was deposed,
and the traitor Jason raised to hold an office which he
disgraced. A gymnasium was built by him in Jerusalem; reverence for Mosaic rites was discouraged.
Both by his example and his active exertions, Jason, the
unworthy successor of Aaron, sought to obliterate the
distinction between Jew and Gentile, and bring all to
one uniformity of worldliness and irreligion. In the
words of the historian : * " The example of a person in his
commanding position drew forth and gave full scope to
the more lax dispositions which existed among the people,
especially among the younger class, who were enchanted
with the ease and freedom of the Grecian customs, and
weary of the restraints and limitations of their own.
Such as these abandoned themselves with all the frenzy
of a new excitement, from which all restraint had been
withdrawn, to the license which was offered to them.
The exercises of the gymnasium seem to have taken their
minds with the force of fascination."

* Dr. Kitto.

To temptations such as these a disposition like that of Abner was peculiarly accessible. His religion had never been the religion of the heart; his patriotism was cold, he prided himself upon being a citizen of the world. Unhappily, after the death of his wife, Abner had become weary of Bethsura, and had gone up to Jerusalem to divert his mind from painful associations. He there came under the influence of Jason, and plunged into amusement in a too successful effort to divert his mind from sorrow.

Ambition soon added its powerful lure to that of pleasure. Abner met the newly-made king shortly after his accession, and at once attracted the attention and won the favour of the monarch. There was nothing but the Hebrew's faith between him and the highest distinctions which a royal friend could bestow. Abner yielded to the brilliant temptation; he parted with his religion (more than nominal it never had been), changed his name to that of Pollux, abandoned all his former friends and pursuits, and attached himself entirely to the Syrian court, then usually residing at Antioch.

Abner, or, as we have called him, Pollux, dared not face his mother after he had turned his back upon all which she had taught him to revere. The apostate never went near Bethsura again; he kept far away from the place where he had passed his innocent childhood, the place where slept the relics of his young Jewish wife.

Abner wrote to Hadassah to inform her of what he termed the change in his opinions; told her that he had given up an antiquated faith, commended his little daughter to her care, and asked her to forget that she herself had ever given birth to a son.

Hadassah, after receiving this epistle, lay for weeks at the point of death, and fears were at first entertained for her reason. She arose at last from her sick-bed a changed, almost broken-hearted woman. As soon as it was possible for her to travel, the widow left Bethsura for ever. She could not endure the sight of aught to remind her of happier days; she could not bear to meet any one who might speak to her of her son. Hadassah's first object was to seek out Abner, and, with all the persuasions which a mother could use, to try to draw him back from a course which must end in eternal destruction. But Abner was not to be found in Jerusalem, nor in any part of the country around it. He had carefully concealed from his mother his new name—the Hebrew was lost in the Syrian—Abner was dead indeed to his family and to his country—and to Hadassah the courtier Pollux was utterly a stranger.

It was long, very long, before Hadassah gave up her search for Abner, and she never gave up either her love or her hope for her son. Affection with her was like the vein in the marble, a part of itself, which nought can wash out or remove. There was scarcely a waking hour in which the mother did not pray for her wanderer; he was often present to her mind in dreams. And the character of Hadassah was elevated and purified by the grief which she silently endured. The dross of ambition and pride was burned away in the furnace of affliction; the impetuous, high-spirited woman refined into the

HADASSAH'S CHARGE.

saint. Exquisitely beautiful is the remark made by a gifted writer :* "Everything of moment which befalls us in this life, which occasions us some great sorrow for which in this life we see not the uses, has nevertheless its definite object. . . . . It may seem but a barren grief in

* Lord Lytton.

the history of a life, it may prove a fruitful joy in the history of a soul."

Hadassah's intense, undying affection for her unworthy son, led her to regard with peculiar affection the child whom he had left to her care. She loved Zarah both for his sake and her own. Zarah was the one flower left in the desert over which the simoom had swept; her smile was to the bereaved mother as the bright smile of hope. Hadassah, as she watched the opening virtues of Abner's daughter, could not, would not believe that the parent of Zarah could ever be finally lost. God would surely hear a mother's prayers, and save Abner from the fate of an apostate. All that Hadassah asked of Heaven was to see her son once again in the path of duty, and then she would die happy. The love for Abner which still lived in the widow's bosom, was like the unseen fires that glow unseen beneath the surface of the earth, only known by the warmth of the springs that gush up into light. Even as those springs was the love of the widow for Abner's daughter.

CHAPTER XXVI

ADASSAH had believed, years previously, that she had suffered to the extreme limits of human endurance—that there were no deeper depths of misery to which she could descend; but the news brought on that fatal night by Salathiel showed her that she had been mistaken. The idea of her Zarah, her tender loving Zarah, in the hands of the Syrians, brought almost intolerable woe. So carefully had the maiden been nurtured, watched over, shielded from every wrong, like an unfledged bird that has always been kept under the warm, soft, protecting wing, that the utter defencelessness of her present position struck Hadassah with terror.

And how—the widow could not help asking herself—how could one so timid and sensitive stand the test of persecution from which the boldest might shrink? Zarah would weep at a tale of suffering, turn faint at the sight of blood. She was not by any means courageous, and her young cousins, Solomona's sons, had been wont to make mirth of her terror when a centipede had once been found nestling under a cushion near her. Could such a soft silken thread bear the strain of a blast which might snap the strongest cable? Hadassah trembled for her darling, and would willingly have consented to bear any torture, to have been able to exchange places with one so little fitted, as she thought, to endure. Sorely tried was the faith of the Hebrew lady: how little could she imagine that the prayers of many years were being answered by means of the very misfortune which was rending the cords of her heart.

In the misery of her soul, all Hadassah's physical weakness and pain seemed forgotten. Before morning she had dragged her feeble steps to the gate of the prison which held her child, with the faithful Anna for her only attendant. In vain Hadassah implored for admission; in vain offered to share the captivity of Zarah, if she might be but permitted to see her. She was driven away by the guards, with insolent taunts, only to return again and again, like a bird to its plundered nest! But no complaining word, no murmuring against the decree of Him who had appointed her sore trial, was heard from Hadassah; only that sublime expression of unshaken faith, *Though He slay me, yet will I trust in Him.*

Then the widow thought of Lycidas the Greek. She had a claim upon his gratitude, and she knew that Zarah had a place in his affections. With his wealth, his talent, his eloquence, might he not help to save her child?

"Anna," said Hadassah to her handmaid, "could we but find the Greek stranger, he might afford us aid and advice in this our sore need. But I know not where he abides."

"Joab would know," observed the Jewess; "and I know the quarter of the town in which he dwells with his mother's sister, Hephzibah; for I have dealt with her for olives and melons. But, lady, you are weary, the heat of the sun is now great; seek some place of shelter and rest while I go in search of Joab."

"There is no rest for me till I find my Zarah; and what care I for shelter when she has but that of a prison!" cried Hadassah.

The two women then proceeded on their quest to a quarter of Jerusalem inhabited only by the poorest of the people. Simple as were the garments worn by the widow lady, she carried with her so unmistakably the stamp of a person of distinction, that her appearance there excited surprise amongst the half-clad, half-starved children that stared at her as she passed along. The street was so narrow that the women, meeting a loaded camel in it, had to stand close to the wall on one side, to suffer the unwieldy beast to pass on the other. Hungry lean dogs were growling over well-picked bones cast forth in the way; evil odours rendered the stifling air more oppressive. But Hadassah went forward as if insensible of any outward annoyance.

Hephzibah, a miserable-looking old woman, with eyes disfigured and half-blinded by ophthalmia, was standing in her doorway, throwing forth the refuse of vegetables, in which she dealt. Anna had frequently seen her before, and no introduction was needed.

" Where is Joab?" asked the handmaid, at the bidding of Hadassah.

The old crone through her bleared eyes peered curiously at the lady, as she replied to the maid, " Joab has gone forth, as he always goes at cock-crow, to lade his mule with leeks and melons, and other vegetables and fruits. He will not be back till night-fall."

Hadassah pressed her burning brow in thought, and then herself addressed the old woman.

" Have you heard from Joab where dwells a Greek— an Athenian—Lycidas is his name?"

" Lycidas? no; there be none of that name in our quarters," was the slowly mumbled reply.

" Has Joab never spoken to you of a stranger, very goodly in person and graceful in mien?" persisted Hadassah, grasping at the hope that the singular beauty of Lycidas might make it less difficult to trace him.

Hephzibah shook her head, and showed her few remaining teeth in a grin.   "Were he goodly as David, I
should hear and care nothing about it," said she.

"The stranger has a very open hand, he gives freely,"
observed Anna.   The words had an instant effect in
improving the memory of the old Jewess.

"Ay, ay," she said, brightening up ; "I mind me of a
stranger who gave Joab gold when another would have
given him silver.   He ! he ! he !   Our mule is as strong
a beast as any in the city, but it never brought us such
a day's hire before."

"When was that ?" asked Hadassah.

"Two days since, when Joab had taken the youth to
his home."

"Can you tell me where that home is ?" inquired
Hadassah with eagerness.

"Wait—let me think," mumbled Hephzibah.

Hadassah thrust a coin into the hand of the seller of
fruit.   Hephzibah turned it round and round, looking
at it as if she thought that the examination of the
money would help her in giving her answer.   It came
at last, but slowly : "Ay, I mind me that Joab said
that he took the stranger to the large house, with a court,
on the left side of the west gate, which Apollonius" (she
muttered a curse) " broke down."

This was clue sufficient ; and thankful at having
gained one, Hadassah with her attendant left the stilling

precincts of Hephzibah's dwelling to find out that of the Greek. Terrible were the glare and heat of the noonday sun, and long appeared the distance to be traversed, yet Hadassah did not even slacken her steps till she approached the gymnasium erected by the renegade high-priest Jason. With difficulty she made her way through crowds of Syrians and others hastening to the place of amusement.

Hadassah groaned, but it was not from weariness; she turned away her eyes from the building which had been to so many of her people as the gate of perdition, and the merry voices of the pleasure-seekers sounded sadder to her ears than a wail uttered over the dead. Precious souls had been murdered in that gymnasium; the Hebrew mother thought of her own lost son!

Almost dropping from fatigue, Hadassah reached at last the place which Hephzibah had described. It was an inn of the better sort, kept by an Athenian named Cimon, who had established himself in Jerusalem. Hadassah had no difficulty in obtaining an interview with the host, who received her with the courtesy befitting a citizen of one of the most polished cities then to be found in the world. Cimon offered the lady a seat under the shadow of the massive gateway leading into his courtyard.

" Dwells the Lord Lycidas here ? " asked Hadassah faintly. She could hardly speak; her tongue seemed to cleave to the roof of her mouth from heat, fatigue, and excitement.

"The Lord Lycidas left this place yesterday, lady," said the Greek.

"Whither has he gone?" gasped Hadassah.

"I know not—he told me not whither," answered Cimon, surveying his questioner with compassion and curiosity. "Months have elapsed since the Athenian lord, after honouring this roof by his sojourn under it, suddenly disappeared. Search was made for him in vain. I feared that evil had happened to my guest, and as time rolled on and brought no tidings, I sent word to his friends in Athens, asking what should be done with property left under my charge by him who, as I deemed, had met an untimely end. Ere the answer arrived, the Lord Lycidas himself appeared at my door, but in evil plight, weak in body and troubled in mind. He would give no account of the past; he said not where he had sojourned; and yester-morn, though scarcely strong enough to keep the saddle, he mounted his horse, and rode off—I know not whither; nor said he when he would return. If the lady be a friend of the Lord Lycidas," continued the Athenian, whose curiosity was strongly excited, "perhaps she may favour me by throwing light upon the mystery which attends his movements."

But Hadassah had come to gain information, not to

impart it. "I cannot linger here," she said; "but if
Lycidas return, tell him, I earnestly charge you, that
the child of one who nursed him in sickness is now the
prisoner of the Syrian king!"

Grievously disappointed and disheartened by her failure,
Hadassah then turned away from the dwelling of the Greek.

"O lady, rest, or you will sink from fatigue!" cried
Anna, whose own sturdy frame was suffering from the
effect of efforts of half of which, a day before, she would
have dreamed her mistress utterly incapable.

Hadassah made no reply; she sank rather than seated
herself under the narrow strip of shade afforded by a
dead wall. The lady covered her face; Anna knew
from the slight movement of her bowed head that
Hadassah was praying.

Presently the Hebrew lady raised her head; she was
deadly pale, but calm.

"I cannot stay here," she murmured. "I must know
the fate of my child. Anna, let us return to the prison."
Even with the aid of her handmaid, the lady was scarcely
able to rise.

The twain reached the gate of the prison. A group
of Syrian guards kept watch there. The appearance of
the venerable sufferer, bowed down under such a weight
of affliction, moved one of the soldiers to pity.

"You come on a fruitless errand, lady," he said; "the
maiden whom you seek is not here."

"Dead?" faintly gasped forth Hadassah.

"No, no; not dead," answered the Syrian promptly. "I know not all that has happened; but the young girl was certainly brought before the king."

"Before him who murdered Solomona and her boys—the ruthless fiend!" was the scathing thought that passed through the brain of Hadassah. "And what followed?" she asked with her eyes, for her lips could not frame the question.

"Belikes the king thought it shame to kill such a pretty bird, so kept it to make music for him in his gardens of joy," said the guard. "All that I can say is, that the maiden was not sent back to prison, but remains in the palace."

"The palace!" ejaculated Hadassah; more distressed than reassured by such information.

"Of course," cried another soldier, with a brutal jest; "the girl was not going to commit the folly of dying for her superstitions like a bigoted fanatic old woman, with no more sense than the staff she leans on! Of course, the maid did what any woman in her senses would do—worshipped whatever the king bade her worship, the Muses, the Graces, or the Furies. Converts are easily made at her age, with all kinds of torments on the one side, all kinds of delights on the other."

Hadassah turned slowly away from the spot. Could the soldier's words be true? had Zarah forsworn her faith as her father had done, though under circumstances so different ?

"Oh! God will forgive her—He will forgive my poor lost child, if she have failed under such an awful trial!" murmured the Hebrew lady, pressing her hand to her side, as if to keep her heart from bursting. But Hadassah was by no means sure that Zarah's resolution had indeed given way. She determined at all events and at any hazard to see the maiden ; and, collecting all her strength, proceeded at once to the palace. The unhappy lady might have guessed beforehand that it would be a hopeless attempt to gain admittance into that magnificent abode of luxury, cruelty, and crime. The guards only mocked at her prayer to be permitted to see the captive Hebrew maiden.

"Then I must speak to the king himself!" cried Hadassah. " I will watch till he leave the gate."

" The king goes not forth to-day," said a Syrian noble who was quitting the palace, and who was struck by the earnestness of the aged widow, and the anguish depicted on her noble features. " But Antiochus rides forth to-morrow, soon after sunrise."

" Then," thought Hadassah, " daybreak shall find me here. I will cling to the stirrup of Antiochus. I will constrain the tyrant to listen. God will inspire my lips with eloquence. He will touch the heart of the king. I may yet persuade the tyrant to accept one life instead of another. Oh! my Zarah, child of my heart, it were bliss to suffer for you!"

A VAIN PRAYER.

Clinging to this last forlorn hope, Hadassah allowed herself at last to be persuaded by Anna to seek the residence of a Hebrew family, with whom she was slightly acquainted; there to partake of a little food, lie down and attempt to sleep. Snatches of slumber came at last to the widow—slumber filled with dreams. Hadassah thought that she saw her son, her Abner, bright, joyous, and happy as he had been in his youth. Then the scene changed to her own home. Hadassah fancied that Zarah had unexpectedly returned; in delight she clasped the rescued maid to her heart, and then, to her astonishment, found that it was not Zarah, but Zarah's father, whom she clasped in her arms! It was strange that dreams of joy should come in the midst of so much anguish, so that a smile should actually play on the grief-worn features of Hadassah. Was some good spirit whispering in her ear, " While you are sleeping your son is praying. Your supplications for him are answered at last " ?

But Hadassah lost little time in sleep. While the stars yet gleamed in the sky, the lady aroused Anna, who was slumbering heavily at her feet. The handmaid arose, and without awakening the household, Hadassah and her attendant noiselessly quitted the hospitable dwelling which had afforded them shelter, and turned their steps again in the direction of the stately palace of Antiochus Epiphanes.

As the two women traversed the silent, narrow, deserted streets, they suddenly, at the angle formed by a transverse road, came upon a young man, whose rapid step indicated impatience or fear. He was moving with such eager speed that he almost struck against Hadassah, before he could arrest his quick movements.

" Ha! Hadassah!"

" Lycidas! Heaven be praised!" were the exclamations uttered in a breath by the Greek and the Hebrew.

" Is it—can it be true—Zarah—captive—in peril?"

cried the young man, whom the tidings of the attack on
Salathiel's dwelling, and the capture of a maiden, had
casually reached that night at Bethlehem, where he
was sojourning, and whom these tidings had brought in
all speed to Jerusalem.   Lycidas had ridden first to the
house of Cimon, where the message left by Hadassah had
confirmed his worst fears.   Leaving his horse, which had
fallen lame on the rocky road, he had hurried off on foot to
the palace, with no definite plan of action before him, but
resolved at any rate to seek an interview with the king.

"Zarah is prisoner in yon palace," said Hadassah;
"you will do all in your power to save her?"

"I would die for her!" was the reply.

Hadassah in few words made known to the young
Athenian her own intention to await at the palace gate
the going forth of Antiochus, and plead with the Syrian
king for the life and freedom of Zarah.   The lady was
thankful to accept the eager offer of Lycidas to remain
beside her, and support her petition with the weight of
any influence which he might have with the tyrant,
small as he judged that influence to be.   Hadassah,
thankful at having found a zealous friend to aid her,
leant on the arm of Lycidas as she might have done on
that of a son.   Difference in nation and creed was for
awhile forgotten; the two were united by one great love
and one great fear, and the Gentile could, with the soul's
deepest fervour, say "Amen" to the Hebrew's prayer.

CHAPTER XXVII

FLIGHT.

T was with a strange sense of happiness mingling with fear that Zarah followed her father out of the apartment which had been her place of confinement. The blessing of Abner lay so warm at the heart of his daughter! Zarah was no longer like one peering into depths of darkness to catch a glimpse of some terrible object below; she had discovered what she had sought, and by the cords of love was, as it were, drawing up a perishing parent into security and light. It was rapture to Zarah to reflect on what would be the joy of Hadassah on the restoration of her son. The maiden could rejoice in past perils, and, with a courage which surprised herself, confront those before her; so clearly could she now perceive that her sufferings had been made a means of blessing to those whom she loved.

With a light, noiseless step, Zarah, obeying the directions of her newly-found parent, and keeping his form

in sight, crossed the first court which they had to traverse. It was paved, surrounded by pillars, and open
to the sky, of which the deep azure was paling into
morning. The place was perfectly silent. Zarah observed that her father glanced up anxiously towards the
building which formed the south side of the court, where
marble pillars, with wreathed columns and richly-carved
capitals, supported a magnificent frieze. Antiochus himself occupied that part of the palace. But no eye peered
forth at that early hour on the forms that glided over
the marble-paved court below.

Under the shadow of the colonnade now reached,
Pollux awaited his daughter;—the first point of danger
was happily passed. Pollux now pointed to a broad,
covered passage to the right, lighted by lamps, of which
some had already burned out, and others were flickering.
Zarah saw at the further end forms of men dimly visible.
The guards, weary with the long night-watch, were apparently sleeping; for they appeared to be half sitting,
half reclining on the pavement, and perfectly still.

Zarah had now to go first, and with a throbbing heart
the maiden approached the soldiers, breathing an inaudible prayer, for she felt the peril to be very great.
The passage at the end of which the guards kept ward
opened into one of the small gardens which adorned the
interior of the extensive edifice, with a tank in the centre,
from which a graceful fountain usually rose from a statuary

group of marble, representing Niobe and her children. The fountain was not playing at this hour, and there was not light sufficient to throw the shadow of the statues upon the still water below.

It was impossible to reach the garden without passing between the two guards. Zarah could not tell whether they were indeed sleeping, and the space left between them was scarcely sufficiently wide to admit of her traversing it. Frightened, yet clinging to hope, Zarah, with her jar on her head, walked slowly and cautiously on. Just as she was gliding by the guards, one of them started and caught hold of her dress.

"Ha, slave! what mischief are you after at such an hour as this?"

"My lord has bidden me dip my jar in yon tank," said Zarah, in as calm a tone as she could command.

"I trow your lord has heated himself with a stronger kind of drink, or he would not need water to cool him now," said the Syrian, releasing Zarah, who, wondering at her own success, rapidly hurried into the garden. She almost forgot, in her haste to escape, that it was needful to dip her jar into the water, as she was still within view of the Syrian. The maiden had to turn back one or two steps, and bend over the brink of the tank. Its cool waters refreshed her, as she dipped her slender fingers therein.

"Now," thought Zarah, "there is a long dark passage to traverse—is it on the right or the left? I scarce can remember my father's directions; and a mistake now might be fatal both to him and to me. Oh, may Heaven direct me!"

As Zarah glanced anxiously on either side, she perceived to the left a narrow opening in the mass of buildings which enclosed the garden. The opening was so utterly dark, that it looked to the trembling girl like the mouth of a sepulchre, and she feared to enter into it. As Zarah stood hesitating, she could hear Pollux behind her giving the password to the sentries. His voice strengthened the courage of his daughter; it was a comfort to know that he was near. Quitting the garden, Zarah entered the gloomy passage. It was not quite so dark within as it had appeared from without. The maiden could dimly distinguish a niche in the wall, in which she deposited her jar, which could now only burden her in her flight.

The passage along which Zarah was groping her way was one merely intended as a back-way, along which slaves carrying viands or other burdens might pass, though it was not unfrequently used by courtiers bound on secret errands. It conducted to a much wider passage or corridor, which crossed it at right angles, and which led direct to a postern-door of the palace, by which four guards kept watch night and day. When Zarah reached the point where the smaller passage opened into the larger, she became aware of the most

formidable obstacle which she had yet had to encounter—
the presence of these guards ; and to the young fugitive
the obstacle seemed insuperable. The door was strongly
bolted, and the soldiers were wide awake ; there appeared to the mind of Zarah not the smallest chance
that they would unbar the door for her, or suffer her
to pass.

The heart of the young fugitive sank within her. It
was terrible to be so near to liberty, and yet have that
impassable barrier between her and freedom ! How
formidable looked the deadly weapons of the soldiers as
they gleamed in the waning torch-light ; how stern the
weather-beaten countenances of the warriors of Antiochus
Epiphanes !

Zarah leaned against the wall of the dark narrow
passage, and listened for the footsteps of her father
behind her. She dared not venture out of the shadow
into the lighted corridor. Presently Pollux was at her
side ; she felt his hand gently laid on her shoulder.

"All will be lost if you attempt to save me, father,"
murmured the trembling girl. "Oh, go on without
me—leave me to God's care ; I can never pass those
guards."

"When I raise my hand, come forward and go forth,"
whispered Pollux. Not like a prisoner escaping, but
with the firm tread of a man who doubts not his right
and power to go where he will, the courtier of Antiochus

strode into the corridor and advanced towards the guards, who saluted, in Oriental fashion, a noble of high distinction, whose person was familiar to them all.

"The word is 'The sword of Antiochus.' Unbar that door, and quickly; I am on business of importance which brooks no delay," said Pollux to the guards in a tone of command.

The order was instantly obeyed. Zarah joyfully heard bolt after bolt withdrawn, and then the creaking of the door upon its hinges; and felt the freshness of outer air admitted through the opening.

Pollux seemed to be about to pass out, when he suddenly raised his hand, as his appointed signal to his daughter. Zarah, gasping with breathless anxiety, obeyed the sign, and glided forward to go forth from the palace. One of the soldiers, however, instantly barred her passage with his weapon.

"Let the slave pass," said Pollux sternly.

The point of the guard's weapon was lowered; but another of the soldiers was about to remonstrate. "It is against orders," he began, when Pollux interrupted him.

"Methinks you are one who served under me in the force of Giorgias," observed the courtier, with presence of mind.

"Ay, my lord," answered the soldier.

"When we next see Maccabeus, we must come to

closer quarters with him," observed the noble. "Here, my brave men,"—he drew forth a purse heavy with gold—"share this among you, and drink success to the brave."

The soldiers could scarcely repress a shout at the unexpected liberality of Pollux. Not one of them so much as looked at Zarah as she glided forth into the open air.

Oh, transporting sense of liberty! How delicious was the breath of early morn on the fugitive's cheek ; how glorious the open vault spread above her, blushing in the first light of dawn! Pollux experienced, though in a very inferior degree, some of the pleasure felt by his daughter, as he joined her on the broad marble steps which led down from the Grecian-built palace of Antiochus to the platform on which it was erected.

"This way, my child," whispered Pollux, as he drew Zarah in the direction of one of the high narrow streets of Jerusalem. "We must put as much space as possible between us and pursuers before sunrise. Would that we had started hours ago! Many dangers yet are before us."

One was nearer than the speaker was aware of. Scarcely had the fugitives entered the nearest street when they encountered a Syrian courtier, splendidly attired, whose unsteady gait betrayed in what manner he had been passing the night. More than half intoxicated as he was, Lysimachus instantly recognized Pollux.

"Ha! whither bound?" exclaimed Lysimachus, standing, or rather staggering, in the narrow path directly in front of the fugitives.

"I give an account of my movements only to such as have a right to demand it," said Pollux haughtily, attempting to pass his rival, while Zarah kept close behind her father.

"The fox has caught sight of the trap—Pollux has found out that I hold his death-warrant," cried Lysimachus; "and that his head must fall at sunrise!"

Pollux started at the words of his enemy.

"He is making his escape!" continued Lysimachus, in a louder voice; "he's falling off to the Hebrews!—but this shall stop him!" and with a quick, unexpected movement, the Syrian plunged a dagger into the breast of Pollux, then himself fell heavily, rolling over into the dust! Lysimachus had been struck down by a blow from the hand of Lycidas, who had been but a few paces behind him.

Zarah had caught sight of the Greek, and of the venerated form of Hadassah at that momentous crisis; her eyes rivetted on them, she had not seen the blow inflicted on her father, who, though mortally wounded, did not instantly fall. For Pollux also beheld his mother; and the sudden, unexpected vision of her from whom he had so long been divided, seemed to have power to arrest even the hand of death. Parent and son met—they

clasped—they locked each other in a first—a last embrace.

"O mother," exclaimed Zarah, "he has saved me!

THE LAST EMBRACE.

He is your own son again, devoted to his country—to
his God!"

Did Hadassah hear the joyful exclamation? If she
did not, it mattered but little, for she had already grasped

with ecstasy all that its meaning could convey; for the
last sentence uttered by Lysimachus ere he fell had
reached her ear.   Her son—her beloved—was "falling
away to the Hebrews," or rather was returning to the
faith which he once had abjured; he was given back—
he was saved from perdition—he was rescuing his child
from death and his mother from despair.   Hadassah's
mind had received all this, conveyed, as it were, in a
lightning flash of joy.   She needed to know no more;—
her son was folded in her arms.

Pollux and Hadassah sank together on the paved way.
The sight of a few drops of blood on the stones first
startled Zarah into a knowledge that Lysimachus had
inflicted an injury on her father.

"Oh, he is wounded!" she exclaimed, throwing herself on her knees beside him.

"Dead!" ejaculated Anna, who was vainly attempting
to raise the head of Pollux.

"No—no—not dead!   O Lycidas!—Lycidas!" exclaimed Zarah in horror, intuitively appealing to the
Athenian to relieve her from the terrible fear which Anna
had raised.

"It is too true," said Lycidas sadly; for he could not
look upon the countenance of Pollux and doubt that life
was extinct.   "We must gently separate the son from
the arms of his mother."

But they who had been so long separated in life could

not be separated in death ; man had now no power to divide them.   Often had Hadassah thought that her heart would break with grief ;—it had burst with joy ! Her day of sorrow was over ; her long Sabbath rest had begun.   The happy smile which had lately played on her lips in sleep, now rested upon them in that last peaceful slumber from which she should never again awake to weep.   She had been given her heart's desire, and so had departed in peace.   Blessed death ; most joyful departure !

CHAPTER XXVIII

LYCIDAS dared not at first break to Zarah the mournful truth that one blow had bereft her of both her protectors, that she was now indeed an orphan, and alone in the world. Zarah saw that her father was dead, but believed that Hadassah had swooned. The subdued wail of Anna over the corpse of her mistress first revealed to the bereaved girl the full extent of her loss. Its greatness, its suddenness, almost stunned her; it was a paralyzing grief.

But this was no time for lamentation or wail. Lycidas remembered—though Zarah herself for the moment entirely forgot it—her imminent personal peril should she be discovered and arrested by the Syrians. To save her precious life was now the Greek's most anxious care. He tried to persuade her to fly; but even his entreaties could not draw the mourner from the dead bodies of

Hadassah and Pollux. It seemed as if Zarah could understand nothing but the greatness of her bereavements. A terrible fear arose in the mind of the Greek that all that the maiden had undergone during the last two days had unsettled her reason.

"What can be done!" exclaimed Lycidas, almost in despair; "if the Syrians find her here, she is lost. The city will soon be astir; already I hear the sound of hoofs!"

A man, leading a large mule with two empty panniers, appeared, trudging on his solitary way. As he approached the spot, Lycidas, to his inexpressible relief, recognized in him Joab, a man whose countenance was never likely to be forgotten by him—being connected with one of the most exciting passages in the life of the young Athenian.

"Ha! the Lady Hadassah!" exclaimed the muleteer, in a tone of surprise and regret, as his eye fell on the lifeless body, round which Zarah was clinging, with her face buried in the folds of its garments.

"I have seen you before; I know you to be a good man and true," said Lycidas, hurriedly. "You risked your life to bury the martyrs, you will help us now in this our sore need. Assist us to lift these bodies on your mule, and take them as secretly and as swiftly as we may to the house of Hadassah."

"I would risk anything for my old mistress," said

Joab; "but as for yon silken-clad Syrian, I care not to burden my beast with his carcass." The muleteer looked with stern surprise on the corpse of Pollux. "Who is he," continued Joab, "and how comes he to be clasped in the arms of the Lady Hadassah?"

"My father—he is my father!" sobbed Zarah.

"Raise them both," said Lycidas; "we cannot divide them, and there is not a moment to be lost."

The united efforts of the party hardly sufficed to raise the two bodies to the back of the mule, which, though a large and powerful animal, could scarcely carry the double burden. Joab took his large coarse mantle, and threw it over the corpses to hide them; then taking his beast by the halter, led it forward in silence.

"Is there no danger from him?" said Anna to Lycidas, pointing to Lysimachus, who lay senseless and bleeding, his head having come into violent collision with a stone.

By a brief examination, Lycidas satisfied himself that the courtier was indeed in a state of unconsciousness, and knew nothing of what was passing around him. The Athenian then went up to Zarah, who, drooping like a broken lily, was slowly following the corpses of her parent and his mother. Lycidas offered her what support he could give; Zarah did not, could not reject it. A deadness seemed coming over her brain and heart; had not Lycidas upheld the poor girl, she must have dropped by the wayside.

With what strange emotions did Lycidas through life remember that early walk in Jerusalem! The being whom he loved best was leaning upon him, too much exhausted to decline his aid; there was thrilling happiness in being so near her; but the uppermost feelings in the mind of Lycidas were agonizing fear upon Zarah's account, and intense impatience to reach some place of safety. Fearfully slow to Lycidas appeared the progress of the heavily-laden mule, terribly long the way that was traversed. The muleteer purposely avoided that which would have been most direct; he dared not go through one of the city gates, but passed out into the open country at a spot little frequented, where a part of the wall of Jerusalem still lay in ruins, as it had been left by Apollonius. Most unwelcome to Lycidas was the brightening day, which awoke the world to life. Every human form, even that of a child, was to him an object of alarm. The brave young Greek was full of terrors for one who in her grief had lost the sense of personal fear.

Partly owing to the skilful selection of paths by Joab, partly owing to the circumstance of the day being still so young, the party did not meet many persons on their way, and these few were of the poorer class, early commencing their morning toils. Inquiring glances were cast at the singular cortege; but at that time of bondage and peril, a common sense of misery and danger taught caution and repressed curiosity.

Only once was a question asked of the muleteer.

"What have you there, Joab, under yon mantle?" inquired a woman with a large jar on her head, who stopped to survey the strange burden of the mule.

"A ripe sheaf of the first-fruits, a wave-offering, Deborah," replied Joab, with significance.

"There will be more—many more—cut down soon," replied the woman gloomily; "may desolation overtake the Syrian reapers!"

Joab saw the Athenian's look of apprehension. "Fear not, stranger," he said; "no Hebrew will betray us; Deborah is true as steel, and knows me well."

There is little of twilight in Judæa; day leaps almost at a bound upon his throne. The world was bathed in sunshine long before the slowly-moving party reached the lonely dwelling amongst the hills. How thankful was Lycidas for the seclusion of that wild spot, which seemed as if it had been chosen for purpose of conceal-ment! Hadassah had left the door fastened when she had quitted the place on the preceding morning, full of anxious terrors on account of the peril of Zarah; but Anna had charge of the key. With what thankful joy would the Hebrew widow have for the last time crossed that threshold in life, could she have foreseen that her child would so soon return in safety, albeit as a mourner, and following Hadassah's own corpse!

The two bodies were reverentially laid on mats on the

floor of the dwelling. Lycidas then went outside the door with Joab, to make such arrangements as circumstances permitted for the burial, which, according to the custom of the land, rendered necessary by the climate, must take place very soon. Joab undertook to find those who would aid him in digging a grave close to that of the martyrs, and promised to come for the bodies an hour after midnight. Lycidas drew forth gold, but the Hebrew refused to take it.

"To bury the martyred dead is a pious office, and acceptable to the Most High," said the brave muleteer; "but as for yon Syrian, son though he may be of the Lady Hadassah, I care not to lay his bones amongst those of martyrs. I trow he was nothing but a traitor."

"He died by the hand of a Syrian, he died saving a Hebrew maiden, he died in his mother's arms," said Lycidas, with tender regard for the feelings of Zarah, who would, he knew, be sensitive in regard to respect paid to the corpse of her parent. "Deny him not a grave with his people."

Joab merely shrugged his shoulders in reply, laid his hand on the halter of his mule, and departed.

On the following night Lycidas found himself again in that olive-girdled spot which he had such reason to remember. He stood under that tree behind the bending trunk of which he had crouched for concealment on the night when he had first seen Zarah.

The ground was very hard from the long drought. Joab, and two companions whom he had brought to assist in the perilous service, had much difficulty in preparing a grave.

"We need the strong arm of Maccabeus here," observed one of the men, stopping to brush the beaded drops from his brow.

"Maccabeus is employed in making graves for his enemies, not for his friends," was the muleteer's stern reply.

Thick, heavy clouds obscured the starless sky; not a breath of wind was stirring; the air felt oppressively close and sultry, even at the hour of midnight. A single torch was all the light which the grave-diggers dared to employ while engaged on their dangerous work. In almost perfect darkness were the remains of Hadassah and her unhappy son lowered into the dust. There was no silver moonlight streaming between the stems of the olives, as on the occasion of the martyrs' burial, nor was Zarah present to throw flowers into the open grave. With her the powers of nature had given way under the prolonged strain which they had had to endure; the poor girl lay in her desolate home, too ill to be even conscious of the removal from it of the remains over which she had watched and mourned as long as she had been capable of doing either.

It was strange to Lycidas to be, as it were, the only

representative of Hadassah's family at the funeral of herself and her son,—he, who was not only no relative, but a foreigner in blood, and in religion an alien; but it was a privilege which he valued very highly, and which he would not have resigned to have held the chief place in the most pompous ceremonial upon earth.

As soon as the displaced earth had been thrown back into the grave of Hadassah and her Abner, the night-clouds burst, and down came the long longed-for, long-desired latter rains. The parched dry sod seemed to drink in new life; the shrivelled foliage revived, all nature rejoiced in the gift from heaven. When the sun rose over the hills, water was again trickling from the stream behind the dwelling of Hadassah; the oleanders were not yet dead, they would bloom into beauty again.

CHAPTER XXIX

SHALL pass lightly over the events of several succeeding months. The summer passed away, with its intense heat and its fierce simooms. Then came heavier dews by night, and temperature gradually decreased by day. The harvest was ended, but few of the inhabitants of Jerusalem had ventured to observe Pentecostal solemnities. The time for the Feast of Tabernacles arrived, but none dared raise leafy booths of palm and willow—to spend therein the week of rejoicing, according to the custom of happier years.

Early in the summer Antiochus Epiphanes had quitted Judæa for Persia, to quell an insurrection which his cupidity had provoked in the latter country. The absence of the tyrant had somewhat mitigated the fierceness of the persecution against such Hebrews as sought to obey the law of Moses ; but still no one dared openly to practise Jewish rites in Jerusalem, and the image of Jupiter Olympus still profaned the temple on Mount Zion.

Judas Maccabeus, in the meantime, still maintained a bold front in Southern Judæa, and the tract of country called Idumea; the power of his name was felt from the rich pasture-lands surrounding Hebron as far as the fair plains of Beersheba on the south-west—or on the south-east the desolate valley of salt. Wherever the Asmonean's influence extended, fields were sown or their harvests gathered in peace; the husbandman followed his team, and the shepherd folded his flocks; mothers rejoiced over the infants whom they could now present to the Lord without fear.

But again the portentous war-cloud was rolling up from the direction of Antioch. Lysias, the regent of the western provinces, by the command of Antiochus had gathered around him a very large army, a force yet more formidable than that which had been led by Nicanor, and Syria was again collecting her hordes to crush by overwhelming numbers Judas and his patriot band.

And how had the last half-year sped with Zarah? Very slowly and very heavily, as time usually passes with those who mourn. And deeply did Zarah mourn for Hadassah—her more than mother, her counsellor, her guide—·the being round whom the maiden's affections so closely had twined that she had felt that she could

hardly sustain existence deprived of Hadassah.   And
much Zarah wept for her father—though in remember-
ing him a deep spring of joy mingled with her sorrow.
A thousand times did Zarah repeat to herself his words
of blessing—a thousand times fervently thank God that
she and her parent had met.   The words of Lysimachus
had lightened her heart of what would otherwise have
painfully pressed upon it.   Those words had told her
that Pollux was a doomed man ; that apostasy on her
part could not have saved his life ; that had he not
fallen by the Syrian's dagger, he would have been but
reserved for the headsman's axe.   And had Pollux
perished thus, there would have been none of that gleam
of hope which, at least in Zarah's eyes, now rested upon
his grave.

Zarah never left the precincts of her secluded dwelling, except to visit her parents' grave—where she went
as often as she dared venture forth, accompanied by the
faithful Anna.   No feet but their own ever crossed the
threshold of their home.   Zarah's simple wants were
always supplied.   Anna disposed in Jerusalem of the
flax which her young mistress spun, as soon as Zarah
had regained sufficient strength to resume her humble
labours.   During the period of the maiden's severe illness, Anna had secretly disposed of the precious rolls of
Scripture from which Hadassah had made her copies, and
had obtained for them such a price as enabled her for

many weeks to procure every comfort and even luxury required by the sufferer. The copies themselves, traced by the dear hand now mouldering into dust, Zarah counted as her most precious possession; her most soothing occupation was to read them, pray over them, commit to memory their contents.

During all this long period of time, Zarah never saw Lycidas, but she had an instinctive persuasion that he was not far away—that, like an unseen good angel, he was protecting her still. The name of the Athenian was never forgotten in Zarah's prayers. She felt that she owed a debt of gratitude to one who had struck down her father's murderer, who had paid the last honours to his remains, and those of Hadassah, and to whose care she believed that she owed her own freedom and life. If there was something more than gratitude in the maiden's feelings towards the Greek, it was a sentiment so refined and purified by grief that it cast no dimness over the mirror of conscience.

But Zarah knew that her life could not always flow on thus. It was a most unusual thing in her land for a maiden thus to dwell alone, without any apparent protection save that of a single handmaid. It was a violation of all the customs of her people, an unseemly thing which could only be justified by necessity. The daughter of Abner was also in constant peril of having her retreat discovered by those who had searched for

herself and her father in vain, but who might at any
day or any hour find and seize her as a condemned
criminal, and either put her to death, or send her as a
captive to Antiochus Epiphanes.

Often, very often had Zarah turned over the subject
of her peculiar position in her mind, and considered
whether she ought not to leave the precincts of Jerusalem, and secretly depart for Bethsura.   There the
orphan could claim the hospitality of her aged relative
Rachel, should she be living yet, or the protection of
the Asmonean brothers, who, being her next of kin,
were, according to Jewish customs, the maiden's natural
guardians.   But Zarah shrank from taking this difficult
step.   Very formidable to her was the idea of undertaking
a journey even of but twenty miles' length, through a
country where she would be liable to meet enemies at
every step of the way.   Zarah had no means of travelling
save on foot, unless she disposed of some of the few
jewels which she had inherited from her parents; and this
she was not only unwilling to do, but she feared to do it,
lest, through the sale of these gems in Jerusalem, she should
be tracked to her place of retreat.   Anna was faithful as a
servant, but could never be leaned upon as an adviser—
she would obey, but she could not counsel; and her young
mistress, timid and gentle, with no one to guide and protect her, felt her strength and courage alike insufficient
for an adventurous journey from Jerusalem to Bethsura.

The possible necessity which might arise of her having to place herself under the protection of Maccabeus, should Rachel be no longer living at Bethsura, greatly increased Zarah's reluctance to leave her present abode. The maiden remembered too well what Hadassah had disclosed of a proposed union between herself and Judas, not to feel that it would be peculiarly painful to have to throw herself upon the kindness of her brave kinsman. Zarah could not, as she thought, tell him why the idea of such a union was hateful to her soul—why she was averse to fulfilling the wishes of Mattathias and Hadassah. While Maccabeus often experienced an almost irrepressible yearning once more to look upon Zarah, whom he believed to be still with Hadassah, of whose death he never had heard, Zarah shrank with emotions of fear from meeting the Hebrew chieftain.

Tender affection also made the orphan girl cling to her parents' grave and the home of her youth. Dear associations were linked with almost every object on which her eyes rested. Those to whom the present is a thorny waste, and the future a prospect darkened by gloomy mists, are wont to dwell more than others on the green spots which memory yet can survey in the past. It is natural to youth to look forward. Zarah, as regarded this world, dared only look back. It was well for her that she could do so with so little of remorse or regret.

> "Not to have known a treasure's worth
> Till time hath stolen away the slighted boon,
> Is cause of half the misery we feel,
> And makes this world the wilderness it is."

When winter was drawing near, when the bursting cotton-pods had been gathered, and the vintage season was over, when the leaves were beginning to fall fast, and the cold grew sharp after sunset, circumstances occurred which compelled a change in Zarah's quiet routine of existence. She could no longer be left to indulge her lonely sorrow; the current of life was about to take a sudden turn which must of necessity bring her amongst new scenes, and expose her to fresh trials.

CHAPTER XXX

NE evening, towards the hour of sunset, as Zarah sat alone at her wheel awaiting the return of Anna from the city, she was startled by the sound of a hand rapping hastily upon the panel of the door. The hand was assuredly not that of Anna, who, from precaution, had adopted a peculiar way of tapping to announce her return. As no visitor ever came to Zarah's dwelling, it was no marvel that she felt alarm at the unexpected sound, especially as she was aware that she had neglected her usual precaution of barring the door during the absence of Anna. As Zarah hastily rose to repair her omission, the door was opened from without, and Lycidas stood before her. The countenance of the Greek expressed anxiety and alarm.

"Lady, forgive the intrusion," said Lycidas, bending in lowly salutation before the startled girl; "but regard for your safety compels me to seek this interview. I was to-day in company with Lysimachus, the Syrian courtier—how we chanced to be together, or wherefore

TIDINGS.

he mentioned to me what I am about to disclose, matters little, and I would be brief. Lysimachus told me that, from information he had received—how, I know not— he had cause to suspect that the maiden who some half-year back had been sentenced by the king to death if she refused to apostatize from her faith, was living secluded in a dwelling amongst the hills to the east of the city. The Syrian declared that he was resolved to-morrow morn to explore thoroughly every spot which could possibly afford a place of concealment to the maiden—whom he intends to seize and send as a prisoner into Persia, to the merciless tyrant whom he serves."

Zarah turned very pale at the tidings, and leaned on her wheel for support.

"You must fly to-night, dearest lady," said Lycidas; "this dwelling is no longer a safe asylum for you."

"Whither can I fly, and how?" murmured the orphan girl. "I have no friend here except"—Zarah hesitated, and Lycidas completed the sentence.

"Except one to whom your lightest wish is a command; to whom every hair of your head is dearer than life!" exclaimed the Athenian.

"Speak not thus to me, Lycidas," said Zarah, in a tone of entreaty; "you know too well the impassable barrier which divides us."

"Not impassable, Zarah," cried the Greek; "it has been thrown down, I have trampled over it, and it separates us no longer. Hear me, O daughter of Abraham! Much have I learned since last I stood on this threshold; deeply have I studied your Scriptures; long have I secretly conversed with the wise and learned who could instruct me in your faith. I am now persuaded that there is no God but one God—He who revealed Himself to Abraham: I have renounced every heathen superstition; I have in all things conformed to the law of Moses; I have been formally received as a proselyte into the Jewish Church; and am now, like Achor the Ammonite, in everything save name and birth, a Hebrew."

Zarah could not refrain from uttering an exclamation of delight. Her whole countenance suddenly lighted up with an expression of happiness, which was reflected on that of him who stood before her—for in that blissful moment Lycidas felt that he must be beloved.

"Oh, joy!" cried Zarah, clasping her hands. "Then have you also embraced the Holy Covenant, and you are numbered amongst the children of Abraham! Then may I look upon you as a brother indeed!"

"Can you not look upon me as something more than a brother, Zarah?" exclaimed the Athenian. "Why should you not fly—since you needs must fly from this dangerous spot—under the protection, the loving, devoted care, of an affianced husband?"

Zarah flushed, trembled, covered her face with her hands, and sank, rather than seated herself, upon the divan from which she had risen on hearing the knock of the Greek. Lycidas ventured to seat himself beside the young maiden, take one of her unresisting hands and press it first to his heart, then to his lips—for he read consent in the silence of Zarah.

But the maiden had none of the calm tranquillity of happiness; she felt bewildered, doubtful of herself; again she covered her face and murmured, "Oh that my mother were here to guide me!"

"Hadassah would not have spurned a proselyte whom the elders have received; she was too large-minded, too just," said Lycidas, disappointed and somewhat mortified at the doubts which evidently disturbed the mind of the maiden. "Listen to the plan which I have formed for your escape, my Zarah. I have already made arrangements with the trusty Joab. He will bring a horse-litter an hour after dark to bear you and your handmaid hence; I will accompany you as your armed and mounted attendant. We will direct our course to the coast. At Joppa we shall, I hope, find a vessel, borne forward by whose white wings we shall soon reach my own beautiful and glorious land, where love, freedom, and happiness, shall await my fair Hebrew bride!"

For some moments Zarah made no reply; how tempting was the vista thus suddenly opened before her—radiant with rosy light, like those seen in the clouds at sunrise! Then Zarah uncovered her face, but without raising it, or venturing to look at Lycidas, she said, in a voice that trembled with emotion, "Hadassah, my mother, would have deemed it unseemly for a maiden thus to flee from her country to a land where her God is not known and worshipped, and under the protection of one who is none of her kindred."

"I thought that you had no kindred, Zarah," said

Lycidas, with uneasiness; "that you had none left of your family whose guardianship you could seek."

"I have—or had—an aged relative, Rachel of Beth-sura," replied Zarah, "who, if she be yet living, will assuredly receive me into her home. But my next of kin are the Asmonean brothers."

"The noblest family in the land!" exclaimed the Athenian. "If it be indeed impossible for you to escape with me into Greece—"

"Not impossible, but *wrong*," said Zarah softly; "it would be disobeying what I know would have been the will of her whose wishes are more sacred to me now than ever."

"Then be mine in your own land," cried Lycidas, "where I may show that I merit to win you. Will the noble Judas and his brothers deem me unworthy to unite with one of their race if I devote my sword to the cause of which they are the champions—a cause as glorious as that for which my ancestor died at Marathon?"

Still the cloud of doubt did not pass from the fair brow of Zarah. There was a difficulty in her mind which she shrank from disclosing to Lycidas. At last she timidly said, her cheeks glowing crimson as she spoke, "Shall I be candid with you, Lycidas? shall I tell all—as to a brother?"

"All, all," replied the Athenian, with painful misgiv-ing at his heart.

"Beloved Hadassah is at rest, I can hear her dear voice no more, but—but I am not ignorant of what were her views and wishes," said Zarah. "I believe—indeed I know"—Zarah could hardly speak distinctly enough, in her confusion, for the strained ear of Lycidas to catch her words—"she had destined me for another; I am not quite certain whether I be not even betrothed."

Lycidas could not refrain from a passionate outburst. "It was wicked—cruel—infamous," he cried, "to dispose of your hand without your consent!"

"Such words must never be applied to aught that she did," said Zarah. "The revered mother ever consulted the happiness as well as the honour of her child. She would never have urged upon me any marriage from which my heart revolted, but she let me know her wishes. And the very last day that we were together" —tears flowed fast from under Zarah's long drooping lashes as she went on—"on that fatal day, ere I left her to attend the Passover Feast, Hadassah charged me, by the love that I bore to her, never to take any important step in life without at least consulting him in whom she felt assured that I should find my best earthly protector."

"And who may this chosen individual be?" asked Lycidas, almost fiercely; a pang of jealousy stirring in his breast as he demanded the name of his rival.

Zarah murmured, "Judas Maccabeus."

"Judas Maccabeus!" exclaimed the young Greek, starting to his feet, more alarmed at the sound of that name than had been the warriors of Nicanor, when hearing it suddenly at night in the death-shout. Lycidas, with all the enthusiastic admiration which noble deeds inspire in a poetic and generous nature like his, had regarded the career of the Hebrew hero. The history of Maccabeus was to the Greek an acted epic; in character, in renown, Judas, in his estimation, towered like a giant above all other men of his generation. Lycidas had met the chieftain but once; but in that one meeting had received impressions which made him idealize Maccabeus into a being more like the demi-gods of whom poets sang, whom worshippers adored, than one of the denizens of earth. He was in the eyes of the young enthusiast, conqueror, patriot, and prince—a breathing embodiment of "the heroism of virtue." The Greek had never thought of Maccabeus before as one subject to human passions, save love of country, and perhaps love of fame; or as one influenced by human affections, who might seek to win a woman's heart as well as to triumph over his foes. The idea of having him for a rival struck the young Athenian with something like despair; it seemed more than presumption to enter the arena against such an opponent as this. Lycidas believed that, had Antiochus Epiphanes laid the crown of Syria at the feet of Zarah, she would have rejected the gift; but breathed

there a maiden in Judæa who could do aught but accept
with pride the proffered hand of her country's hero—of
him who was to all other mortals as snow-capped Lebanon
to a mole-hill ?

Zarah felt that her disclosure had inspired more alarm
in the mind of Lycidas than she had intended, or than
was warranted by the true state of the relations between
her and the Hebrew leader. She hastened to relieve the
apprehensions of the Greek. "I reverence Maccabeus,"
said the maiden ; "I would repose the greatest confidence
alike in his wisdom and his honour ; but, personally,
Judas is no more to me than any of his brothers."

Lycidas drew a deep sigh of relief. Grateful for the
encouragement which he drew from this avowal, the
Greek resumed his place by the side of Zarah. "What
course will you then pursue towards Maccabeus?" he
inquired.

"I must consult him, as Hadassah bade me consult
him," said the maiden : "he must know all that most
nearly concerns me ; it seems to me as if he stood to me
now in the place of a father."

The spirits of Lycidas rose at the word ; again his
heart was buoyant with hope.

"Our first object now, beloved one," said he, "must
be to place your person in safety. . As you will not seek
refuge in Attica, we will bend our course southward—if
such be your wish—and find out your aged relative at

Bethsura. I would fain that she dwelt in any other direction; for Bethsura itself holds a Syrian garrison, the army of Lysias is advancing, and Southern Judæa is so infested by armed bands that travelling is scarcely safe. Have you no friends, no relatives, in Galilee, or on the sea-coast?"

Zarah shook her head. "I know not of one," she replied. "Rachel dwells not in Bethsura, but near it, and in a spot so retired that the enemy is scarcely likely to find it out. If the country be infested by armed bands—they are the followers of Maccabeus, and from them we have nothing to dread."

Though Lycidas was not a little disappointed at having to give up his first scheme—that of bearing off Zarah to the coast, and thence to Attica—he could not but respect her scruples, and own that the course upon which she had decided was not only the most dutiful but the most wise. It was agreed therefore that Zarah, under the escort of Lycidas, should start at the hour which the Greek had first proposed; but that, instead of Joppa, her destination should be Bethsura — at which place, by travelling all night, she might hope to arrive before dawn.

While Zarah was concluding these arrangements with Lycidas, Anna returned from Jerusalem. The face of the faithful servant expressed anxiety; a warning dropped in her ear by a Hebrew acquaintance had rendered her uneasy on account of her mistress. "Beware! dogs are on the scent of the deer." Heartily glad was the handmaid to find that the Athenian lord had come to aid the escape of Zarah ; his talents, his courage, the gold which he so lavishly spent, would, as she thought, clear away all difficulties attending their flight.

The Greek soon left the lady and her attendant to make needful preparations for a journey so sudden and unexpected as that which was before them.

CHAPTER XXXI

THE enforced hastiness of Zarah's departure rendered it perhaps less painful than it would otherwise have been. Zarah had little time to indulge in tender regrets on leaving a spot which memory still peopled with loved forms, giving a life to lifeless objects, making the table at which Hadassah had sat so often, the wheel at which she had spun, the plants that she had nurtured, things too precious to be parted from without a pang. There was little which Zarah could take with her in a litter; save the parchments, some articles of dress and her few jewels, all must be left behind.

Yet at this time of peril, while the wound inflicted by bereavement was yet unhealed, Zarah felt a spring of happiness which she had believed could never flow again, rising within her young heart. "Lycidas is an adopted son of Abraham! Lycidas, one of God's chosen people!"

That thought sufficed to make Zarah's soft eyes bright and her step buoyant, to flood her spirit with hope and delight. Not that Zarah forgot Hadassah in her new sense of happiness; on the contrary, the memory of the sainted dead was linked with each thought of joy, and served to make it more holy.

"How Hadassah would have praised and blessed God for this!" reflected Zarah. "Her words were the seeds of truth which fell on the richest of soils, where the harvest now gladdens her child. It was she who first saved the precious life of my Lycidas, and then led his yet more precious soul to the Fount of Salvation! Had Lycidas never listened to the voice of my mother, he had been an idolater still!"

It was with more of pleasure than of apprehension that Zarah, timid as was her nature, anticipated the journey before her. Lycidas was to be her protector, Lycidas would be near her, his presence seemed to bring with it safety and joy.

"And may it not be thus with all the future journey of life?" whispered hope to the maiden. "Will Judas Maccabeus make any very strong opposition to the union of his kinswoman to a proselyte, when he finds that her happiness is involved in it, and that Lycidas will be a gallant defender of the faith which he has adopted as his own?" Zarah felt some anxiety and doubt upon this question, but nothing approaching to despair. The

maiden had little idea of the intensity of the affection
concentrated upon herself by one who was wont to re-
strain outward expression of his feelings; she feared that
Judas might be offended and displeased, but never im-
agined that she had the power of making him wretched.
Was such a mighty hero, such an exalted leader, likely
to care for the heart of a simple girl? Love was a
weakness to which Zarah deemed that so calm and lofty
a being as Maccabeus could scarce condescend. But is
the forest oak less strong and majestic because spring
drapes its branches with thousands of blossoms; or are
those blossoms less truly flowers because their hue is too
like that of the foliage to strike a careless beholder?
Maccabeus, with his thoughtful reserved disposition,
would as little have talked of his affection for Zarah as
he would of the pulsations of his heart; but both were
a part of his nature, a necessity of his existence.

Joab was punctual to his appointment. An hour
after dark the clatter of horses' hoofs was heard on the
lonely hill-path which led to the house of Hadassah.
Anna cautiously unclosed the door, peering forth
anxiously to see whether those who came were friends
or foes.

"It is my Lord Lycidas!" she joyfully exclaimed, as
the horseman who rode in front drew his rein at the
door.

The Athenian found Zarah and her attendant ready to

start, and in a few minutes the two were seated in the
horse-litter conducted by Joab, the crimson curtains
were drawn, and the travellers departed from the lonely
habitation upon their perilous journey.

A NIGHT JOURNEY.

The weather at this advanced season was cold, almost
frosty, at night; but Lycidas was glad of the cessation
of the heavy rains which had, as usual, heralded the
approach of winter. The night was cloudless and clear,
the azure vault was spangled with stars.

After some windings amongst the hills, the party
entered the long valley of Rephaim, rich with corn-fields,
vineyards, and orchards. The corn had long since been
garnered, the grapes had been gathered, but the fig-trees

were still laden with fruit. Zarah noticed little of the
scenery around her, though brilliant starlight rendered
it faintly visible. The rough motion of the litter over
rocky roads precluded conversation, even had Zarah been
disposed to enter into it with her attendant. The rocking of the litter rather invited sleep, and after the maiden
had been for about an hour and a half slowly pursuing
her journey, drowsiness was stealing over her, when she
was startled by a sudden shock, which, though not
violent, was sufficient somewhat to alarm, and thoroughly
to arouse her. "Has anything happened?" asked the
maiden, partly drawing back one of the crimson curtains
of her litter. Lycidas had dismounted, and was at her
side in a moment.

"It is a trifling matter," he said; "be not alarmed,
dear lady. One of the thongs has given way; Joab will
speedily set all to rights; I only regret the delay."

"Where are we now?" asked Zarah.

"Close to the village of Bethlehem," was the
Athenian's reply.

"Ah! I must look upon Bethlehem again!" cried
Zarah with emotion, drawing the curtain further back,
so as to obtain a wider view of the dim landscape of
swelling hills and soft pastures. "My loved mother
Hadassah was wont to bring me every year to this place;
she called its stones the Memorial of the Past, and the
Cradle of the Future."

"I know that Bethlehem is a place of great historical interest," observed Lycidas, glancing around; "it was here that David, the anointed shepherd, watched his flock, and encountered the lion and the bear. And it was here that the gentle Ruth gleaned barley amongst the reapers of Boaz." The young Greek was well pleased to show his recently-acquired knowledge of sacred story.

"Yes; my mother was wont to point out to me the very spots where events took place which must ever render them dear to the Hebrews," observed Zarah. "But Hadassah always said that the chief interest of Bethlehem lies in the future rather than in the past. It is here"—Zarah reverentially lowered her voice as she went on—"it is here that Messiah the Prince shall be born, as has been revealed to us by a prophet."

"One would scarcely deem this village to be a place likely to be so honoured," observed Lycidas.

"Ah! you remind me of what my dear mother once said in reply to words of mine, spoken several years ago, when I was very young," said Zarah. "'It will be a long time before the Prince can come,' I observed, 'for I have looked on every side, and I cannot see so much as the first stone laid of the palace in which He will be born.'—'Think you, child,' said Hadassah, 'that a building ten thousand times more splendid than that raised by Solomon would add a whit to His glory? The presence of the king makes the palace, though it should

be but a cave. Does it increase the value of the diamond
if the earth in which it lies embedded show a few
spangles of gold dust?'—I have never forgotten that
gentle reproof," continued Zarah, "and it makes me look
with something of reverence even on such a building as
that mean inn which we see yonder, for who can say
that the Prince of Peace may not be born even in a
place so lowly!"

As Joab was still occupied in preparing the thong,
Lycidas, standing bridle in hand beside Zarah's litter,
went on with the conversation.

"The mind of Hadassah," he observed, "seemed
especially to dwell upon humiliation, suffering, and sacrifice in connection with the mysterious Being for whose
advent she looked—we all look. If her view be correct,
it may be possible that not only the death, but the
earthly life of the Messiah may be one long sacrifice from
the cradle to the grave."

The conversation then turned to themes less lofty, till
Joab had succeeded in effecting the slight needful repairs.
Lycidas then remounted his horse, and the party resum-
ing their journey, Bethlehem was soon left behind them.

It is unnecessary to describe that night-journey, or
tell how Lycidas and his companions passed the site of
King Solomon's pleasure-grounds, his "gardens, and
orchards, and pools of water;" or how the road then led
over the succession of barren hills which extend south-

ward as far as Hebron. Travelling was slow and tedious, the road rough, and the horses grew weary. Lycidas was too anxious to place his charge in safety to permit of a halt for refreshment and rest on the way. The Greek's uneasiness on Zarah's account was increased as, towards dawn, they met parties of peasants fleeing, as they said, from the Syrians, who, like a vast cloud of locusts, were carrying devastation through the land. Lycidas felt that danger was on all sides; he knew not whether to advance or to retreat; responsibility weighed heavily upon him, and he almost envied the stolid composure with which the hardy Joab trudged on his weary way. The Athenian would not disturb the serenity of Zarah's mind by imparting to her the anxious cares which perplexed his own. Lycidas was touched by the implicit confidence placed by the gentle girl in his power to protect and guide her; and he was thankful that while with him eye, ear, brain, were strained to the utmost to detect the most remote approach of danger, the weary Zarah in her litter was able to enjoy the refreshment of sleep.

CHAPTER XXXII

"OLD! stand! who are ye, and whither go ye?" was the stern challenge, the sound of which startled Zarah out of a pleasant dream. The motion of the litter suddenly ceased, a strong hand was on the bridle of the horse which Lycidas was riding, a weapon was pointed at the breast of the Greek. There was not yet sufficient light to enable him to distinguish whether those who thus arrested the further progress of the party were Syrians or Hebrews.

"We are quiet travellers," said the Athenian; "let us pursue our journey in peace. If gold be your object, I will give it."

"If we want your gold we can take it," cried the leader of the band that now surrounded the litter. "Are you a follower of Antiochus Epiphanes?"

"No," replied Lycidas boldly. To speak the simple

truth is ever the manliest, and in this instance it also proved the safest course to pursue. The grasp on the Greek's bridle was relaxed, the point of the weapon was lowered, and in a more courteous tone the leader inquired, "Are you then a friend of Judas Maccabeus?"

"May he be given the necks of his enemies!" exclaimed Joab, before Lycidas had time to reply. "It is his kinswoman whom we are taking in this litter to Bethsura, that we may put her in safety out of reach of the tyrant who has sworn to slay her because she will not burn incense to his idol!"

"What, the Lady Hadassah?" asked one of the men.

"No; it is more than six months since that mother in Israel departed to Abraham's bosom," replied Joab, lowering his tone.

An exclamation of regret burst from more than one of those who surrounded the litter, and he who had first spoken observed, "These will be sorry tidings for Maccabeus and his brethren."

Lycidas now addressed a Hebrew who appeared to be of superior condition to the others. "In this litter," he said, "is the grand-daughter of the Lady Hadassah. She is fleeing from persecution, and seeks an asylum in the home of an aged relative who dwells near Bethsura."

"Ah! Rachel the widow; we know her well," was the reply.

"Then you can guide this lady to her abode."

"Guide her into the wolf's den!" exclaimed the Hebrew ; and one of his companions added with a laugh, "The only way to reach Rachel's dwelling from hence is over the corpses of defeated Syrians, as mayhap we shall do ere to-morrow."

Alarmed at finding that he had conducted Zarah to the scene of an expected deadly conflict, Lycidas inquired with anxiety, "Where then can the lady and her attendant find shelter and protection ?"

"For protection, she has all that our swords can give —our fate must be her fate," replied the Hebrew whom the Greek had addressed. "As for shelter, there is a goatherd's hut hard by. Some of our men have passed the night there, though our leader slept on the ground."

There was some whispering amongst the Hebrews, and Lycidas caught the words, uttered in a half-jesting tone, "An awkward matter for Maccabeus to have this his fair kinswoman coming on the eve of a battle on which the fate of Judah depends."

"I pray you show us this hut at once," said the Greek, annoyed at Zarah's being exposed to such obser-vations, and impatient to remove her as soon as possible to a place of as much retirement as could be found in the camping-ground of an army. "The lady has travelled all night, and is weary."

"I will lead her to the hut," said one of the Hebrews ; "and do you, Saul," he continued, addressing a com-

panion, "go at once and announce to our prince the
lady's arrival."

Again the litter of Zarah moved onwards, and the
weary horses were guided to a hut at no great distance.
One of the Jewish soldiers ran on before to give notice,
that the dwelling might be vacated of its warlike occu-
pants, and put into such order for the reception of a
lady as circumstances and haste would permit. The
Hebrews who had passed the frosty night under the
roof of the goatherd's dwelling quitted it at once to
make room for the lady and her handmaid, leaving a
portion of their simple breakfast for the newly-arrived
guests.

A homely care occupied the mind of Zarah on her
way to the hut.

"Anna," she said to her attendant, "we are much
beholden to Joab, and I have no shekels wherewith to
pay for the hire of the litter and horses, or to requite
him for his faithful service. It is not meet that the
Lord Lycidas should be at charges for me. Let Joab
speak to me when I quit the litter, or do you give him
this jewel from me."

The jewel was a massive silver bracelet, which had
been worn by the unhappy Pollux. Zarah had selected
this from the other ornaments which had belonged to
her parents, on account of the weight of metal which it
contained. There was also something heathenish in the

fashion of the bracelet itself, which made the Hebrew maiden care not to keep it as a remembrance of her father.

"Joab is not here," said Anna, glancing from between the curtains; "he has given up the guidance of the horses to one of the Hebrew warriors."

Joab had in fact gone off with Saul, being eager to be the first to carry to Judas Maccabeus intelligence of what had occurred in Jerusalem since they had parted beside the martyrs' grave, and especially of the momentous events which had occurred in the family of Hadassah.

"If I cannot see Joab himself," observed Zarah, "I must ask the Lord Lycidas to find him and do this my errand, for the muleteer must not go unrewarded by me."

Accordingly, after the maiden, assisted by Lycidas, had descended from her litter, and explored with Anna the goatherd's abode, she bashfully asked her protector to execute for her this little commission, and with the heavy silver bracelet requite her obligation to Joab. "To yourself," added Zarah with downcast eyes, "I can proffer but heartfelt thanks."

The spirits of Lycidas had risen : with him, as with nature, the gloom of night was now succeeded by the brilliance of morning. The rebound of a mind lately weighed down with intense anxiety and the pressure of heavy responsibility was so great, that it seemed as if every care were flung off for ever. Lycidas had accomplished his dangerous mission; he had placed his beloved charge under the care of her relatives; and he felt assured that her heart was his own. The clang of martial preparation which he now heard around him was as music to the ardent spirit of the Greek. He was now going to join in a brave struggle under a heroic commander, to deserve Zarah, and then to win her! The heart of the gallant young Athenian beat high with hope.

"Nay, Zarah," said Lycidas gaily, in reply to the maiden's words; "I may one day claim from you something better than thanks. As for the bracelet, rest assured that I will well requite faithful Joab; he shall be no loser if I keep the jewel in pledge, and never part with it, save to my bride." Lycidas clasped the bracelet on his arm, as with a proud and joyous step he quitted the goatherd's hut.

"Stay, Lycidas," expostulated Zarah, following him over the threshold; but then arresting her steps, and watching his receding form for a moment with a smile as radiant as his own. "How could *he* fear a rival!" was the thought flitting through Zarah's mind as she gazed. She then turned to re-enter the hut, and saw before her—Judas Maccabeus!

CHAPTER XXXIII.

THE LEADER AND THE MAN.

IN the unsettled state of the Holy Land, where its brave sons had to maintain a kind of guerilla warfare against the powerful enemy who held its strongholds and ruled in its capital — where communication between places not far remote from each other was difficult and dangerous, and a written letter was a thing almost unknown — the Asmonean brothers had been in ignorance of many events which have occupied a large space in these pages. Joab, therefore, on his arrival in the camp of the Hebrews, had much to tell that was to them entirely new.

Judas with thrilling interest had listened to the muleteer's account of Zarah's peril and escape from the palace of Antiochus, and the deaths of Hadassah and Pollux. The fount of tenderness which lay concealed under the chief's usually calm and almost stern exterior was stirred to its inmost depths. Grief, admiration, love, swelled his brave heart. Maccabeus could hardly wait to hear the end of Joab's narration. Zarah was near him—his beauteous, his beloved, his chosen bride —she who had so suffered and so mourned—the tender orphan maiden bereaved of all love, all protection save his own—but dearer in her poverty and desolation than she could have been had she brought him the dowry of an empire.

It was thus that Maccabeus thought of Zarah, as, with an eagerness of impatience which could not have brooked an instant's longer delay, he strode rapidly towards the hut which sheltered his treasure. He soon beheld her—could it indeed be she? No desolate, weeping, trembling fugitive met the gaze of the chief; but a maiden bright and fair as the morn, with a blush on her cheeks and a smile on her lips, her whole countenance beaming with hope, and her eyes fixed with a lingering look on a Greek who was disappearing from view in a direction opposite to that by which Judas had approached her! The depths of the leader's feelings were again stirred, but this time as by a bar of glowing red-hot iron.

"Who is yon Gentile?" was the sudden fierce exclamation which burst from the warrior's lips.

Never before had her kinsman looked so terrible to Zarah as when he startled her then by his sudden appearance.   It was not because she now saw Maccabeus for the first time arrayed in the harness of battle, his tall powerful frame partly sheathed in glittering steel, and a plumed helmet on his head, giving him a resemblance to the description which she had heard from Lycidas of the fabled god of war; it was the eye, the manner, the tone of Judas that changed the smile of the maiden in a moment to a look of embarrassment and fear.   Antiochus himself, on his judgment-seat, had scarcely appeared more formidable to the trembling captive before him, than did the kinsman who had come to welcome her, and who would have died to shield her from wrong!

Maccabeus repeated his stern question before Zarah found courage to reply.   "That is Lycidas, the Athenian lord," she faltered; "he whom you spared by the martyrs' tomb.   He has well requited your mercy.   He protected and aided Hadassah to the end, and paid the last honours to her dear remains; he struck down the Syrian who slew my father.   Lycidas has embraced the Hebrew faith, and has come to fight, and, if need be, to die in the Hebrew cause!"

The maiden spoke rapidly, and with a good deal of nervous excitement.   She did not venture to glance up again into the face of her kinsman to see the effect of her explanation, for all the false hopes regarding his indifference with which she had buoyed herself, had vanished like a bubble at a touch. Maccabeus did not at once reply. Silently he led Zarah back into the hut, and motioned to her to take her seat upon a low heap of cushions which Anna had removed from the litter, and placed on the earthen floor for the accommodation of her young mistress. He then dismissed the attendant by a wave of his hand. The profound gloomy silence of her kinsman was by no means reassuring to Zarah, who felt much as a criminal might feel in presence of a judge—albeit in regard to her conduct towards Lycidas her con-science was clear.

Maccabeus stood before Zarah, the shadow of his form falling upon the maiden, as he towered between her and the light, gloomily gazing down upon her.

"Zarah," he said at last, "there must be no conceal-ment between us. You know in what relation we stand to each other. You have told me what that Gentile has been to Hadassah, and to Abner your father; tell me now, What is he to *you?*"

Zarah struggled to regain her courage, though she knew not how deeply her evident fear of him wounded the spirit of her kinsman. She did not dare to answer his question directly. "Lycidas is *not* a Gentile," she said; "he is, as you are, a servant of God, a true be-liever; he has been fully admitted into all the privileges held by our race."

JUDAS AND THE MAIDEN.

"Even the privilege of wedding a Hebrew maiden?" inquired Maccabeus with slow deliberation.

Zarah fancied that his tone was less stern, and was thankful that Judas had been the one to break ground upon so delicate a subject.

"Hadassah would not have blamed us," she said simply, blushing deeply as she spoke.

Notwithstanding what had just passed, Zarah was utterly unprepared for the effect of what was in fact an artless confession. It was not a groan nor a cry that she heard, but a sound that partook of the nature of both ; a sound that the last turn of the rack could not have forced from the breast that uttered it now ! It was the expression of an agony which few hearts have affections strong enough to feel, fewer still could have fortitude to sustain. No death-wail, no cry of woe, no shriek of pain that Zarah had ever listened to, smote on her soul like that sound ! She heard it but once—it was never heard but once—and before she had recovered from the shock which it gave her, Judas had rushed forth from the hut. He was as one possessed ; so fierce were the demons of jealousy and hatred that for a space held reason, conscience, every power of mind and soul in subjection. One wild desire to kill his rival, to tear him limb from limb, seemed all that had any definite form in that fearful chaos of passion. It was well for Lycidas that he did not then cross the path of the lion !

Maccabeus plunged into the depths of a wood that was near, seeking instinctively the thickest shade afforded by evergreen trees. He would fain have buried his anguish from the sight of man in the darkest cavern— in the deepest grave ! The very sunlight was oppressive !

All lost—all rent away from him for ever ! What hope had clung to, what love had treasured through the long, long years of waiting, giving new courage to the brave, new energy to the weary ! Youth, happiness, the cup of joy just filled to the brim by the coming of Zarah, without one moment's warning dashed from the lips of him who loved her, and the last drops sucked up by the thirsty sand! The miseries of a long life seemed to be crowded into the few minutes during which the leader of the Hebrews, the hope of Judah, lay prostrate on the earth, clinching the dust in his despair.

Hatred and jealousy raged within; and a yet darker demon had joined them, one whose presence, above all others, makes the soul as a hell! Like burning venom-drops fell the suggestions of rebellious unbelief upon the spirit of the disappointed man. "Is it for this that you have washed your hands in innocency, and kept your feet in the paths of truth? Is it for this that you have devoted all your powers to God and your country, have shrunk from no toil, and dreaded no danger? He whom you were faithfully serving hath not watched over your peace, nor guarded for you that treasure which you had confided to his care? What profit is there in obedience, what benefit in devotion? Prayer has been but vanity, and faith but self-deception!"

Such moments as these are the most terrible in the experience of a servant of the Lord. They afford a glimpse of the depths of guilt and misery to which the noblest human soul would sink without sustaining grace; they show that, like the brightest planet, such soul shines not with light of its own, but with an imparted radiance, deprived of which it would be enveloped in

utter darkness.   An Abraham, left to himself, could lie ;
a David stain his soul with innocent blood.   All need the
Sacrifice of Atonement, all require the grace which comes
from above.

But Judas Maccabeus was not left unaided to be carried away to an abyss of crime by his own wild passions.
They were as a steed accustomed to obey the rein of conscience, that, smitten with agonizing pain, has taken the
bit into its teeth, and rushed madly towards a precipice.
But the hand of its rider still grasps the bridle, his eye
sees the danger in front, and the frantic animal beneath
him has but for a brief space burst from his master's
powerful constraint.   If the rider cannot otherwise stop
his wild steed, he will strike it down with a heavy blow,
that by a lesser fall the greater may be avoided ; and so
he leads it back to its starting-place, quivering, trembling in every limb, the sweat on its flanks, the foam on
its bit, but subdued, submissive, under command.   Even
so with the Hebrew chief, conscience regained its habitual
sway over the passions ; as soon as the anguish of his
soul found vent in prayer, the crisis of danger was past.
Maccabeus rose from the earth, pale as one who has received a death-wound, but submissive and calm.

"Shall one who has been so favoured, beyond his
hopes, far beyond his deserts, dare to repine at the
decree of Him who orders all things in wisdom and
goodness ? "   Thus reflected the chief.   " Who am I,

that I should claim exemption from disappointment and loss? Shame on the leader who gives way to selfish passion, and at such a time as this! We shall shortly close in battle; and if in that battle I fall" (the thought brought strange consolation), "how shall I look back from the world of spirits on that which for a time could almost shake the trust of this unworthy heart in the God of my fathers? If I survive the perils of the day, better it is that there should be no selfish hopes, no selfish cares, to prevent me from concentrating all my energies and thoughts upon the work appointed me to do. I have been wasting my time in idle dreams of earthly enjoyment; I have been rudely awakened. O Lord of hosts, strengthen Thy servant to arise and gird up his spirit to perform fearlessly and faithfully the duties of the day!"

Then, with slower step and calmer aspect, Judas Maccabeus returned to his camp.

CHAPTER XXXIV.

FANATICISM.

WE will now glance at the encampment of the Hebrew warriors, upon a wild expanse of undulating ground, in view of the towers of Bethsura, a strong fortress rebuilt by the Edomite settlers on the site of that raised in former times by Rehoboam. Bethsura is now garrisoned by the Syrians, and its environs occupied by the countless tents of their mighty host.

On a small rising ground near the centre of the Hebrew camp stands, as on a rostrum, an old Jew, clad in a camel-hair garment, with long gray unkempt hair hanging over his shoulders. His manner is excited, his gestures vehement, and the shrill accents of his voice are so raised as to be heard to a considerable distance. A gradually increasing circle of listeners gathers around him—stern, weather-beaten men, who have toiled and suffered much for their faith. What marvel if with

some of these warriors religion have darkened into
fanaticism, courage degenerated into savage fierceness?
It is the tendency of war, especially if it be of a guerilla
character, to inflame the passions and harden the heart.
Only terrible necessity can justify the unnatural strife
which arms man against his brother man. Even the
most noble struggle in which patriot can engage in
defence of his country's freedom, draws along with it
terrible evils, of which a vast amount of human suffering
is not perhaps the greatest.

"Yea, I do charge you, Joab, I do charge you, O son
of Ahijah, with having brought a spy, a traitor, into our
camp!" almost shrieked the wild orator Jasher, as he
pointed with his shrivelled finger at the sturdy muleteer,
who stood in the innermost rank of the circle. "Was
not this Greek, by your own showing, present at the
martyrdom of the blessed saint Solomona?—was he not
tried for his life at her grave, where he was discovered
coiling like a serpent in the darkness?—is he not one
of a race of idolaters, worshippers of images made by
man's hand?"

"All that I can say," replied Joab doggedly, "is, that
whatever Lycidas may have been, he is not an idolater
now."

"Who are you that you should judge, you Nabal, you
son of folly?" exclaimed the excited orator. "Mark
you, men of Judah, mark you the blindness that falls

on some men—ay, even on a reputed saint like the Lady
Hadassah! Joab has learned from her handmaiden the
astounding fact that for months this Lycidas, this viper,
was nurtured and tended in her home, as if he had been
a son of Abraham! Doubtless it was this act of worse
than folly on the part of Hadassah that drew down a
judgment on her and her house. Mark what followed.
The warmed viper escapes from her dwelling, and the
next day—ay, the very next day—Syrian dogs beset
the house of Salathiel as he celebrates the holy Feast!
Who guided them thither?" The question was asked
with passionate energy, and the feelings of the speaker
were evidently beginning to communicate themselves to
the audience. "Who then lay a bleeding corpse on the
threshold, slain by the murderous Syrians?" continued
Jasher, with yet fiercer action; "who but Abishai, the
brave, the faithful, he who had denounced the viper, and
had sought, but in vain, to crush it—it was he who fell
at last a victim to its treacherous sting!" Jasher ended
his peroration with a hissing sound from between his
clinched teeth, and the caldron of human feelings around
him began, as it were, to seethe and boil. Fanaticism
stops not to weigh evidence, or to listen to reason.
Joab could hardly make his voice heard amidst the roar
of angry voices that was rising around him.

"Lycidas was present and helped at the burial
of the Lady Hadassah; he has risked his life to

protect her daughter," cried the honest defender of the Greek.

"Ha! ha! how much he risked we know not, but we can well guess what he would win!" exclaimed Jasher, with a look of withering scorn. "He has crept into the favour of a foolish girl, who forgets the traditions of her people, who cares not for the afflictions of Jacob, who prefers a goodly person"—the old man's features writhed with the fierceness of his satire—"to all that a child of Abraham should regard with reverence and honour! But what can we expect from the daughter of a perjured traitor, an apostate? Had she not Abner for a father; and can we expect otherwise than that she should disgrace her family, her tribe, her nation, by wedding an accursed Gentile, a detestable Greek?"

"Never, never!" yelled out a hundred fierce voices. And one of the crowd shouted aloud, "I would rather slay her with my own hand, were she my own daughter!"

"I cannot believe Lycidas false!" cried out Joab, at the risk of drawing the tempest of rage upon himself.

"You cannot believe him false, you son of the nether millstone!" screamed out the furious Jasher, stamping with passion; "as if you were a match for a wily Greek, born in that idolatrous, base, ungrateful Athens, that banished her only good citizen, and poisoned her only wise one!" The fierce prejudices of race were only too

easily aroused in that assembly of Hebrew warriors, and
if Jasher were blamed by some of his auditors, it was
for allowing that any Athenian could be either wise or
good.

"Yet hear me for a moment—I must be heard,"
cried Joab, straining his voice to its loudest pitch, yet
scarcely able to make his words audible; "Lycidas has
been admitted into the Covenant by our priests; he can
give proofs—"

"Who talks of proofs?" exclaimed Jasher, stamping
again on the earth. "Did you never hear of the proofs
given by Zopyrus? Know you not how Babylon, the
golden city, fell under the sword of Darius? Zopyrus,
minion of that king, fled to the city which he was
besieging, showed its defenders his ghastly hurts—nose,
ears shorn off—and pointed to the bleeding wounds as
proofs that Darius the tyrant, by inflicting such injuries
upon him, had won a right to his deathless hatred.*
The Babylonians believed the proofs, they received the
impostor, and ye know the result. Babylon fell, not
because the courage of her defenders quailed, or famine
thinned their numbers; not because the enemy stormed
at her wall, or pestilence raged within it; but because
she had received, and believed, and trusted a traitor,
who had sacrificed his own members to gain the oppor-

* The student of history need not be reminded that the fall of Babylon through the
stratagem of Zopyrus was quite distinct from and subsequent to its conquest by Cyrus
(See Rollin's "Ancient History.")

tunity of destroying those who put faith in his honour!
Hebrews, a Zopyrus has now come into our camp! Will
ye open your arms, or draw your swords, to receive
him?"

A wild yell of fury arose from the listening throng,
so fierce, so loud, that it drew towards the spot Hebrews
from all parts of the encampment. It drew amongst
others the young proselyte, who came eager to know the
cause of the noise and excitement, quite unconscious
that it was in any way connected with himself. As
Lycidas made towards the centre of the crowd, it divided
to let him pass into the immediate presence of Jasher,
his accuser and self-constituted judge, and then ominously
closed in behind him, so as to prevent the possibility of
his retreat.

Lycidas had come amongst the Hebrew warriors with
all the frank confidence of a volunteer into their ranks;
and the Greek's first emotion was that of amazement,
when he found himself suddenly the object of universal
indignation and hatred. There was no mistaking the
expression of the angry eyes that glared upon him from
every direction, nor the gestures of hands raising javelins
on high, or unsheathing keen glittering blades.

"Here he is, the traitor, the Gentile, led hither to die
the death he deserves!" exclaimed Jasher.

"What mean ye, Hebrews—friends? Slay me not
unheard!" cried Lycidas, raising on high his voice and

his hand. "I am a proselyte; I renounce my false gods—"

"He has their very effigies on his arm!" yelled out Jasher, pointing with frenzied action to the silver bracelet of Pollux worn by the Greek, on which had been fashioned heads of Apollo and Diana encircled with rays.

Here was evidence deemed conclusive; nothing further was needed. "He dies! he dies!" was the almost unanimous cry. The life of Lycidas had not been in greater peril when he had been discovered at the midnight burial, or when he had wrestled with Abishai on the edge of the cliff. In a few moments the young Greek would have lain a shapeless trampled corpse beneath his murderers' feet, when the one word "Forbear!" uttered in a loud, clear voice, whose tones of command had been heard above the din of battle, stayed hands uplifted to destroy; and with the exclamation, "Maccabeus! the prince!" the throng fell back on either side, and through the ranks of his followers the leader strode into the centre of the circle. One glance sufficed to inform him sufficiently of the nature of the disturbance; he saw that he had arrived on the spot barely in time to save his Athenian rival from being torn in pieces by the crowd.

"What means this tumult? shame on ye!" exclaimed Maccabeus, sternly surveying the excited throng.

LYCIDAS IN PERIL.

"We would execute righteous judgment on a Greek—
an idolater—a spy!" cried Jasher, pointing at Lycidas,
but with less impassioned gesture; for the fanatic quailed
in the presence of Maccabeus, who was the one man on
earth whom he feared.

"He is a Greek, but neither idolater nor spy," said
the prince. "He is one of a gallant people who fought
bravely for their own independence, and can sympathize

with our love of freedom. He has come to offer us the aid of his arm; shame on ye thus to requite him."

"I doubt but he will play us false," muttered one of the warriors, giving voice to the thoughts of the rest.

"We shall soon have an opportunity of settling all such doubts," said Maccabeus; "we shall attack the enemy at noon, and then shall this Greek prove in the battle whether he be false man or true."

The prospect of so soon closing with the enemy was sufficient to turn the attention of every Hebrew warrior present to something of more stirring interest than the fate of a solitary stranger. Jasher, however, would not so easily let his intended victim go free.

"He's an Achan!" exclaimed the fanatic; "if he fight amongst us, he will bring a curse on our arms!"

"He is a proselyte," replied Maccabeus in a loud voice, which was heard to the furthest edge of the crowd; "our priests and elders have received him—and I receive him—as a Hebrew by adoption, a companion in arms, a brother in the faith!"

The words of the prince were received with respectful submission, if not with satisfaction. Maccabeus was regarded with enthusiasm by his followers, not only as a gallant and successful leader, but as one whose prudence they could trust, and whose piety they must honour. No man dare lay a finger upon him over whom the chief had thrown the shield of his powerful protection.

Lycidas felt that for the second time he owed his life to Judas Maccabeus. There was a gush of warm grati- tude towards his preserver in the heart of the young Athenian; but something in the manner of the prince told Lycidas that he would not listen to thanks, that the expression of the Greek's sense of deep obligation would be regarded as an intrusion. Lycidas therefore, com- pelled, as it were, to silence, could only with fervour ask Heaven for an opportunity of showing his gratitude in the coming fight by actions more forcible than words.

"Now, sound the trumpets to arms," exclaimed Maccabeus, "and gather my troops together. If God give us the victory to-day, the way to Jerusalem itself will be open before us! Here will I marshal our ranks for the fight." Maccabeus strode to the summit of the rising ground from which Jasher had just been address- ing the crowd, and beckoned to his standard-bearer to plant his banner behind him, where it could be seen from all parts of the camp. Here, with folded arms, Maccabeus watched the movements of his warriors as, at the signal-call of the trumpet-blast, they hastened from every quarter to be marshalled in battle-array, by their respective captains, under the eye of their great com- mander. With rapid precision the columns were formed; but before they moved on to the attack, Maccabeus, in brief but earnest supplication, besought the Divine bless- ing on their arms.

CHAPTER XXXV.

THE BATTLE-PRAYER.

YCIDAS was a native of the very land of eloquence; he had been, as it were, cradled amidst "thoughts that breathe, and words that burn." He had studied the philippics of Demosthenes, and felt the spirit of the dead orator living in them still. Lycidas had listened to the eloquence of the most gifted speakers of his own time, expressing in the magnificent language of Greece thoughts the most poetic. But never had the Athenian listened to any oration which had so stirred his own soul, as the simple prayer of Judas Maccabeus before the battle of Bethsura. There was no eloquence in it, save the unstudied eloquence of the heart; the Hebrew but uttered aloud in the hearing of his men the thoughts which had made his own spirit as firm in the hour of danger as was the steel which covered his breast.

There was much in the scene and in the congregation

to add to the effect of the act of worship on the mind of
Lycidas.   He beheld adoration paid to no image formed
by man's art—no fabled deity, capricious as the minds
of those in whose imaginations alone he had existence—
but to the holy, the high and lofty One who inhabiteth
eternity, "whose robe is the light, and whose canopy
space."   And it was in no building raised by mortal
hands that Maccabeus bent his knee to the Lord of
Hosts.   He knelt on the soil of the glorious land which
God had given to his fathers—the one spot chosen out
from the expanse of the whole mighty globe to be the
scene of events which would influence through eternity
the destinies of the world.   On the verge of the southern
horizon lay Hebron, where had dwelt the father of the
faithful—where the ground had been trodden by angels'
feet, and the feet of the Lord of angels, with whom
Abraham had pleaded for Sodom.   It was that Hebron
where David had reigned ere he was hailed king over all
Israel.   And the nearer objects were such as gave thrilling interest to the prayer of the Asmonean prince : the
view of the towers of Bethsura which he was about to
assail—the hosts of the enemy whom he, with far inferior numbers, was going to attack,—this, perhaps, even
more than associations connected with the past, made
every word of Maccabeus fall with powerful effect on
his audience.

    And that audience was in itself, probably, the noblest

that could at that time have been gathered together in any land, not excepting Italy or Greece. It was composed of men whom neither ambition nor the lust of gold had drawn from their homes to oppose an enemy whose force greatly exceeded their own. In face of the trained warriors of Syria were gathered together peasants, artizans, shepherds, animated by the purest patriotism and the most simple faith in God. Every man in that kneeling army knew that he carried his life in his hand, that in case of defeat he had no mercy to expect, and that victory scarce lay within the verge of probability according to human calculation; yet not a countenance showed anything but undaunted courage, eager hope, firm faith, as the weather-beaten, toil-worn Hebrews listened to and joined in the supplications of their leader.

But it was the character of that leader himself which gave the chief force to his words. If Maccabeus the Asmonean received the lofty title of " Prince of the sons of God," it was because his countrymen acknowledged, and that without envy, the stamp of a native royalty upon him, which needed not the anointing oil or the golden crown to add to its dignity. Any nation with pride might have numbered amongst its heroes a man possessing the military talents of a Miltiades, with the purity of an Aristides—one whose character was without reproach, whose fame was unstained with a blot. Simple,

earnest faith was the mainspring of the actions of Maccabeus. The clear, piercing gaze of the eagle, energy like
that with which the strong wing of the royal bird
cleaves the air, marked the noble Asmonean; for the
soul's gaze was upward toward its Sun, and the soul's
pinion soared high above the petty interests, the paltry
ambition of earth. As there was dignity in the single-
mindedness of the character of Judas, so was there
power in the very simplicity of his words. I will
mar that simplicity by no interpolations of my own,
but transfer unaltered to my pages the Asmonean's
battle-prayer.

"Blessed art Thou, O Saviour of Israel, who didst
quell the violence of the mighty man by the hand of
Thy servant David, and gavest the host of strangers into
the hand of Jonathan the son of Saul, and his armour-
bearer. Shut up this army in the hand of Thy people
Israel, and let them be confounded in their power and
horsemen. Make them to be of no courage, and cause
the boldness of their strength to fall away, and let them
quake in their destruction. Cast them down with the
sword of them that love Thee, and let all those that
know Thy Name praise Thee with thanksgiving."

When the tones of the leader's voice were silent, there
was for a moment a solemn stillness throughout the
martial throng: then from their knees arose the brave
sons of Abraham, prepared to "do or die."

CHAPTER XXXVI

HER brief but momentous interview with Maccabeus had left a very painful impression upon
the mind of Zarah. It had disclosed, to her
distress as well as surprise, the depth of the
wound which she was inflicting upon a loving heart; for Zarah had none of that miserable vanity
which makes the meaner of her sex triumph in their
power of giving pain. Zarah's apprehensions were also
awakened on account of Lycidas: she could not but fear
that very serious obstacles might arise to prevent her
union with the Greek. Generous as Maccabeus might
be, it was not in human nature that he should favour
the claims of a rival; and determined opposition from
her kinsman and prince must be annihilation to the
hopes of the maiden. There would be in many Jewish
minds prejudices against an Athenian: Zarah was aware
of this, though not of the intense hatred to which such

prejudices might lead.   The short interview held with
Maccabeus had sufficed to cover Zarah's bright sky with
clouds, to darken her hopes, to distress her conscience,
to make her uneasily question herself as to whether she
were indeed erring by giving her heart to a stranger.
Had she really spoken truth when she had said, " Hadassah would not have blamed us" ?

But when Anna, pale with excitement, brought tidings
to her young mistress that the Hebrews were marching
to battle—when Zarah heard that the decisive hour had
come on which hung the fate of her country, and with
it that of Lycidas—all other fears yielded for a time to
one absorbing terror.   On her knees, with hands clasped
in attitude of prayer, yet scarcely able to pray, Zarah
listened breathlessly to the fearful sounds which were
borne on the breeze—the confused noises, the yells, the
shouting—which brought vividly to her mind all the
horrors of the scene passing so near her.   It was not
needful for her to look on the raging torrent of war :
imagination but too readily pictured the streams of
opposing warriors, like floods from opposite mountains,
mingling and struggling together in a wild whirlpool of
death—chariots dragged by maddened horses over gory
heaps of the slain—the flight of hurtling arrows—the
whirl of the deadly axe—the crash—the cry—the
rush—the retreat—the rally—the flashing weapons,
now dimmed with blood ;—Zarah in thought beheld

them all, and covered her eyes with horror, as if by so doing she could shut out the sight.

For hours this agony lasted. The excitement of conflict may bear brave hearts through a battle with little sense of horror and none of fear. Warriors, even the generous and humane, can see and do things in hot blood from which their souls would revolt in calmer moments; but the woman whose earthly happiness is on the cast of the die, who cannot shield the being dearest to her upon earth from the crushing blow or the deadly thrust,—to her the day of battle is one of unmixed anguish. Suspense is agony; and yet she dreads to exchange that suspense for knowledge which might bring agony more intolerable still.

The maiden found some slight alleviation of her distress in the occupation in which she and her handmaid engaged —that of making such preparations as circumstances permitted for the comfort of the wounded; though they knew too well that if the Syrians should win the day, there would be no wounded Hebrews to tend—the conqueror's sword would too thoroughly do its hideous work.

Judas Maccabeus had displayed his accustomed judgment in choosing to be himself the assailant, instead of awaiting the assault of the myrmidons of Syria. His sudden, unexpected attack threw the enemy into some confusion, and gave an advantage in the commencement of the battle to the slender forces of the Hebrew prince.

His men rushed to the conflict as those assured of success.   Had they not measured swords with the warriors
of Apollonius and Seron ?   Had they not scattered the
thousands of Nicanor, and made Giorgias seek safety in
ignominious retreat ?   Was not Maccabeus their leader,
and saw they not the light flashing from his helmet in
the fore-front of the battle ?   Yet was the struggle obstinate ; and when the Syrians were at last forced to retire
before the Hebrew heroes, a number of the troops of
Lysias threw themselves into the fortress of Bethsura,
to rally their forces behind its walls, and gather strength
to renew the combat on the following day.

But it was no part of the plan of their active adver-
sary to leave such a rallying-point to the Syrians, or suffer
them from thence to harass his rear, should he press
onwards towards Jerusalem.   His victory must not be
incomplete ; Bethsura must be his ere darkness should
put an end to the conflict.

"See you yon Syrian banner waving from the
tower ?" cried Maccabeus.   "Who will be the first to
tear it down ?"

He was answered by a shout from his men.   "To the
walls ! to the walls ! " as the Hebrews pressed hard upon
their retreating foes.

Bethsura was not a place of much strength, though
the height of its towers gave to their defenders the
power to annoy and distress assailants with a shower of

arrows and other missiles as they rushed to the assault. Maccabeus, foreseeing that Bethsura itself must become the scene of the closing struggle, had had scaling-ladders in readiness, roughly constructed by his own men from trees hewn down by their battle-axes. With cries and shouts these were now borne onwards towards the bulwarks of Bethsura, and notwithstanding the fierce opposition of the Syrians, two of them were planted against the wall. Who would mount them, who would be the first to climb upwards through the death-shower of darts, the first to meet the fierce downward blows and thrusts of those who stood to the defence of the beleaguered fortress?

Lycidas had borne himself bravely in the battle, he had well maintained the honour of the land that had withstood the gigantic power of Xerxes; now his foot was the first on one of the ladders. It was a perilous moment. The rough spar, with branches fastened transversely at intervals across it, on which Lycidas was mounting, swayed backwards and forwards with the struggle between those above to fling it down, and those below to sustain it, and it was with extreme difficulty that the climber could keep his footing. Stones and arrows rattled on the shield which the young Greek held with one arm above his head, as he used the other in climbing; but Lycidas neither flinched nor paused.

" Well done!—bravely done!" shouted the Hebrews who were rushing on from behind.

" He is no Gentile, though he be a Greek ! " cried the wild shrill voice of Jasher.   " Onwards—upwards, warriors of Judah !   One struggle more, and Bethsura is ours!"

Almost at the top of the ladder, almost close to the wall, gasping, straining, bleeding, struggles on the young Greek.   A stone strikes his shield, smashes it, stuns, disables the left arm which upheld it ; slain by a dart, the Hebrew just behind him falls crashing from the ladder !   The brain of Lycidas is dizzy, his ears are filled with wild clamour, he is conscious only that honour and most probably death are before him, still he mounts, he mounts !   Two powerful Syrians have seized the upper end of the ladder ; with an effort of gigantic strength they thrust it back from the supporting wall with its living burden of clambering men, all but one— the foremost !   Lycidas feels the ladder beneath him failing.   With a tremendous effort of agility he springs as it falls at the wall, catches hold of it with his right hand, and flings himself up on the parapet.   But not one moment's breathing-space is given him to start to his feet, or grasp the sword which he has carried hung round his neck.   He cannot rise, he cannot resist ; swords are gleaming above him ; those who have thrown down the ladder seize the Greek to hurl him after it ! A thought of Zarah flashes across the reeling brain of the young man, is it not his last ?—no, a broad shield is suddenly thrust between Lycidas and his assailants, they

AN EVENTFUL CRISIS.

shrink back from the sweep of a terrible sword; up the other ladder the strong and brave have pressed with irresistible force; Judas Maccabeus himself has planted his foot on the bulwarks, has driven back step by step

their defenders before him, and has arrived at this crisis
in the fate of Lycidas to preserve for the third time the
life of his rival!

The banner of Maccabeus is planted on the highest
tower of Bethsura, and as it waves in the light of the
evening sun, such a loud wild shout of triumph rises
from the victors, as might be heard for miles around!
It reaches Zarah in her hut, and sends a thrill of hope
and exultation through her heart, for she knows the
shout of her people, and none but conquerors could have
rent the air with such a cheer as that! It is followed
by the cry, "Jerusalem, Jerusalem!" as from the
Hebrew heroes, in that their hour of success, bursts that
name of all earthly names most dear to the sons of
Israel! Jerusalem, their mother, will be free, her
liberty from a galling yoke will be the crowning reward
of their labours and perils, no foe will now dare to oppose
the conqueror's onward march towards the holy city.

Maccabeus joins in the shout, and shares in the exultation; he tramples his own private griefs under his
feet, that they may cast no gloom over the triumph
which God has vouchsafed to the arms of his people.
The prince raises his helmed head and his victorious
right arm towards heaven, and cries aloud, not with
pride, but with glad thanksgiving, "Behold! our
enemies are discomfited! Let us go up to cleanse and
dedicate the sanctuary of Zion!"

CHAPTER XXXVII.

HERE are joys as well as sorrows into which the stranger cannot enter, and which baffle the attempt of the pen to describe: such was that of Lycidas and Zarah when they first met after the battle of Bethsura. The maiden had her happiness tempered indeed with something of anxiety and even alarm, for she beheld the young Greek pale with loss of blood, exhausted by excessive fatigue, and with his left arm in a sling; but her mind was soon relieved, for Lycidas had sustained no serious or permanent injury. The young proselyte was rather glad than otherwise to carry on his person some token of his having fought under Judas Maccabeus, and been one of the foremost of those who had stormed Bethsura.

With Zarah and her attendant for his deeply interested listeners, Lycidas gave a graphic and vivid description of the fight. Zarah held her breath and trembled when

the narrator came to that thrilling part of his account
which described his own position of imminent peril, when
he would have been precipitated from the top of the
wall, had not Judas Maccabeus come to his rescue.

"I deemed that all was over with me," said Lycidas,
"when the prince suddenly flashed on my sight! Had
I not long since given to the winds the idle fables that
I heard in my childhood, I should have deemed that
Mars himself, radiant in his celestial panoply, had burst
from the cloud of war. But the hero of Israel needs no
borrowed lustre to be thrown around him by the imagination of a poet—he realizes the noblest conception of
Homer."

"And Maccabeus was the one to save and defend
you! Generous—noble!" murmured Zarah.

"Ay; it seems destined that I should be overwhelmed
with an ever-growing debt of obligation," cried Lycidas,
playfully throwing a veil of discontent over the gratitude
and admiration which he felt towards his preserver. "I
would that it had been my part to play the rescuer;
that it had been *my* sword that had shielded his head;
and that Maccabeus were not fated to eclipse me in
everything, even in the power of showing generosity to
a rival. But I must not grudge him the harvest of
laurels," added the young Athenian, with a joyous
glance at Zarah, "since the garland of happiness has
been awarded to me."

On the morning after the battle of Bethsura, Simon and Eleazar, the Asmoneans, both visited their youthful kinswoman in the goat-herd's hut, where she and Anna had remained during the night. They regarded her still as their future sister, and offered her their escort to the house of Rachel, which was at no great distance from the fortress of Bethsura. As Zarah desired as soon as possible to place herself under the protection of a female relative, she gladly accepted the offer. The horse-litter was brought to the door of the lowly hut; and with the curtains closely drawn, the maiden and her attendant proceeded to the dwelling of old Rachel, who joyfully welcomed the child of Hadassah. Zarah, on that morning, saw nothing of Lycidas, and Judas Maccabeus avoided approaching her presence. The chief could not trust himself to look on that sweet face again.

Through the Hebrew camp all was bustle and preparation. Tents were struck—all was made ready for the coming march to Jerusalem; the tired warriors forgot their weariness, and the wounded their pain, so eager were all to gather the rich fruits of their victory within the walls of Zion.

But amidst all the excitement and confusion, with so many cares pressing upon him from every side, the mind of the prince dwelt much upon Zarah. He felt that she was lost to him—he would have scorned to have claimed her hand when he knew that her heart was another's; but he resolved at least to act the part of a brother towards the orphan maiden. Painful to Maccabeus as was the sight of his successful rival, the chief determined to have an interview with Lycidas, that he might judge for himself whether the stranger were indeed worthy to win a Hebrew bride. Lycidas had proved himself to be a brave warrior—he had won the admiration even of the fanatic Jasher; but would the Greek stand firm in his newly-adopted faith when fresh laurels were no longer to be won, or fair prize gained by adhesion to it?

"The most remote hope of winning Zarah," mused Maccabeus, "were enough to make a man espouse the cause of her people, and renounce all idolatry—save idolatry of herself. I must question this Athenian myself. I must examine whether he have embraced the truth independently of earthly motives, and, as a true believer, can indeed be trusted with the most priceless of gems. If it be so, let him be happy, since her happiness is linked with his. Never will I darken the sunshine of her path with the shadow which will now rest for ever upon mine."

It was with no small anxiety that Lycidas obeyed the summons of the prince, and entered his presence alone, in one of the apartments of the fortress which he had aided to capture. The Greek could not but conjecture that his fate, as regarded his union with Zarah, might hang on the result of this interview with his formidable rival.

The interview was not a long one : what occurred in it never transpired. Not even to Zarah did Lycidas ever repeat the conversation between himself and the man whose earthly happiness he had wrecked. As the Greek passed forth from the presence of Maccabeus, he met Simon and Eleazar, who had just returned from escorting their young kinswoman to the dwelling of Rachel.

The Asmonean brothers frankly and cordially greeted the stranger whom they had seen for the first time in the thick of the conflict of the preceding day. The bandage round his temples, the sling which supported his left arm, were as credentials which the Athenian carried with him—a passport to the favour and confidence of his new associates in the field.

"You have leaped into fame with one bound, fair Greek !" cried Eleazar. "You had reached the highest round of the ladder ere I could plant my foot on the lowest. I could fain envy you the honour you have won."

Eleazar, accompanied by Simon, then passed on into the presence of Maccabeus, while Lycidas pursued his way. The smile with which the young Hebrew had spoken was still on his lips when he entered the apartment in which the prince sat alone, but the first glance of Eleazar at Judas banished every trace of that smile.

"You are ill!" he exclaimed anxiously, as he looked on the almost ghastly countenance of his brother; "you have received some deadly hurt!"

The chief replied in the negative by a slight movement of the head.

"The weight of responsibility, the lack of sleep, the exhaustion of yesterday's conflict, are sapping your strength," observed Simon gravely. "Judas, you are unfit to encounter the toils of the long march now before us."

"I was never more ready—never more impatient for a march," said Maccabeus, rising abruptly, for it seemed to him as if violent physical exertions alone could render life endurable.

"I marvel," said Eleazar, "if our graceful young proselyte will bear hardships as bravely as he has proved that he can encounter danger. Methinks he shows amongst our grim warriors as a marble column from Solomon's palace amongst the rough oaks that clothe the hill-side. If Lycidas is to be—"

"He is to be—the husband of Zarah," interrupted Maccabeus. His voice sounded strange and harsh, and he turned away his face as he spoke.

"The husband of Zarah!" re-echoed Eleazar in amazement; "why"—Simon's warning pressure on the

young man's arm prevented his uttering more. The
brothers exchanged significant glances. That was the
last time that the name of Zarah was ever breathed by
either of them in the hearing of Maccabeus.

Zarah found that her residence in her new home
would be but a brief one, and that she was likely to
return to Jerusalem far sooner than she could have
anticipated when she had set out on her night journey
so short a time before. Rachel—a woman who, though
well stricken in years, had lost none of the energy and
enthusiasm of youth—was filled with triumphant joy at
the victory of Bethsura, and declared to Zarah her
intention of starting for the city in advance of the
army.

"I have a vow upon me—a solemn vow," said the
old Jewess to the maiden. "Long have I mourned over
the desolation of Zion; and I have promised to the
Lord that if ever holy sacrifices should again be offered
up in the Temple at Jerusalem, my heifer, my fair white
heifer, should be the first peace-offering. I have vowed
also to go up myself to the holy city, and make there
with my own hands wafers anointed with oil, to eat
with the sacrifice of thanksgiving. The time for keeping my vow has arrived. We will go up together, my
daughter, and my bondsman shall drive the white heifer
before us. My soul cannot depart in peace till I have
looked upon the sanctuary in which my ancestors wor-

shipped, and with a thankful heart have performed this my vow to the Lord."

Zarah made no opposition to the wishes of her relative, which, indeed, coincided with her own. Arrangements for the proposed journey were speedily made. The horse-litter in which Zarah had travelled to Bethsura would avail for the accommodation of both the ladies on her return to the city. The faithful Joab would resume his office of attendant, and Anna join company with the handmaidens of Rachel. It was under joyful auspices that the travellers would set forth on their way to the city of David.

CHAPTER XXXVIII

THE VICTOR'S RETURN.

S there a more glorious, a more soul-stirring sight than that of a brave nation bursting from foreign bondage, casting from her the chains that bound and the sackcloth that covered her, rising victorious and free—free to worship the one God in purity and truth?   Even so, when the shadow of the eclipse is over, the moon bursts forth into brightness, to shine again in beauty in the firmament of heaven.

It was thus with Jerusalem when Maccabeus and his followers went up to the holy city which they had delivered, through God's blessing on their arms.   The town was in a delirium of joy, which there was now no need to conceal.   The voice of thanksgiving and rejoicing was heard in every street; women wept for very happiness; and while the younger inhabitants made the walls ring with their shouts, the old men blessed God that they had been spared to see such a day.   The

advanced season forbade any profusion of flowers; but
on every side palm branches were waving, doors and win-
dows were decked with evergreens, and goodly boughs
were strewed in the way. Every trace of heathenism
was eagerly destroyed in the streets, and the very children fiercely trampled under foot the fragments of idol
or altar.

Again was the song of Miriam heard, "Sing ye unto
the Lord, for He hath triumphed gloriously;" and
women went forth with timbrels to welcome the
warriors of Judah. Though it was the month of
Casleu,* the sun shone with cheerful radiance and
warmth, as if Nature herself shared in the general
rejoicing.

Up Mount Zion they come, the brave, the true, the
devout; they who through much tribulation have kept
the faith; they who have never bowed the knee to idol,
nor forsaken the covenant of God. Maccabeus is foremost now in glory as once in danger. Press ye to see
him, children of Judah! shout to welcome him, sons of
the free!

A group of matrons and maidens surrounded the
entrance to the Temple. Zarah and Rachel were
amongst them.

"You should stand foremost, my daughter, to greet

* Answering to December. Of this time of the year, Dr. Kitto tells us: "Gumpen-
berg in Jerusalem, on the 6th, 10th, 11th, and 16th, experienced weather which he
describes as almost equal to that of May in our latitudes."

the conquerors," cried Rachel to her fair young companion, who was rather inclined to shrink back. "The Asmonean blood flows in your veins; you are kinswoman to our prince; and you have yourself nobly suffered persecution for the faith. What! tears in your eyes, maiden, on such a morning as this!"

"Oh that my beloved mother, Hadassah, had lived to behold it!" thought Zarah. "She would have deemed this glorious day a type and forerunner of that even more blessed time when *the ransomed of the Lord shall return to Zion with songs and everlasting joy upon their heads: they shall obtain joy and gladness, and sorrow and sighing shall flee away* (Isa. xxxv. 10).

Yes; as that bright, warm day in winter, soon to be succeeded by frosts and storms, was in regard to the long, glorious summer, so was the happiness of Judæa under the sway of her first Asmonean princes, compared to the glory which will be hers when her many ages of tribulation shall be ended. In the time of Maccabeus and his successors, the "discrowned queen" had arisen from the dust; but she has not yet, even at this late period, mounted her throne. More fearful judgments, more terrible desolation, were to succeed an interval of prosperity and freedom in the history of Zion. The Romans, more formidable even than the Syrians, were to give Jerusalem's sons to the sword and her temple to the flames; and God's ancient people were to be scattered throughout all nations, to be a by-word and a hissing amongst them. But the glory is not departed for ever. We may—or our descendants must—see the Vine brought out of Egypt, budding into new beauty and life at the breath of the promised Spring.

"He comes, he comes! Maccabeus, our hero!" Such were the shouts which burst from every side as the war-worn victors appeared, with palm-branches in their hands. Was not exultation in the heart of Maccabeus at that moment? Perhaps not. Perhaps he would gladly have exchanged the shouts of all the people for a loving welcome from one dear voice. Judas caught a glimpse of Zarah. Hers were the only eyes in all the crowd that were not fixed upon himself. She was eagerly looking at the form of one a little way in the rear of the chief—the form of her betrothed husband, the Gentile proselyte whom she loved.

The conquerors entered the Temple of Zion. They came, not only to worship, but to purify. No sacrifice could be offered in the sanctuary till what the heathen had defiled the Hebrew should cleanse. With indignant horror Maccabeus and his followers beheld the image of Jupiter, which for years had desecrated the Temple. Since the departure of Antiochus, no worshipper indeed had bowed down before the idolatrous shrine: the edifice had been deserted and left to neglect. The place had now an appearance of wildness and desolation, as if the curse of God were upon it, and presented such a contrast to what it had been in former days as struck sadness into the hearts of Maccabeus and his warriors. In the words of the historian : " When they saw the sanctuary desolate, and the altar profaned, and the gates burned up, and shrubs growing in the courts as in a forest or in one of the mountains, yea, and the priests' chambers pulled down, they rent their clothes and made great lamentations, and cast ashes upon their heads, and fell down to the ground upon their faces, and blew an alarm with the trumpets, and cried towards heaven."

But no long time was given to lamentations. With all the energy of his nature, Maccabeus at once set about the work of restoration. He chose out the most zealous and virtuous of the priests to cleanse the sanctuary, destroy every vestige of idolatry, carry away even the stones that had been defiled, and pull down the altar which had been profaned. New vessels were made, shew-bread and incense were prepared, all in the renovated sanctuary was made ready, for the joyful Feast of Dedication. This festival was appointed by Judas Maccabeus to be annually held ; and it was from thenceforth celebrated from year to year for more than two centuries—till her darkest, most lengthened trial came upon Jerusalem. Who shall now keep the Feast of the Dedication of the Temple when that glorious Temple has itself become a thing of the past ?

CHAPTER XXXIX

LOUD was the burst of joyous music from citherns, harps, and cymbals—Mount Zion rang with songs of gladness—when in the early morning the worshippers of the Lord of Hosts appeared in His Temple, to offer sacrifices of thanksgiving ! The front of the building was decked with crowns of gold, and with shields ; and, in the forcible language of the ancient historian, " thus was there very great gladness among the people, for that the reproach of the heathen was put away."

Then—emblem of thanksgivings from thousands of hearts—rose clouds of delicious fragrance from the altar of incense. Judas Maccabeus stood beside it—more pale and pensive, perhaps, than seemed to suit the occasion—watching the light curling smoke as it ascended and lost itself in the perfumed air. Presently the prince took something from his arm, and cast it into the flame. The

movement was so quiet that it was noticed but by few
by-standers; and none knew what that was which

JUDAS' SACRIFICE.

blazed brightly for a moment, and then left not even
visible ashes behind.   It was but a few threads of flax,
which had bound up flowers long since withered; it
seemed a worthless sacrifice indeed; but when, a few
years later, Judas Maccabeus poured out his life's-blood
on the fatal field of Eleasa, the steel which pierced his
brave heart inflicted not on him so keen a pang.

And here will I close my story, leaving the hero of
Judah a victor over his enemies, and a victor over him-
self.   Let the picture left on the reader's mind be that of
Jerusalem in the hour of her triumph and rejoicing—

when the Lord had turned again the captivity of Zion, and her exulting citizens were like unto them that dream!

But, ere I lay down my pen, let me crave leave for a few moments to address my readers, both Christian and Hebrew. And to the first I would say: Think not of the record of the lives of Judah's heroes, and the deaths of her martyrs, as something in which we have no personal interest—merely to be admired, like the courage of the Greeks at Thermopylæ, or the devotion of Regulus at Rome. Rather let us honour the children of Abraham who fought or died for the Covenant as our brethren in faith, heirs of all the promises on which we rest our hopes, as well as of some others peculiarly their own. Their Scriptures are our Scriptures—they guarded them at hazard of their lives; their Messiah is our Messiah, though he visited earth too late for them—as too early for us—to behold Him. Christianity rests on such Judaism as was held by Hebrew saints and martyrs; Christianity is in regard to the ancient religion as the capital to the column, the full-blown flower to the bud, as the cloud floating high above the sea is to the waters from which it drew its existence. Laws and rites which passed away when types had been accomplished and prophecies fulfilled, are as the salts which are necessary component parts of the sea but not of the cloud; when it rose on high it left them behind.

It is an interesting subject for thought to inquire whether, if Daniel's weeks had run out in the times of the Maccabees, and the Messenger of the Covenant had then come suddenly into His Temple, Christ would not have found adoring worshippers instead of fierce perse-cutors—a throne instead of a cross? Would he not then have been welcomed by the heroes of Emmaus and Bethsura, instead of being despised and rejected of men? Would he not, humanly speaking, have escaped the scourge, the nails, and the spear? But how then shall the Scriptures be fulfilled (Matt. xxvi. 54) that Christ should suffer these things? (Luke xxiv. 26.) The Sacrifice must be slain, that the sinner may be pardoned and live.

And if—as I would fain hope—some Hebrews peruse these pages, how earnestly would I desire power to speak to their hearts! Countrymen and countrywomen of Maccabeus, ye whose fathers fought side by side with the Asmonean brothers, does the history of their deeds rouse none of their spirit of patriotism in your breasts? Can ye, amidst the cares and toils of this working-day world, be indifferent to the state of your own land, your own city—yours by divine right—yours by a deed of gift signed and sealed by God himself! Is it no grief to you that the mosque stands on the site of your holy Temple; that—under a corrupt form of so-called Chris-tianity—idolatry is practised at this day in the city of

David? *Ye that make mention of the Lord keep not silence, and give Him no rest, till He establish, and till He make Jerusalem a praise in the earth!* (Isa. lxii. 7, 8.)

If Gentile Christians are longing and praying for that time, shall not Hebrews long, pray, and strive to hasten its coming? Shall they not search their hearts and ask, "Wherefore is it so long delayed? Wherefore are the heathen still suffered to prevail; the followers of the false prophet to hold the holy city in subjection? For what transgression doth the Lord God of Israel still hide His face from His people; what hath brought upon them a judgment enduring so much longer than Egyptian bondage, or Babylonish captivity, or the tyranny of an Antiochus Epiphanes?" Seek for the answer to this momentous question in your own Scriptures; read them in the light thrown by your own history;—that history will in the future flash into greater brilliancy than even in the days of the Hebrew heroes; we Christians are assured of this, because we, like yourselves, believe those Scriptures, and know that God's Word is pledged for your restoration, and that *the Word of the Lord endureth for ever!*

www.ingramcontent.com/pod-product-compliance
Lightning Source LLC
Chambersburg PA
CBHW031336070726
47496CB00017B/1131